IN DANGEROUS WATERS

By

David O'Neil

W & B Publishers
USA

W & B Publishers

For information:
W & B Publishers
Post Office Box 193
Colfax, NC 27235
www.a-argusbooks.com

ISBN: 978-0-6923503-6-2
ISBN: 0-6923503-6-5

Book Cover designed by Dubya

Printed in the United States of America

Dedication

For Isabella

Chapter one

Taking the strain

Portsmouth 1940

The ML motored quietly through the murky waters of the harbour, the film of old fuel adding its sheen of shifting colour under the lights of the dockside traffic. As they made way round the sterns of the ships packed into the crowded harbour, Sub Lieutenant Peter Woods stretched his arms above his head, tired from the long day's activity.

His skipper, Paul Evans, looked at him, and jeered, "Look at yew, great big feller, and you knackered already, why, man, we have hardly dropped the buoy."

The Welsh accent grated in Peter's ears. The fact was that he, Peter Woods, had spent the entire day fixing the boat which had been damaged the night before by his bloody skipper, a point that seemed to have by-passed Evans. As it was, he has only had time to get out of his overalls and shower before coming back on board to report for this patrol.

He said nothing. The little Welshman in command of the boat had decided to punish his 2nd in command for being a skilled yachtsman, a member of the pre-war RNVR, and son of a wealthy man – *Possibly for being tall as well,* Peter thought, as he stood behind the man in the cramped bridge of the Fairmile 'A'.

The helmsman, Leading Seaman Johnston, was below in the wheelhouse, whistling silently through his teeth. Chief P/O Toby Hebden stood beside the engine controls chewing on a piece of gristle from the pork at teatime, thinking about Caroline, and the last time they met. A week ago they had called in at the cinema. It was some movie she had been keen to see. As they sat waiting for the feature to start, she had squeezed his hand and whispered, "I'm free for the weekend. Can you get time off?"

Last Friday he had a pass for the weekend. They had spent most of it in her bed. He heard the order and automatically repeated it, "Engines full ahead together, sir," as he thrust the controls forward together. "Watch your steering there," he said automatically to the helmsman.

Equally automatically, Johnson replied, "Yes, Chief." As the boat surged forward into the increasing swell, he corrected the tendency for the head to swing at the bite of the increased speed from the propellers.

Ninety minutes later Evans stood searching the night with his glasses glued to his eyes. The boat was silent, engines off, rocking in the long swell coming in from the Atlantic.

Peter leaned over the screen, listening to the slap of the water against the hull, eyes roaming over the surface of the water, glinting in the patches of moonlight periodically appearing and disappearing through gaps in the clouds.

An object appeared, drifting closer to the boat. It caught his eye, a wooden dinghy. "Boat in sight. Port side, forward." He called, low-voiced to Evans.

The Chief appeared beside him, boathook in hand. They waited. Then the PO leant over, caught the thwart with the hook and hauled the dinghy in. As

Peter watched, he saw a figure in the bottom of the boat. There was water there as well. The boat was half full of water, from bullet holes. The Chief called the gunner down from the twin Brownings on the fore deck. Between them they hauled the figure from the boat while Peter held it alongside.

"He's breathing, Chief." Watts, the gunner, said.

The ML whispered forward once more, with the dinghy hauled on board and the rescued man dried off, and wrapped in blankets. Peter left him with the wireless operator, L/S 'Dingle' Bell, who doubled as medic, and returned to the bridge. "Any sign of where our guest comes from?" Evans said quietly, still searching the horizon with no success.

"Not so far, sir. He's still unconscious. He'll probably wake when he warms up a bit. I left Bell to keep an eye on him. Any signs of our convoy yet?"

As soon as he had said it Peter realised it would bring a sarcastic answer. He braced himself for the expected acid comment. He was surprised therefore when Evans said mildly, "There you are, my lovelies, just where you should be, give a mile or two. Action stations, Number one. Quietly now."

Peter felt the jolt of adrenaline as he passed the order on. His experience so far had been on a mine-sweeper. They had never fired a gun in action whilst he had been aboard. He had been posted to MLs on promotion from Midshipman to Sub Lieutenant, and up until now they had not been on an offensive patrol. Having been damaged three weeks before Peter arrived, her first test run had disclosed a steering fault which had damaged her once more, resulting in the night and day efforts to prepare for tonight's patrol.

At the three pounder gun aft, Archie Maddox stood with his loader, Able Seaman Murphy. As the speed increased Murphy muttered, "Here we go again."

"Once more into the 'breech'," Archie mis-quoted. "Got the bricks ready, Paddy."

"Of course. Haven't I always?" Archie smiled, same old question, same old answer. He shrugged, and spat over the side into the white flush of foam alongside. At the stern, Torps' checked the settings on the depth charges for the third time. There had been an occasion when he has set the charges at 6 feet instead of 60 feet which still haunted him some-times. It had been a mistake and nobody had been hurt, but it had been pure luck at the time. He re-called that it had been the first time he had set the charges at minimum depth. The MTB had been in a minefield which they had strayed into while chasing a U boat. The setting should have been sixty feet, not shallow. The explosions had set off three mines in the vicinity, shocking everyone, but it had warned the skipper and saved the boat. L/Torpedoman, William Steven Fforbes-Smith, had been extra careful ever since.

The exercise tonight was to ambush a German coastal convoy. The ML's, escorted by MGB's in case there were E-Boats about, were to disable the convoy, sink what they could, then leave the rest for the RAF.

As they approached the convoy the MGB's made for the escorts, guns blazing, triple Rolls Royce Merlin engines pouring power to their screws as they worked up to full speed. Peter watched as they flew past the slower ML, spray flying, a great moustache of white foam at their bows.

Evans was watching the convoy. He shouted, "They are turning. Give me all you've got, Chief. The need for caution now over, the Chief thrust the engine controls to full and the stern sank as the ML rapidly accelerated to her full 25-knot speed.

The five ships in the convoy were now firing at the approaching ML's. The armed trawlers and the flak ship escorting the convoy had their hands full with the MGB's. Peter saw the lead ML falter. Smoke appeared from the centre of the craft, but the boat recovered and continued toward the enemy ships.

Evans shouted, "Open fire!" The three pounder gun immediately started its regular thud-thud as the team went into action. The twin .303s opened up from its mounting on the fore-deck in front of the bridge. Evans called "Bring her round, Chief. Close alongside." They neared the lead coastal freighter, Peter crouching, watching, then "Depth charges, shallow setting." He called to Torps crouched beside the racks.

As they passed close to the freighter two charges dropped from the port side rack. The ML raced on to the second in line. Peter looked back at the freighter. The charges had exploded within a few feet of the propeller of the unfortunate ship. Their effect was to blow the stern and prop shaft to twisted metal. The rudder was bent out of shape and locked to starboard. But the death blow had been to breach the boiler-room. The surge of icy water had caused the boiler to blow and the ship immediately settled inexorably by the stern. He turned to the next ship in line, which was firing all the guns she could find at the approaching ML.

Archie was shouting at Paddy, who was laughing as he slid the shells into the breech in a smooth, regular flow. Peter could see the shells' impacting on the bridge structure of the ship, brief flares of fire as the wheelhouse caught fire. The .303 was chattering madly from the bows and, as Peter watched, one of the guns on the target ship stopped firing. Then they were in position. The ship, now out of control, started to turn into the speeding ML.

"Standby, Torps, shallow setting. Fire two." Once more the depth charges went over but, as they veered away from the ship, though the charges blew the screw and the steering, the ship's stern lifted at the explosion, but remained afloat. The guns on the stricken ship continued to fire as the ML made a turn to port to return and finish the job.

The calm voice of the chief came through the headphones. "Number one, report to the bridge!"

Peter turned, calling to the gun crew. "You're on your own." He made his way to the bridge where Evans was sitting, white faced, with a bloody patch on his chest and Dingle Bell, with his first aid kit, trying to stop the bleeding.

"Take over, will you, Peter." Evans gasped. It was the first time he had called him Peter. "Let us finish this job, nice and tidy, eh."

Peter looked up. The freighter was turning a great lazy circle. Elsewhere the other members of the convoy showed as bright fiery exclamation marks against the dark sky.

"Steer to cross her stern. We'll take her on our starboard side." His voice was steady. He felt completely calm and assured.

"Aye, aye, skipper. Starboard side to."

Surprised, Peter turned to Evans. Dingle shook his head. "He's gone, sir."

The calm voice of the chief came up the voice pipe. "When you are ready, sir."

Peter turned back to the job in hand. The stern of the ship was approaching fast. "He spoke through his headset. "Torps, two depth charges, starboard side, shallow setting. Fire."

He could feel the thud of the firing charges as the two lethal canisters were sent over beneath the stern of the freighter. The turning ship found itself directly over the exploding charges and the stern disintegrated. The huge hole in her hull absorbed the greedy waters of the channel taking the ship down by the stern, sinking fast. As they turned away from the shattered convoy, Peter saw that the senior boat was still smoking though it maintained speed. Two of the MGB's were gone.

***

When the boats were moored alongside the pontoons, Commander David Osborne DSO was standing waiting for his brood to return.

As they carried the body of Evans ashore, the Chief, standing at Peter's elbow, said, "He was a good skipper. You would have got to know him, if there had been time."

Peter remembered Evans sitting on deck dying. He had called him Peter, "I wish we could have had time."

The survivor from the dinghy was also carried ashore and taken in the waiting ambulance, presumably to Haslar Hospital.

Turning to the chief, Peter said, "I need to report, so I'll leave you to get the boat cleared up. I'll be back as soon as I can. I suppose there will be a new skipper to get to know."

He turned and strode off along the pontoon toward the admin building. The chief watched and he saw Lieutenant Harry Warrender, RNVR, skipper of

No1 boat, join Peter as he walked up to the offices to report.

In the office, Lieutenant Commander Norman Marker DSC.RN sat checking brief details off a list. Peter stepped forward in turn. "Sub Lieutenant Peter Woods, ML3. Report two men dead, two injured."

"Where is Lieutenant Evans?" The rude question surprised Peter and, for a moment, he was unsure what to say. Then he said, "The Lieutenant is unable to attend, sir."

"Why is he unable to attend?" The impatience in the officer's voice, expressed his opinion of these amateur sailors playing at being naval officers."

"He is dead. Sir!" Peter's words dropped into the silence like stones in a pool.

The voice of Commander David Osborne broke the silence. "Sub Lieutenant Woods! My office!"

Peter entered the CO's office and stood in front of the desk at attention.

The Commander looked up and waved to a chair, "Take a pew. Peter, isn't it?"

"Yes, sir."

"So, young Evans didn't make it! That is bad news. Apart from anything else, we have no boat CO's available to take his place. You will have to come out with me for the next job. Hopefully, we'll get a replacement for Evans later this week. Meantime, can I leave it to you to get the boat ready and restored?"

"Of course, sir."

"Good. It does me good to get out now and again. It's too easy to lose touch with what you people are up to. Between you and me, our next trip will be a Pickford, so make sure the hand weapons are clean and loaded with plenty of spare mags."

He looked up, his quick blue eyes giving the man in front of him a once over. "Very good, Peter. I'll be down on the boat later this afternoon."

Peter left the office, not a slight bit dazed at the speed of events.

***

When the Commander came down the pontoon, the boat was ready for operations once more.

When the chief heard that their next op would be a Pickford, he had opened up the small arms locker and removed all the guns for cleaning and oiling.

From him Peter learned that a Pickford was a collection and delivery trip, anything from people to guns and provisions.

Chapter two

Living dangerously

David Osborne puffed at his pipe with enjoyment. The towel round his neck was still dry, and though the wind of their passage was blustery, his hat was firmly jammed down and his all-weather jacket buttoned to the neck. Seated, jammed in the corner of the bridge swaying easily to the swell, he reflected, *There is nothing quite like just messing about in boats.* He felt very close to Ratty in 'Wind in the Willows' sometimes.

He thought about the passengers below. The four men seemed normal enough. He thought he should be worried about the woman. She seemed so young. It was only when she looked him in eye that he realised that she was older than she looked, and she knew exactly what she was doing. David Osborne had never felt so sad for anyone in his life. Whatever she had been through, it had left its mark inside.

There were other things to be dropped off and three people to be collected. In coastal forces terms, 'a milk run.'

***

The early evening light was fading to the west as the two ML's motored through the slate-coloured waters of the Channel. The No-1 boat, skippered by Lieutenant Harry Warrender kept station to starboard, occasionally throwing up a shower of spray as the bow hit the odd cross wave. Both boats carried the small blue light which allowed them to keep in touch in the encroaching darkness.

It had been over two months since David Osborne had last taken part in one of these operations, and he was finding it surprisingly difficult to keep his attention from straying. His naval career had begun in 1920 as a midshipman. As a Lieutenant Commander, he had missed his first promotion chance. It had come as a shock to find himself shifted sideways to a training position, having been sea-going up to that time.

His promotion to Commander had occurred almost one year to the day later.

In 1938 rumours of war in newspapers were coming and going, but in the inner circle of the services, there was little doubt that it would happen.

***

The boat bounced, and the hand carrying the mug of tea swore as he nearly lost it. "Chief sent up a mug of warmers, sir."

The Commander stirred and received the mug gratefully. "Just the ticket," he said. "Thank the chief, Watson!"

"Aye-aye, Sir," Watson disappeared below once more.

Peter Woods appeared and joined him on the bridge, "This could be a long night." He commented.

The Commander smiled and said "After sitting in an office waiting to see how many of your people have been lost during an operation you have personally devised, a long night is just what the doctor ordered."

"I didn't mean...I didn't intend to imply..." Peter stumbled over his words thinking he had in some way put his foot in it.

Osborne turned to him, "Don't fuss. I was just commenting on the fact that I have been stuck in an office for far too long. It is a relief to get out and feel the wind in my face for a change. For good measure, it also good to share the tasks I set out every day, and share the risks for once." He stopped and collected his thoughts, in a quieter voice he added. "That is always the worst bit, sending people off into danger and having to live with the casualties afterwards."

Peter was silent, realising suddenly for the first time that the perils of life as crew in coastal forces were just one end of the story. At least they were actively doing something, able to react to changes – physically if necessary. The pressure on the people who sent them out had to be, in many ways, worse. They were helpless to do anything at all once the boats left harbour. Just sit and wait for the return of the boats, hoping.

***

As they approached the first landing site, Peter watched the signal light on shore as it flashed the code letters to the two ML's.

The dinghy was prepared. He helped the landing party down into boat. The woman was for this drop, accompanied by one of the men. The woman sounded French. The man sounded English. Peter ran the electric motor and set them ashore where the reception party waited.

A man and a woman were helped into the boat for the return trip to the ML. Back on board, the two boats crept quietly round the headland into the rivermouth and across the three-mile wide estuary to the south side. The shore was cluttered with the remains of two coasters, run aground under attack by dive bombers when hostilities commenced one year ago. The wrecks on what had once been an open beach had created an altered formation throwing up shadows and creating gulley's where the tides had ripped the sands into shapes caused by the presence of the wrecks.

Peter watched while the No. 1 boat nosed in to make the rendezvous with the local agents. He was suddenly made aware of the woman agent who had boarded them at the other pick-up point. She was standing watching the shore through binoculars.

He moved to make a little more space at the rail beside him.

The woman made no sign that she was aware of his presence. When she spoke it was a surprise. "That is a trap! Stop them!"

Peter reacted, calling to the Commander. "Skipper it's a trap!"

David Osborne did not hesitate. "Fire a red flare and a white, over the rendezvous!" He snapped to the signaller beside him.

The two flares shot up from the launcher, exploding over the rendezvous point. The shoreline was lit up as the combined effect of the flares created an eerie pink light. The line of German soldiers stationed along the beach at the upper tideline was revealed. The three people at the water's edge dropped immediately into the shallow water.

In No. 1 boat, Harry Warrender reacted fast. The twin Brownings opened fire on the line of troops even as the troops opened fire on the ML. The boat reversed in a flurry of foam, still over 100 yards offshore. The dinghy, ready for use in the pick-up, was drifted on a rope toward the three figures swimming away from the shore. All three managed to get hold of the grab ropes on the sides of the dinghy. The retreating ML dragged the dinghy away from the beach and the three escaping people were hauled out of the water by the crew as soon as they were brought alongside.

Both ML's reversed course and made their best speed out of the estuary. David Osborne realised that there would be some form of ambush arranged for the boats, and he just hoped that the warning had been in time for them to clear the confines of the two headlands before it could be effected.

They made it. Two E boats appeared from the north as they cleared the headland to the south. The eight-mile gap was just too far for the chasing boats to make up.

***

The two boats made it back three hours later. There had been a sighting of an aircraft on the way, but it had not appeared to have spotted them as they stopped to prevent their distinctive wake showing up against the grey waters of the early morning sea.

In Portsmouth the de-briefing was tense. The three agents recovered had been unaware of the trap for which they were bait.

The leader of the trio suggested that the betrayal had been by one of their French volunteers, a member of the resistance. "Most of them are exactly what they say they are, but the Gestapo have a nasty way of blackmailing people, holding the threat of reprisals over the families of their informers."

The other two people were silent on the subject. The woman appeared to be under some strain, judging from her appearance while the de-brief was under way.

Peter noticed particularly because he had the feeling he knew her from somewhere. She was probably in her early twenties, with fair hair and blue eyes. Her clothes were shapeless and bulky but he had the impression that she was slim. Her name had been given as Clarice, but he was aware that all the agents used names that were not their own.

It came to him as they, broke for lunch – the identity of the informant still a mystery. Her name was Chris DeNeuve, and she had crewed for her brother in the cup races at Cowes in 1938. He had asked his friends about her but had been told she was at the Sorbonne and was returning to France after the racing week. They had spoken briefly at a party after one of the races. But, though he had asked if he could see her again, she had smiled gently and pointed out that she was leaving in the morning to return to her studies in Paris. The sad shrug of the shoulders said it all.

Taking a chance, Peter sat beside her at the table for lunch. The group of people had been milling about but she slipped away from the others and sat at the far end by the wall. He joined her with a smile and a brief "May I?"

She did not look up, just murmured, "Of course."

As he sat down he said quietly, "Chris DeNeuve? How is your brother?"

She turned and looked at him. "You know my brother?"

"We raced at Cowes 1938, the cup races. You were crewing for Henri, studying at the Sorbonne, I believe."

"Peter Woods, you asked me out!"

"And you turned me down, very kindly I recall."

"I am sorry I did not recognise you." She lifted her hand and indicated his nose. "It has been straightened." She grinned. "It is an improvement, and now you are in the Navy driving small boats."

"Absolutely. It seemed the right thing for me to do." Peter acknowledged. "Once more I am asking you out, if it is possible, of course?"

"Oh dear. I'm afraid I have to say no for the second time. I am due to return to London this evening, then I will be returning for another posting, I fear. I have no idea where that will be."

"In that case, if you have an address, I can write to you. That way we can keep in touch wherever we are."

Chris looked at him properly. "Peter, we hardly know each other. This is only our second meeting, and our first lasted, what, ten minutes."

"That is the problem I intend to overcome. Given the chance I would have taken you out. If things had gone well I would have taken you out again. If things were still going well between us, we would have become boyfriend and girlfriend. As we grew older, as things continued to improve between us, I would have asked you to marry me. Hopefully, you would have accepted my proposal. We would marry and over the next few years probably had at least two, possibly three, children and lived happily ever after. So keeping that particular scenario in mind, do I get your address?"

"When you put it like that how could a girl refuse." Peter noticed, when Chris smiled, her face lit up and he felt the warmth and humour envelope him. She reached into her handbag and retrieved a small notebook. Taking his proffered pen she wrote a name and address on one of the pages, tore it out and gave it to him.

"Who is Alice Worth?"

"She is my best friend and a colleague in the service. We share a flat in London when I am there. She is based in London and will pass on any letters so that they do not pass through the office."

They had finished the meal and the others were rising from the table to resume the briefing. Chris took Peter's hand and said quietly for his ears only. Don't trust Monroe, our leader. He is holding something back. I think he knew the troops were there last night. If Ceasar had not pulled him into the sea along with me, we would have been captured and perhaps you would have lost your boats. I have no proof, but you are warned."

Peter nodded slowly acknowledging her warning. She released his hand, and was gone. In the mess that evening Peter encountered the Commander who drew him aside for a moment. "Peter, I noticed you talking to the younger of the agents. Have you met her before?"

Peter looked at his skipper seriously. "We raced on competing boats at Cowes in 1938. I knew her brother well. Skipper, she warned me that she did not trust that man, Monroe. She was convinced that he knew there was a trap laid for us all on that beach. Her companion, Caesar, dragged them down into the water and allowed them to escape. Monroe was pulling back. He was taken by surprise by Caesar's action."

The Commander looked keenly at Peter Woods. "What did you think?"

"I think she was telling it as it happened. I did not get a chance to speak with Caesar so I cannot comment on his reaction."

The Commander smiled grimly. "I did. His feeling was the same as your girlfriend's."

"Oh!" Peter looked a little surprised but pleased as well.

"Did you expect to have to persuade me?"

"Frankly, yes!"

"Well, my opinion went with the agents on their return to London. I have heard nothing since, nor am likely to. Perhaps your friend may let you know sometime.

Peter nodded. "Perhaps she will!"

Chapter three

In harm's way

Ranger Lee was a surprise to Peter and a shock to the squadron. The American, who arrived with a roar of power from his Indian motorcycle, carried the insignia of the Royal Canadian Navy on his shoulders. The Lieutenant reported to Lieutenant Commander Norman Marker, DSO RN who was not impressed by the appearance or the demeanour of the replacement skipper for the No. 4 boat.

"We have not had any colonial officers here up to now so I will expect you to set a good example for any future drafts we receive. By the way, that motorcycle. Please find another place to park, preferably behind the wardroom where it will be out of sight. The parking in front of the building is for motor cars only."

As Ranger Lee explained afterwards, "It was not what he said. It was the way he said it that pissed me off. Colonial indeed?"

"So!" Harry Warrender said, "Where do you come from?"

Lee looked both ways in a theatrical manner, "Why, I am from El Paso, Texas."

"How come you are a boat driver rather than a donkey walloper,(cavalryman)?" Joe Handiman of Boat No. 2 asked.

"My Dad was a PO on a gunboat in China. I guess when he retired to El Paso it was to get away

- 19 -

from the sea, but it was too late for me. I read just about every sea adventure story I could get hold of. When Dad discovered my feelings on the matter, he said, if ever I actually went to sea, to make sure I became an officer. I started racing boats on Lake Michigan when I was sixteen."

"Were you any good?" Harry asked.

"I won a few cups," Ranger said modestly.

Peter looked at him keenly. "How few?"

"42 in total. Thirty-six firsts. Made enough money to allow my dad to retire, and keep me in booze for a few years yet."

"A few years?"

Ranger grinned. "Mebbe a lot. Actually." And that was all he would say.

By universal agreement, Ranger Lee became Texas. As Harry pointed out, with a name like Ranger, what else could it be.

However flamboyant Ranger Lee was he certainly knew boats. On their first shakedown he made boat No. 3 do most things, apart from submerge. As the chief put it, he could probably have done that too, if necessary.

His laughingly disparaging comments about the speed and mobility of the boat by comparison with the PT boats he had trained on in Canada were offset by the fact that the Fairmile was not inundated by a continual fog of high octane fumes from the fuel required to fire the Packard engines of the said PT boats. The five knot disparity in top speed was also offset by the range and the armament of the British boat.

The first operation under their new skipper was uneventful. A simple search and rescue operation for a downed Walrus aircraft off St Albans Head was accomplished in medium seas on a summer evening.

They found the amphibian still afloat, it having touched down to pick-up a ditched pilot in his one-man dinghy. While hauling the pilot aboard, a freak splash of wind-driven spray had stalled the plane's engine, the battery had shorted at the same time.

They passed a tow, and began towing the aircraft to the safety and calmer waters of Poole Harbour. The lively comment that passed between pilot and skipper ended with the suggestion that the skipper should speed up the tow while the plane's prop freewheeled. Then, when sufficient revs had built up, they could flip the mag switches and open the throttle for a running engine start.

Realising the speed of tow required would probably rip out the bow of the Walrus, common sense prevailed and they cruised sedately past Shell Beach into the calm waters of Poole Harbour. They left the aircraft in the hands of a tender, and with promises of a joint booze-up in the future when possible, they departed for their home base.

The shorter nights of the summer made secret operations difficult. The cover of darkness being a major element in approaching the enemy coast without giving their presence away. However, there were always convoys to protect and search and rescues to be done, so the life on a ML was a lot more varied than in the more specialised branches of Coastal Forces.

The boat quickly settled to a routine. Peter Woods found that Texas was happy to leave certain duties to him, which meant that Peter found his confidence in the handling of the boat and the men that ran it.

A long evening in the middle of June found boat No. 3 cruising, with Peter on the bridge. They were searching for a small dinghy or launch that had been spotted south of the Isle of Wight. Texas was down below in the cabin studying the search area on the chart.

Texas thought for a few moments, then poked his head through the hatch. "Peter, you sailed these waters, I believe, in Cowes week before the war. Do you know what the effect of the trend of the sea is in this area? I know where the currents run but we are seeking a lightweight boat with little in the way of navigation gear."

"I would be inclined to run down channel for a few miles and toward the French coast. In a small boat it is difficult to take into account the true effect the current and wind have." Peter spoke, carefully running through his mind the ideas he had put to the skipper earlier. The zone suggested for the search had never really felt right to him, having heard the circumstances and timing of the boat's race for freedom.

Texas said, "Let's get on it. I agree we are in the wrong place. Take us to where we should be. Let her rip; we've wasted enough time already."

Thrilled at the chance, Peter called, "All engines, full ahead. Course south by southwest."

"South by southwest. Full speed ahead. Aye-aye sir."

The boat swung on to the new course and the bow rose as the Fairmile worked up to her full speed of 25-knots, racing to her new search location.

Peter stood balancing against the pitch and roll of the fast-moving boat, trying to keep his binoculars focussed. He called for a reduction in speed after half an hour and the boat settled back. The bow dropped and the stern rose as the speed bled away. The lookouts all found the quieter motion helpful and the pattern of search was established.

It was late in the evening when the boat was spotted. The occupants were lying in the bottom which had made it more difficult to spot. As they approached a German launch loomed out of the dusk. It was armed with a deck-mounted machine gun, flying the Nazi flag and it was obviously searching for the same boat. The French coast was no more than fifteen miles away by this time. The deck-mounted machine gun on the enemy boat spat fire at the ML as she increased speed to intercept her before she reached the small boat. The foredeck-mounted twin Brownings opened fire, creating a line of spray running up to and disappearing into the foredeck of the German launch.

The German gun stopped abruptly. As the ML swung past the small boat into the path of the launch, the three pounder opened up, to join the machine guns, making the life uncomfortable for the German vessel. It lurched to a stop, with smoke seeping from the engine compartment. Texas was on the bridge standing beside Peter. "Collect our people. Then see if the Germans would like to join us for tea!"

Startled, Peter had been unaware of the arrival of his captain It took a few moments to take in that he had handled the entire action. He gave the orders for the pick-up. Then called the Chief PO to prepare to take the German survivors prisoner.

The three people in the small boat were suffering from exposure and all needed warming up in a hurry. Despite the time of year, two nights at sea had taken their toll, in addition to being soaked by spray.

The Germans came almost quietly. Three were garrison soldiers grabbed to provide support for the crew of the launch. The machine gun had been mounted by the launch skipper, a Naval reserve Petty Officer who had been killed while operating it. The crew were two civilians who operated the pilot launch at Wilhelmshaven. They had been pressed into service to operate the launch in the harbour at Cherbourg. Following a series of sabotage events, for which the original crew had been blamed, their summary execution had meant a more trustworthy crew was needed. One of the soldiers had been injured and another had been rendered senseless when he had objected to the surrender of the boat.

Peter left the bridge and went below to help with the three people from the small boat. 'Dingle' Bell was working on one of the men. Another was already stripped and wrapped in blankets. Peter went to the third person, shivering visibly, though apparently unconscious. He stripped off the jacket and tie and gathered a heated towel ready to dry off the man as soon as he was undressed. The trousers seemed a bit oversized. Peter presumed that clothing would be difficult to obtain in occupied countries, and yanked them off, grateful that the size made them easy to pull off. He threw one of the towels over the exposed legs of the man, undid the shirt and hauled it off, over his raised head. It was then he realised he was stripping a woman. Shocked, he found he was looking at her breasts through the thin cloth of her vest.

Bell looked over at him, then at his patient. "Get on with it, boss. She needs to be dry and warm whoever she may be. Somebody has to do it."

Peter shook off his momentary shock and got on with it, trying without much success to avoid looking too closely at what he was doing while he removed the rest of her clothing.

He then got to work with the towels, scrubbing the cold body with them until she was dry enough to wrap in the waiting blankets. As he laid the woman down on the bunk and tucked her in, her eyes opened. "Thanks, love," the woman said quietly. "Nice and snug." Then promptly closed her eyes, and fell asleep, just the occasional shiver interrupting the even rise and fall of her chest under the blankets.

A small charge left in the German boat exploded as the ML left the scene. It disintegrated and disappeared beneath the waters of the Channel

Two Messerschmitts found them before they reached the Isle of Wight. The Brownings in their rotating turret opened fire as the two aircraft attacked the now jinking ML. Texas was swearing picturesquely and noisily as he manoeuvred the ML at increasing speed back and forth while keeping to the mean course they were following. They had been hit in several places before three Hurricanes' appeared and drove the Messerschmitts off.

Peter went below to check up on their guests.

The woman was sitting up sipping a mug of something hot, with a lacing of rum he suspected, judging from the scent in the air of the cabin.

She looked at Peter who blushed, remembering her naked figure. She smiled, "I presume you are the man who stripped me."

"Yes. I am afraid I am." Peter said hesitantly.

"You are my first." The mischievous look she gave him robbed the remark of any offence. "You are the first man to see me naked since I was a baby. I hope it wasn't too disappointing?"

"Oh, no. You are beautiful." Peter suddenly realised what he was saying and blushed bright red. "I …I did not mean, I did not intend…"

"You did what you had to do. Otherwise I would have been down with pneumonia by now. I'm sorry. I was pulling your leg. You must have been most embarrassed?"

Peter grinned at her, "Embarrassed? Yes. Privileged also. In fact my first and only sight of .the female form unclothed which was not made of marble."

"Well, I trust it has not disillusioned you and put you off women for life? By the way, I understand you are Peter Woods. My name is Karen Sullivan. How do you do?" She held her hand out to him and he reached forward to take it. She leaned forward and kissed him. The blanket slipped revealing her breast. She ignored it and slipped her arms round his neck and made a proper job of the kiss, which Peter found disturbing and surprising. When she let go she took her time retrieving the blanket saying, "You've seen me before, after all."

Peter blushed once more. This lady was affecting him in more ways than one. He looked at her. She was pretty with dark hair and green eyes. A little thinner than she should be, but shapely in all the right places. A little older than he had first thought, perhaps 27-28 years, maybe even 30.

"Do I pass?" She asked.

With a start he realised he had been staring. "Oh, sorry. I was miles away for a moment there."

"The answer is yes. I live in an apartment in Southsea, and I would like you to take me out to dinner one night, during next week."

Bell appeared at that point in the conversation.

Confused, Peter was at a loss for a moment. Karen smiled, and said, "Friday, would be fine. I'll call you."

Peter nodded and beat a hasty retreat.

Bell looked at Karen and grinned. "He's a good lad, just a bit shy."

"Not one of your failings then?" Karen said with a laugh. She stood and walked over to the pile of dry clothes piled on the bunk opposite. She turned and looked at Bell pointedly.

He got the message and left, closing the door behind him.

The chief commented, "Is he fixed up?"

Bell nodded, "I believe he is. Wow, I envy him. She is something special."

The chief looked at him. "The Sub's time is overdue. You are a randy git who has managed to remove more girls' knickers than Woolworths sell. Just stand back and give someone else a chance."

Bell sighed. "I'd be wasting my time there, Chief. He was the only one there as far as she was concerned."

"That I should live to see the day. Get off back to work, you idle bugger." The chief shook his head sadly. The younger generation was a cause for despair to the 32 year old Chief Petty Officer.

Chapter four

Manoeuvers

On the bridge the Skipper stood, gazing at the green island they were passing as they entered the Solent. Peter joined him on the bridge. "Ah, you are back. How are our three passengers?"

"The woman is up and about and one of the men. The other was shot, and is feeling the effects, so he is still under observation. Bell is with them now."

"Can I come up on the bridge?" Karen appeared at the hatch.

Texas looked at Peter. "Take her in for me, Number one. I'll go below and check up on the others." He turned to Karen with a smile. "Please be my guest. I'll leave you with Sub Lieutenant Woods if you don't mind."

Karen stood beside him as they approached Gosport, entering the channel through to the harbour itself. She spoke quietly so that only he could hear, "Did I shock you, inviting you out like that?"

Peter grinned. "Frightened the daylights out of me actually. I'm so pleased you did though. I could not think of a way to ask you out for myself."

"You'll be coming out then?"

"It's too late to back out now. Of course I would love to take you out. You did say Friday?"

They drew alongside the pontoon at the base. The stretcher with the injured man was carried ashore, followed by the second man who was able to manage without assistance. Karen stirred, "I must go," she pressed a piece of paper into his hand and gave him a quick peck on the cheek. I'll ring you, or call me. Otherwise Friday, okay?"

Peter smiled, "Okay!"

He followed her down to the main deck and handed her ashore. Leading Seaman Bell appeared with a bag containing her own clothes. "Here you go miss, all dried and ready to iron."

"Thanks, Dingle." She said quietly, "Look after him for me?"

"Will do!" Dingle Bell said. "Like a brother."

He watched the trim derriere of the lady in the Middy's britches as she progressed up the hard to the offices. With a sigh, he returned to his duties clearing up his area, after his nursing efforts with the rescued agents and the German prisoners.

***

Peter attended the meeting in the Commander's Office with his skipper, Ranger Lee. They were seated along with the executive officer Lieutenant Commander Norman Marker. The Commander entered, ushering a stranger in plain clothes along before him.

When seated, the Commander introduced him as Michael Forbes, and went on to point out that he was the man they had brought home from the dinghy on Peter's first mission, the one that cost the life of his skipper, Lieutenant Paul Evans.

"There is a matter Mr Forbes has brought to our attention which we have to confirm. He needs to be taken back to the French coast to the same spot, but importantly he also has to be brought back. The task will have to wait for the dark of the moon. That means waiting until Saturday next week.

"It will also mean that Mr Forbes must not land alone. He must be accompanied to make sure there is at least someone to bring out the information he will be verifying. It means that Sub Lieutenant Woods will need to accompany Mr Forbes ashore, with perhaps one other man as back-up." He looked keenly around the small group. To Ranger Lee he said, "There will be diversionary action for the ML's that night and you will be needed to drop off the landing party and rejoin the diversion. The pick-up will be 90 minutes after the drop-off. The other boats will be in support at that time."

He had risen from his chair while delivering his instructions. Now he seated himself once more and said, "Questions?"

Texas spoke first. "Why is Peter needed to go ashore?"

"We, in this room, are the only people who are aware that there is a secret on the coast. We need to verify it before we can involve the other services. The reason we need to go back is that Mr Forbes was wounded in his escape. He lost his notes and we need to reconnoitre the site to make sure that what he has seen is what he thinks it was. Also that it is feasible to make a raid, and remove parts of the equipment he spotted on his first visit."

"Do we know what this special equipment is?" Marker asked pettishly.

"That information is classified." Forbes said, speaking for the first time.

Peter thought that Forbes had an accent sounding almost German to his untutored ear.

Marker looked as if he was going to take issue on the matter, but was stopped by the Commander who noticed. "Well, there are several days to wait until the exercise can be run. The long term weather forecast is still holding. There will be some training for the people involved. He indicated Peter. "Please hang on for a few minutes after the others leave. I have some information for you alone."

The meeting broke up and Peter waited for the Commander to return, after seeing their guest off.

"Sit down, Peter. What I have to tell you is for your ears only. Do you understand?"

"Yes. Of course." Peter answered.

There was a pause while the Commander collected his thoughts. "Peter, have you ever killed anyone?"

"Not to my knowledge."

"If you are faced with capture when you are in France, you will need to kill Mr. Forbes. He knows far too much about his subject and our use of his expertise to allow the Gestapo to get hold of him. In addition he is a German Jew. His treatment will be savage at their hands and he is fully aware that he will be unable to prevent them finding out all he knows."

"Why send him if it is so critical?"

"Because he is the best qualified to judge if the equipment you are going to examine is as good as he thinks it is. Only he knows enough to make the judgement. In fact only he knows exactly where to look."

"Surely it would make sense to send a squad of Marines with him?"

"Need to know. It is not an option! Now, you will be sent to Hamworthy, the Royal Marine base on Poole harbour. They will train you to use the small canoe you will take for the landing and the pick-up. They will also give you a course in small arms. You report this evening. You should be back by Wednesday. You can have a pass for Friday/Saturday.

Weather permitting you will be carrying out the operation on Sunday night."

He looked at Peter keenly, "Any questions?"

Peter shrugged. There was nothing to say. It would be either him, or some other poor bugger. "No questions just now, sir. I had better get my kit together for Hamworthy."

Commander Osborne rose to his feet and held out his hand. Peter took it. "Good luck, Peter. I'll see you next week."

"Thank you, sir. Next week." He saluted, left the office, and made his way to his cabin in the accommodation block.

***

The small Navy staff car taking him to Hamworthy was a pre-war Austin ten, and, despite its vintage and its already high mileage, it made good time through the summer evening traffic. The roads were pretty quiet. Most of the traffic was official, of one sort or another. The driver was a girl who looked about fifteen but drove with the easy confidence of a veteran.

Her WRNS cap was set square in top of her head. The neatly trimmed hair, made a straight line across the back of her neck.

Peter read the order transferring him to Hamworthy. He was required to report to Major Stuart McNeil RM. His orders were to wear civilian clothes.

"I'm sorry, I don't know your name. Do you know the Marine Barracks at Hamworthy?" he asked.

"Yes, sir. It's one of my regular haunts most nights. I am Leading Wren Amy Lucas." The voice was soft, the faint London accent subdued.

There was a vague familiarity about the name, he could not pin it down. He shrugged. It would probably occur to him in the middle of the night. Ignoring it, he commented, "I beg your pardon. Did you say 'your regular haunt'?"

She giggled. "I'm sorry, sir. I mean I am based there. I have the impression that, when I tell people that, they think I am the only woman in among fifteen hundred Marines, give or take. It seems to convey the wrong image. I make a joke of it for that reason."

Peter laughed. "Wow, your off duty life must be interesting?"

"I really have no time to get about unless I have a pass. Then I normally head home if I an. My fiancé is in the Air Force, stationed in Essex. We meet when we can, at my home in Wimbledon."

"I am due to report at 2100. Have we time for me to make a phone call, and still get there on time?"

"We have time for you to stop for a quick one at Ringwood. We'll be there in a minute or two. There will be a phone at the pub."

***

The thatched building just off the road looked exactly what it was, a warm welcoming coaching inn, windows open and tables in the garden beside bar. There were few customers. As the barman explained most people tried to get home before they were caught out in an air raid. "They are getting fewer these days." The barman volunteered. "Reckon they bit off a bit more that they can chew this summer." He served Peter with a pint of beer and directed him to the phone booth beside the toilets at the end of the public bar. He gave Amy the lemonade she had ordered, and wandered off to chat to one of his cronies in the corner of the room.

Peter came back with a smile on his face and joined Amy with his beer.

"Do you know the Major?" He asked.

"Everyone on the base knows the Major," she spoke in a low voice, a habit she had developed when in a public place. "He is the sort of man you turn to when there is a problem, whatever the problem!"

"He's popular then?"

"Respected and trusted rather," Amy said after a little thought. "I like him."

Peter finished his beer, "Shall we get on then?"

They shouted goodbyes to the barman and set off once more.

Peter sat in the back of the car wondering what he had let himself in for. His call to Karen had been to let her know he had a pass for Friday and Saturday. Was there anything she might like to do, would be free to do even? There had been a few moments silence at his words and he had wondered if he had been too forward in suggesting she might spend the time with him.

To his surprise she had suggested he bring an overnight bag and they could visit her sister at Bosham.

"My boat is moored there and I can maybe check up on its moorings if we have time while we are there.

"That sounds perfect then. I've got the firm's car. I'll collect you first thing Friday at the Dockyard Gate. 0800 don't be late!" She sounded happy as she gave her instructions. Peter was, he believed, pleased though apprehensive at the same time.

"Was she pleased to hear from you?" Amy asked.

"Who… Oh yes, I think she was. I have a two day pass after my visit to Hamworthy. She suggested we spend the two days at her sister's place in Bosham. My boat is moored there, so I suggested we could check up on it while we were there. She sounded happy about it."

"Sounds good to me." Amy said. "What sort of boat have you got?"

"Forty foot sloop, four berth. I race her when I can."

"Wow, that sounds serious. You skipper her yourself?"

"Yes I do. Do you sail yourself?"

"I've crewed for a couple of boats from the Blackwater in Essex. My fiancée races *Catchpole*" She said simply.

"*Catchpole*. Now I think of it, I seem to recall racing against her in the Estuary series in 1938. I thought your name was familiar. You were nominated to helm for the cup at Cowes in the cancelled series. I think you are a little more than a crew-dog, young lady."

Peter wrote down the details of his yacht at Bosham. "She is called *Salamander*. If you and your fiancé are looking for somewhere to be together, be my guest. Give the yard manager this note and he'll let you through."

"That is very kind of you. I would love to see her if nothing else."

***

They arrived at the Marine Barracks in time for Peter to dump his bag in the Officers' Mess, before reporting to Major McNeil's office at 2100 precisely.

The Major turned out to be smart, stocky, and sandy haired, with icy blue eyes.

"I like punctuality." He said briskly. From his
desk he took a leather belt and holstered gun. He
pushed it into the hands of the rather surprised naval
officer. "You will live with that. For the next five
days you will wear it all times. Eat with it, sleep with
it, and use it as often as it is possible. In five days'
time you will wonder how you have lived all this
time without that gun by your side. It is a Browning
automatic, bored for 9mm ammunition. I took it from
a German officer who had it altered to his own speci-
fication. You will notice it has no identification numbers. It therefore does not exist. While you are here
neither do you."

He came around the desk and held his hand
out, taking and shaking Peter's.

The bemused Sub Lieutenant was led from the
room, gunbelt in hand, by the major.

***

The indoor range was lit so that the ten, and
twenty yard, targets were highlighted.

At the shooting point, there was a big man in
overalls waiting at ease. He snapped to attention
when they arrived.

"He's all yours for the next ninety minutes."
He turned to Peter. "Colour Sergeant Edwards will
issue you with overalls. You will wear them at all
times in this barracks. Here you will be known as
Captain Cotton. Your mess room is in that name. If
you believe that we are being ultra-cautious, it is because we are. You are not the first spook we have
trained."

Peter made to correct the Major, then realised it
made no difference and the secrecy was for his benefit.

The Major left and the Colour Sergeant took over. "Your overalls, sir."

Peter removed his jacket and slacks, and stepped into the overalls. They were multi pocketed and they had three sewn pips denoting the rank of captain on the shoulders. There was a Marine beret tucked into the breast pocket.

He turned to the Sergeant and waited. The gunbelt was held out to him. He accepted it and wrapped it round his waist. The dull leather holster hung at his hip. The automatic was retained by a snap strap across the butt, so that it would not jolt out of the holster in a tumble or when he ran.

"When you are on operations you secure the bottom of the holster with the tie around your leg. It stops the gun sticking in the holster when you need it in a hurry. Now draw your weapon…"

***

In the mess Captain Cotton found that there were several others about. But Stuart McNeil preempted any contact by joining him and suggesting an early night. He would start the day in Poole Harbour getting to know his kayak.

Early, in the Royal Marines, meant 0600. The bugle was not blown until 0700. That was normal time. Captain Cotton was on the quay at 0615, wishing he was still in Portsmouth. His weapon was on his hip with snap closed, and ties in place around his leg.

On the quay lay two canvas bundles which, he was assured, were boats. The man assembling them was adept at the task making it look easy. Peter was not fooled. He foresaw the problems that he would encounter, and quailed at the thought.

He was fed at 0715, and immediately returned to the battle with the folboats as they were called. By 1600 he was opening and closing the folboat as if he had been doing it all his life.

"Three rounds, rapid fire! Change hands. Left hand, single action, at your target in front, three rounds rapid fire."

In his bed that night he could hardly get to sleep. That relentless voice seemed to be shouting in his ear. He was shocked to find it was. He leapt out of bed and dragged on his overalls grabbing his gun he made for the range on the run. Once there, with his gunbelt in place, he was called to shoot 24 rounds at the targets.

Three days later he was scoring maximums while still half asleep. The kayak was assembled and in the water in two minutes. His skill with the paddle was still suspect but regarded as adequate, though it was suggested for future operations the course in boatmanship be extended.

On Wednesday evening Leading Wren Amy Lucas, drove him back to Portsmouth. The overalls were packed in his small suitcase. Peter was back in civilian clothes. His shirt was loose and his waist-band benefitted from the support of the gunbelt from which the holstered gun had been removed, safely wrapped with the overalls in the case.

"How was the course?" Amy asked.

"Exhausting!" Peter answered.

"Shall I let you sleep?" She suggested.

"Rather not. What has been happening for the last few days?"

"Graham remembers you and your boat. He said thanks for the offer. If he can, he will take you up on it."

Chapter five

The dark of the moon

Sub Lieutenant Peter Woods RNVR lay, fully clothed, on his bunk as the ML made its way across the Channel to its appointed drop point. He was recalling the past two days, spent at Bosham. Karen's sister had not been in evidence when he arrived. There had just been time to drop off his bag before they drove down to the moorings where his boat *Salamander* was moored. They had rowed out to her in a borrowed dinghy and climbed aboard. The cabin was pleasantly warm, a small greenhouse heater keeping the damp at bay. They threw open the hatches to let the fresh air in, and Peter switched on the engine to run it and power the electric stove. Karen looked around admiringly, "This is some boat, comfortable accommodation, too. She bounced on the double bunk in the forward cabin.

Peter was looking in lockers to see what tinned and dried food there was, when a bare arm slipped over his shoulder. The soft voice that accompanying it murmured, "Look what I've found." As he turned, he realised that the arm was attached to a naked body hauling him towards the bed. The other hand was undoing his shirt. In the circumstances there was only one thing a gentleman could do.

***

The two days passed too quickly for Peter, but there was no doubt they were enjoyable. He had been stunned when he parted company with Karen. Her pragmatic attitude at first shocked him, though he admitted as he made his way back to the naval base, that he was relieved.

Pleased for her that her fiancé was due on leave, but secretly delighted that she had chosen to introduce him to making love, that part of his education had been sadly lacking up to now. He had to admit that he had been attracted by Karen, but his disappointment when she had mentioned her fiancé was just that, disappointed! Not heartbroken.

He was brought down to earth in a hurry. The door crashed open to reveal Dingle Bell with a mug of kye. "Time to rise and shine, sir. Skipper says 40 minutes to drop point."

Peter took the mug. "Thanks, Dingle. I'll be there pronto."

***

The ML engine muttered quietly as the boat slipped between the headlands. Despite the lack of moonlight the loom of the near headland could be made out from water level. The northern headland was eight miles away. All that could be seen in that direction was the odd whitecap created by the wind flirting with the odd wave top. .

On the fore deck the two-man folboat lay already braced and locked ready for its passengers to take it ashore. The slate colour of the material made it easier to hide among the rocks on the foreshore. In the red-lit cabin Texas was looking at the chart of the area. He indicated a small creek. "That could be the best place for you to land. The rest of the frontage looks pretty open."

Michael Forbes smiled. "I agree, Captain. We plan to use the creek to get past the immediate shoreline. It is guarded about 400 metres inland, at the bridge taking the road along the coast. It is still the best place for us to make for. There are holiday homes and beach huts on both sides of the creek. We can conceal the folboat under one of the many boat piers on the way to the bridge.

Peter broke in. "It could also be a place where we could conceal a raiding party in the future. But for tonight I suggest we stick to the briefing. We need to be in and out without giving the enemy any warning that we are aware of what goes on here."

The voice of CPO Hebden interrupted the discussion. "We are coming up to the launch point, sir."

"Very good, Chief. We'll be up directly." The American accent of the skipper made the terribly English response sound odd, but nobody laughed.

Ranger Lee looked at the two men dressed in waterproof coveralls, over their civilian clothes. "If you have everything, gentlemen. Time to go."

On deck the folboat was dropped alongside. The two overalled men slid down and secured the waterproof aprons, preventing water getting into the boat around their seated figures. Peter took his double-bladed oar and secured the tether to one of the tie-downs on the deck. A second oar was passed down to Forbes in the forward seat, He secured it also, but he made no attempt to use it. Peter accepted a push off from the ML, took a look at his shielded compass, and started paddling. The sea was not rough and he soon fell into the rhythm. He had learned painfully at Hamworthy. Every thirty strokes he stopped and checked the compass, ensuring that he was keeping in roughly the right direction. They reached shore in twenty minutes. They found the river mouth almost immediately. Against the loom of the skyline the break showed up even on such a dark night. Carrying the boat between them the deposited it in the garden of the nearest deserted house. The long grass concealed it effectively.

Michael Forbes took the lead. Finding a small path up and over the dunes behind the beach he led Peter for half a mile through an orchard and over a field to a wire mesh fence.

As they approached the fence, the first real sign of extra security, in the form of a German soldier, appeared. The odd shape of his helmet caused Forbes to swear under his breath. "He is a paratrooper. They have brought in the elite troops to guard the place."

They lay there until it became obvious that, special troops or not, guarding this establishment was not a favoured task for the elite troops. They watched the man out of sight on his patrol line and waited for him to reappear. He took five minutes. When he departed again, Peter ran forward and – using his bolt cutters – he made two cuts in the base of the fence. Replacing the cut section in place he returned and waited with Forbes until the next circuit. After the guard passed once more, they both crawled through the cut section of the fence and made their way to the top of the slope. There they had a view of the basin below. Apart from the building, it was deserted as far as they could see.

Peter slid over the top of the slope and lay on the downslope out of the line of sight of the guard. He grabbed Forbes and yanked him over the top with him.

Ahead, outlined against the sky, was an angular shape. It appeared to be rotating. There was a flash of light as someone opened a door on the opposite side of the building below them. In that instant Peter realised the depth of the depression in the ground. They were lying on the slope with the whole of the object in view. The base was an octagonal concrete block-house with doors and windows all blacked out. From the centre of the roof projected what appeared to be an upright, mattress-shaped object rotating smoothly on bearings.

It was difficult to see clearly in the darkness, though it was not quite so intense within the depression. Peter realised that there was a leakage of ambient light which, once his eyes became accustomed to it, allowed him to see minimally at least. The mattress assembly glinted as it turned and Peter saw that there was an array of cones like loudspeakers in rows over the face of the assembly.

Michael Forbes studied the arrangements, pointing a small instrument at it. It beeped quietly every time the face of the array pointed in their direction.

Finally, Forbes put the instrument away and started to slide back up the slope. Peter stopped him, looking around carefully checking for the guard. He waited until the sentry passed them and only then slid down with Forbes.

At the fence Peter took care to replace the wire carefully, making sure that the cut section was not obvious.

The footpath back seemed to take longer than when they used it earlier. They reached the estuary. There they had to stop and wait while several soldiers crossed the road to the bridge. Then they located their boat and carried it round to the open beach, where they launched at the water's edge.

Using his compass once more, Peter paddled towards the open sea. Beyond the southern headland there was obviously some action taking place, the sound of machine guns and the odd flash of light from a heavier gun. Forbes started pointing a small torch ahead of them and flashing the light, keeping it shielded from the shore behind them. After Peter had paddled for twenty minutes, he checked the compass and listened. He moved the boat's head round to starboard and started paddling once more.

A few minutes later the sound of the muted engine of the ML could be heard.

***

The ML rounded the headland and joined in the general melee creating the diversion. The four other boats involved were circling a flak-ship, its guns silent. Flames were spurting from the superstructure, and she was settling in the water. As they watched, a lifeboat was dropped over the side and several bodies tumbled into it. As it pulled away, the stricken craft seemed to sink lower into the water. The boat exploded with a massive roar and scattered parts of its structure over a wide area of sea. The survivors in the lifeboat disappeared in the process. The stunned silence was broken by the cool voice of the skipper. "Time to go home, lads. Our Flotilla Leader is flashing even as I speak."

The laconic voice of Ranger Lee had its effect. Everyone came out of their temporary trance to carry on at their action stations. The group of ML's and MGB's formed up and set off across the channel, at 20 knots. "We are expecting to be intercepted on the way home, so make yourselves comfortable at your action station. It will be getting light during the next hour. From then on, it could be busy."

Forbes looked at the Skipper nervously, "Are we likely to be attacked?"

"I would say yes, the chances are pretty good that we will be. I am told that the RAF will be paying a call as the sky gets lighter. We may also have a visit from the Luftwaffe, hopefully the visits will coincide."

Forbes did not look reassured. He went below and sat in the cabin looking miserable.

Peter stripped off his overall, got back into his working gear and joined the skipper on the bridge.

"Everything go all right?" Texas asked.

"I think so. Forbes seemed pleased."

"Am I allowed to ask what you were looking at?"

Peter grinned. "I could tell you. But then I would have to kill you, I'm afraid."

"I noticed the tied-down holster. Can you use that thing?"

In his best Texas accent Peter said, "If I had notches for all the targets ah killed, there would be no buttplates left on mah gun."

The Skipper chuckled, "If yew try thet accent out on me agin, ah'l hev tew haul out mah own smokepole 'n put yew in boot hill."

"On that note I will organise sandwiches and tea for the staff, before I assume my normal role." Peter went below and called Dingle Bell to make sandwiches and a brew, while it was still quiet.

***

To the horror of Michael Forbes, the Luftwaffe lived up to expectation and appeared shortly after dawn. To his relief the RAF arrived three minutes later, after the guns of the flotilla had opened up. The ensuing dogfight strayed back toward the French coast leaving the boats to continue unchecked toward Portsmouth.

There was no more activity recorded for the rest of the journey. Forbes was delivered along with

Peter Woods into the hands of Intelligence Officers from London.

***

Having been ordered to London at short notice, Peter grabbed his overnight kit and, remembering Chris DeNeuve and the address she had given him, he joined Michael Forbes in the car laid on for them. Forbes spent most of the journey buried in his notes, so Peter checked with the driver the location of the address he had for Chris and her friend, Alice Worth.

"Dolphin Court, it's on our way to the Embankment. I'll point it out as we pass. It's not far from Millbank, where I deliver you both."

In due course they arrived. After a brief interview, Forbes, having been hastily taken away as soon as their documents were checked, Peter was instructed to report the following day to a room in the Millbank building. Meanwhile he was told to make himself scarce until then.

The rather precious, army Captain actually said, "Just bugger off until tomorrow old chap. Report at 1100, and for god's sake don't turn up stinking of booze."

At that rather odd point, Peter saluted and left the building.

***

It was a pleasant afternoon so he turned and strolled back up the road along the riverside to Dolphin Court.

He studied the address, shrugged his shoulders and entered the building. The receptionist looked up at the tall Naval Officer before her and, deciding he looked nice, smiled and asked "Is there anything I can do for you, sir?"

"Yes, I believe there is Miss Worth and a Miss DeNeuve living here. I wondered if I could be directed to apartment 7?"

"I will call and see if they are in. Who shall I say is calling?"

"Peter Woods, for Miss DeNeuve."

She dialled a number and, after a few moments, spoke quietly. Peter could not hear what she said, but she nodded, put the phone down, and pointed to double doors on the right of the lobby. "Down the corridor, the last door on the right." She smiled. "Good luck," she said for no reason at all.

Peter found the door ajar when he reached it. So he knocked and was told to come in.

He closed the door behind him and found himself in a lounge area, fitted carpet and settee arm chairs and coffee table, a sideboard by the wall and a small dining table and chairs in the window bay. The door at the rear of the room opened and Chris appeared, looking fresh and even more beautiful than he had remembered. She stopped and noticing his bag, asked, "Just arrived in town? Bathroom is through here. Sorry about the washing. There is nowhere else to hang it."

Peter went through into the bathroom trying to avoid looking at the line of underwear suspended above the bath. He splashed some water on his face, used the toilet and turned to leave, having knocked more underwear to the floor from the towel rail. Despite being alone, he blushed as he picked up the silky knickers and replaced them on the towel rail.

Back in the lounge still flushed, he pointed to his bag and said, "I called before I checked in at the Club."

Chris grinned, "You were anxious to see me. I understand."

Peter noticed the twinkle in her eye. "I could not wait to see my future fiancée once more would be more accurate."

He was rewarded by her reaction. She went pink at his words, then stepped up to him, "Don't I even get a kiss?"

He seized the moment and kissed her folding her into his arms to make the most of the moment.

He was startled by her reaction, feeling her arms slip round his neck, and her body relax against him.

They parted when breathing was becoming difficult. At least that was the way it seemed to Peter.

Chris laughed nervously and produced her compact to check her makeup. "Well, now the formalities are over, shall we go out?"

Peter picked up his bag and opened the door. As he closed it Chris lifted a tissue and wiped the lipstick from his mouth. "There. Now that little minx in reception will have less to talk about. Taking his arm they walked down the corridor side by side like old friends.

They dropped his bag off at the Union Jack Club, and went to the Trocadero for an early dinner, followed by a show.

***

Walking back to Dolphin Square, they found they could relax in each other's company without the need to force conversation. The warmth, which seemed to have just happened between them, persisted and seemed to deepen the longer they were together. He found there had been a fiancé, but it had not worked out. She found that he had occasional girlfriends but there was no one current.

The twinkle was back in her eye when she asked, "Does this mean you are preparing the way for our future engagement and perhaps marriage?"

Peter immediately replied, "Of course. Did you ever doubt it?"

"Just checking." Chris replied. "When did you anticipate announcing our engagement."

"It did occur to me that I should probably clear it with your parents before I went to that stage. Otherwise there is only the ring to negotiate. Did you have any thoughts on the matter yourself?"

"The parents are probably a good idea. Might be as well not to rock the boat too much, I suppose. The ring should not be too difficult. There are several jewellers still open in London. How long can I have you for?" She said innocently.

"Well, I'm supposed to be here for three days. And I don't report until 11:00 tomorrow."

"Ah." She said.

"What does that mean?" He asked quickly.

"Oh, nothing really. Just that I will have to wait until tomorrow, I suppose."

Peter stopped suddenly and faced her. He pulled the ring from his little finger, and lifted her left hand. Slipping the ring onto the third finger of her hand, he said, "There. Until I get the real thing tomorrow. We are engaged."

She looked at him suddenly serious. "But...."

"But what? Am I serious? Am I making fun of you?"

"Well, are you?"

"How about you? Have you been pulling my leg, leading me on?"

Chris thought for a moment, "Actually, no!"

Peter smiled ruefully. "Oops. I am hoist with my own petard it seems, whatever that is. I walked right into that one, I guess I will have to marry you after all!"

"What is it to be? Will you marry me? Or is this just a joke that went wrong?"

Chris looked at Peter seriously. "I believe I will. Yes. The answer is yes."

Peter looked at her stunned for an instant, then he swept her up in his arms, and kissed her.

Her enthusiastic acceptance of his kiss was an affirmation of the offer made and accepted.

By mutual agreement they agreed to keep it between them until there was more time to arrange things. As they continued on their way, Chris turned the ring on her finger. It was a wedding ring, just a little too big for her. "Where does this ring come from?" She asked.

"It was my grandmother's."

"I will have it altered a little when we get married, if that is all right. Meanwhile, I will keep it on a chain around my neck. An engagement ring can wait until we make a formal announcement. What do you think?"

"I think that is a very good idea, and I am delighted that you are going to keep Granny's ring."

They reached the apartment block and entered the lobby. The night porter on duty greeted Chris, "Good evening, Miss DeNeuve. Miss Worth left a message." He passed over the note.

"Thank you Charlie, come on in, Peter." She opened the note and read it. "We won't be disturbing Alice at least. She is away till next week."

In the apartment, Chris disappeared into the bathroom while Peter put the kettle on in the small kitchenette. Chris returned. "Don't bother with the kettle. I've got some gin here and tonic in the fridge."

Peter joined her on the settee as she prepared the gin and tonic. She placed the glasses on the table and seated herself next to him. She fingered the ring, then looked up at him. "Did you really mean what you said tonight?"

"What particular thing are you talking about?" He said innocently.

She looked at him warningly.

He gave in. "All right. Yes. I meant every word, and I can tell you now. On the day we first met and I mentioned our possible future, I had already decided that it was the future I wanted. So there it is. I fell in love when I first saw you. Nothing since has caused me to change my mind."

Chapter six

The Raid

The training facility at the Royal Marine Base at Hamworthy was busy. In one small gymnasium a special course of training was being undertaken by a special group of trainees.

Peter Woods had not volunteered for this course. But since he had volunteered to take part in the raid on the site identified by Michael Forbes, he accepted the need for an additional training program.

The other members of the course were preparing to be dropped in Europe as part of the SOE, the army of men and women supporting the underground organisations in Axis-occupied countries. Whilst his earlier training had already fitted him with new skills, this was an extension of that course entailing instruction in survival and included killing in a hand-to-hand situation. This meant learning to face and overcome your enemy, using the famous commando knife, the invention of William Fairburn, former Shanghai Police officer. The Fairburn knife was designed solely for killing, and as such, used by commandos, and in this case by the SOE.

In addition to his weapons' training with gun, knife and garrotte, Peter had to undergo the infamous assault course, which entailed training of a different sort. Every afternoon for the entire two weeks was spent on exhausting runs, carrying varying loads of rocks in a rucksack. Peter had been fit before he arrived at Hamworthy. At the end of the first week he was exhausted. By Friday of the second week he realised that his afternoon runs were no longer torture. The assault course on Saturday was not a picnic, but nor was it a killer. He accomplished it in the time, and shot a reasonable score at the end of it. Of the SOE operatives sharing the course, none took the afternoon training.

***

He boarded ML3 at the Marine base in Poole Harbour. A platoon of Royal Marines was split between ML3, Ranger Lee's boat, and Norman Warrender's No. 1 boat. Michael Forbes appeared and joined the party.

The two boats rendezvoused with the mixed group of MGB's, ML's, and MTB's. It was the biggest flotilla that Peter had been involved with.

They set off in the early evening, then split into three groups ready to rejoin later for the attack on a coastal convoy, which included an escort of three German destroyers.

The two ML's with the assault group made directly for their target. They needed to arrive in time for the commencement of the convoy attack.

Unlike the last visit, the weather at the French coast was overcast. So there was not even starlight to give the raiders even minimal help with locating their target. The rubber dinghies used held eight men. As on the first occasion, Peter was sharing the folboat with Michael Forbes. They followed the first dinghy. The others followed.

At the beach Peter held off, while the advance party landed and signalled that the beach was clear using a small shaded light.

Between them they hauled the folboat up the beach, and left it against the foot of the wall with the first boat.

Peter stayed with Forbes as they followed the leading group through the silent houses of the deserted village, then over to the location of the odd building with what Peter described as a rotating mattress. He had been told in secret that it was an RDF unit.

The Marine Lieutenant, Alec Stuart, checked his men at the wire fence. Peter waited for the sentry to make his circuit, and then went forward to see if his cut section had been discovered.

He had difficulty finding it at first. But when he did he was not surprised that the cuts had not been discovered. The long grass grew unchecked all around the area. He whispered to the Marine officer. "Over here!" Stuart and Forbes arrived together. The Marine signalled his men and, assigning one man to stay at the wire to see the others through, led the others through, followed immediately by Forbes and Peter.

Inside the wire, Peter took the lead and showed the group where to position themselves to see the target.

It was with some relief that Forbes, after checking with his small meter, verified that nothing had changed. Their last visit had not been discovered.

The remainder of the men joined them, the sentry having been removed. The first group now went to cover the door of the building. The rotating mattress made a creaking noise as it turned. Stuart opened the door carefully. A streak of light appeared, so he flung the door wide and dashed in sten-gun up and ready.

Inside the building was one big room, with four men seated at desks and two soldiers seated on a bench against the far wall. There was a box with a red button on the wall near the bench. The Lieutenant shouted, "Nein!" But the soldier ignored him, and went for it. Three bullets hit his chest and he collapsed to the floor dead.

The others in the room held their hands up. Peter came in with Forbes who immediately started to examine the equipment, deciding what to take and what to leave. Peter stared to disconnect units at his direction.

Forbes turned to Lieutenant Stuart. "All these people go with us. Have all the papers here gathered. We will take them with us as well. When we leave there must be an explosion and the entire place destroyed. Nothing must survive. Do you understand?"

Stuart nodded, indicating the man who was placing small blocks of material joined together with wires all around the walls, "That his job. He knows what he is doing."

Apparently satisfied, Forbes returned to his assessment of the equipment. Peter assisted the unit sergeant tying up the operators. The surviving German soldier was already bound and gagged.

Elsewhere in the room two of the Marines had tipped a cabinet on its back and were loading all the paperwork they could find into it. At the far end of the wall the explosives expert lit a fuse. A ring of fire appeared all around the door of the round safe they had found behind a picture of Adolf Hitler. Having lit the fuse, he turned back to the job of rigging the place to explode, ignoring his handiwork with the safe.

The door of the safe fell off and dropped the floor with a clang. Forbes went to the safe and, taking care to avoid the still-smoking-burnt door frame, he withdrew several files and packages. A glance at the files was enough for him to place them in his bag. Peter collected all the other contents, placing them in his own bag.

The various machine parts selected from the blockhouse, were now all on their way back to the beach. The prisoners having been linked together with a rope started out for the boats. Forbes went with them.

When all were gone except Alec Stuart and Peter, they looked at each other and by mutual agreement turned and left the building.

On the way out Stuart shut the door. He waited listening, heard the click of the timer, the circuit having been completed by the closing of the metal door.

"What happens if someone opens the door now?" He asked.

Stuart grinned. "Kerbooooomb!" He said and turned to lead the way back to the beach.

***

The two ML's joined the others in the dying moments of the convoy attack. The lead destroyer had hit a mine and had sunk before the attack had got started. One of the others was still firing her main armament at the elusive power boats dashing in and out of the convoy, using the ships as cover. Several of his shells missed, to the extent of hitting the shore line. When the target blew, the explosion was just one of many at the time. The other destroyer was down by the head, her screws, creating a heap of white water as she struggled to make way. Her guns still in action, but with her head sinking deeper, her fate was sealed. The attacking force had lost two MGB's. An ML was dead in the water, receiving a tow line from another boat. Of the others, none was without scars or injury of one sort or another. The convoy however had really suffered. Three of the ships were sinking. Another was blazing from stem to stern, heeling over at an alarming angle, the waters around littered with the bodies from its cargo of troops. The stern was all that could be seen of the fifth. The sixth was suffering from a damaged rudder. It was running at twelve knots pointing its bow at the headland, directly ahead. Men were leaping into the water, despite the speed of the ship. They were too late to save themselves. As the tanker struck, the tanks full of aviation fuel exploded, and the entire area of sea around it seemed to burst into flame. It engulfed the trail of fuel that had spilled from holes in the tanks.

The unfortunate crew men who had jumped were all engulfed in the burning fuel.

Michael Forbes looked at the savage scene and went below, sickened and horrified.

Peter Woods joined the skipper on the bridge with a mug of kye. "It's been a busy night all round it seems."

Texas looked at him over the rim of his mug. "Weren't you bothered, chasing around the country in the dark." He amended it. "Enemy country, that is!"

Peter thought about it. "You know, I didn't think about it. As far as I was concerned, the training they insisted on was so bloody brutal, it made performing the actual operation a piece of cake."

Texas shrugged. "Well, as far as I am concerned, I will stick to the boats. Will you be back with us soon?"

"Not at the moment I understand. But I do believe this boat will be first choice for any spy dropping or collecting in future."

***

It was Amy who drove Peter back to Portsmouth. The de-brief for the operation had been held in Hamworthy. The boats had dropped the landing party, their loot and the prisoners at the Marine Base and then returned to Portsmouth.

Forbes and the captured operators from the site disappeared immediately, vaguely toward London. Peter and the Marine party stayed to be questioned on the base. They released Peter to return to Portsmouth, after lunch the following day.

Amy was not her normal cheery self. Peter noticed, as soon as they set off.

"What's up, Amy? He asked quietly.

In a weary voice she said, "Oh, it's the old story I'm afraid. I received a 'Dear Amy' letter from Graham yesterday."

"Ouch! That was unexpected. What was his excuse?"

"I suppose it's the usual thing these days. Life expectancy short, local girl on the spot, long-distance romance not enough." Her voice broke, "It's not fair. I did not expect that from Graham."

Peter could hear the break in her voice. "Can we stop at the pub on the way?" He asked.

"Yes, alright." Amy said shortly. "Got a phone call to make, I suppose?"

She sounds a touch bitter, Peter thought.

***

They were silent until they reached the pub. There she pulled over and sat waiting while he got out. Amy made no attempt to move.

Peter opened her door, "Out!" He said.

Startled, she looked up at him. He gestured. So she got out of the car. He took her arm and steered her through the door into the bar.

"Hullo, you two. Back again, I see." The landlord realised that there was something wrong from the look on Amy's face. Guessing she may have lost somebody close to her, he quietly said, "What can I get you today?"

Peter looked at Amy. "Brandy?"

She shook her head. "Perhaps a sherry, no more."

The barman turned and drew a small sherry from the small barrel behind the bar and a pint of bitter for Peter.

As Peter went to pay for it, the landlord said quietly, "On the house." He left them to it.

At their table, Peter sat beside Amy and said quietly, "Right. Tell me all about it."

Amy took a sip of the sherry and grimaced, "There is nothing really to tell." She reached into her pocket and produced a folded letter. "See for yourself."

Opening the folded paper, Peter smoothed it out and started to read.

Dear Amy,

I'm sure you must feel as frustrated as I have been over the past few months. I used to miss you terribly, all the time. Last time we got together I realised that we were growing apart, and I got back to base feeling unhappy. I found I was not alone in my misery.

One of the WAAF officers here, Janice, had just found out that her fiancé stationed at Biggin Hill had got a local girl pregnant. He had written to her and broken off the engagement. One thing led to another and we found we had a lot in common.

And, to put it in a nutshell, we have become engaged. We have arranged to get married on Thursday.

Sorry to break it like this but I could not think of any other way.

I hope things work out for you. I'm sure they will.

Best wishes,
Graham

He read it again, then folded it up and passed it back to Amy. There was nothing really to say, but he found some words anyway. "You may not realise it at the moment, but just think about it as a lucky escape. Suppose you had been married. It seems that there are some people in this world who never recognise a good thing when it's staring them in the face. It's his loss."

He took her hand. It was cold, so he warmed it between his two. "You have friends here, in Hamworthy, and in me. We are still here and, however bad things look at the moment, you are needed, doing your job. You are important to all of us. And don't forget I'll need a crew for *Salamander* when we get a chance to sail her again. The offer, to use her when you have time off, still stands by the way."

Amy took her hand back. "Thanks Peter. You do have a way with words. I may well take you up on the boat offer one of these days. We had better drink up. We need to get going again."

The barman came round to see if they needed more drinks. Amy got up and kissed him on the cheek. "Thanks for the drinks. We will be back."

"You'll be welcome." A little bemused, but feeling rather pleased with himself, the landlord saw them off.

Chapter seven

In the midst of life

Back in harness, Peter was soon involved in the normal routine of patrols, convoy escorts and the odd raid. Over the next months, he had small chance to see Chris. They spoke on the phone as often as they could. There were several secret drops made in Europe during that time. As he anticipated, when a landing in France was scheduled, the Number 3 boat was usually detailed for the task, He was designated as landing officer, whenever one was required, and was required to do regular training sessions as a result.

It was no real surprise when Chris appeared in her role as SOE operative, in charge of a group of three agents, one of whom was Monroe.

An opportunity came to speak to her, on the deck of the boat out of the hearing of the others. After exchanging a discrete hug and a kiss he asked, "What is Monroe doing with your party?" He asked. "I thought he was suspect?"

"They decided we were mistaken. Since he is an expert in locks, and speaks fluent German and French, they decided to take a risk."

"What about you? How do you feel about it?"

"I'm not sure, but I have my eye on him. Caesar, my partner is very quick and expert, and never trusted him in the first place. So he will be there if things go wrong."

Peter took her hand as they stood by the rail, overlooking the white wash of water marking the boat's progress through the water. She squeezed his hand. "We should be able to meet in two weeks. I will be back by then, I am told by air. If you can get away that is."

Peter smiled grimly. "I'll make a point of it."

"Just in case, call Alice. You have the number." She kissed his cheek salty with spray. "I'll see you then."

He saw her down to the main cabin and looked at his watch. To the landing party he said, "We'll be there in 30 minutes. Please collect all your gear ready to load into the dinghy. We will not be able to hang about tonight. Moonrise could catch us out if we delay."

***

Back on the bridge, Texas turned to him. "Got news for you, now you've managed to tear yourself away from that gorgeous lady."

Peter grinned. "Please tell me that you, the 'Adonis' of Portsmouth nightlife, are not jealous of your poor young sidekick?"

"Listen, 'Quimo Sabe.' The Lone Ranger is jealous of nobody. Get it! I am just acknowledging that there are other beautiful women in this world whom I have not yet got round to. Does that answer your question?"

"So what is this news you have for me, sir?" Peter said formally.

"Well, against my better judgement in the circumstances, you will be told tomorrow anyway. Your second stripe has been gazetted, and you will be transferred and given a command of your own. I believe you will be part of a new flotilla. You'll learn all about it from the Commander." He checked his watch in the light of the compass repeater. "We are approaching Wimereux just about now, I believe. Get them ashore as quick as possible. Moonrise was three hours ago and though this overcast is forecast for twelve hours, they have been known to be wrong."

***

The dinghy dropped into the water with a soft splash. The gear of the landing party as dropped and stowed, before the three members of the SOE group seated themselves. The small electric outboard motor murmured into life. In the bows LS Watts crouched with his Thompson sub-machine gun ready for any nasty surprises as they stepped ashore.

The landing was smooth and unopposed. All three were loaded up with their gear while Watts stood guard. Peter accompanied them to the roadside, where transport waited to take them on to their first port of call.

The van was where it was expected to be, so Peter said, "Good luck," and left the party to take the van. He turned with Watts to go back to the dinghy. They were out of sight of the van when they heard the altercation behind them. Peter turned back to see what was going on.

In the distance a vehicle was approaching the van from the south, another from the north. The group were standing in the road. Caesar shouted to the other two to be quiet and stand still.

Peter watched from the shadows on the road verge, unseen by the trio. Caesar had his gun in his hand pointing at the other two. As he watched, Caesar shot Monroe with a silenced pistol. "I don't need you," he said. He turned to Chris. The pistol lined up, keeping Chris covered, he said, "I've got you at last. My masters will be pleased."

Peter, without thinking, lifted the 9mm from his holster and in one smooth movement, shot Caesar. The two vehicles were approaching fast, so Peter called to Watts, "Get back to the boat. I'll try and signal for pick-up at our last landing spot."

While Watts scrambled back to the beach, Peter ran across the road calling to Chris. "Are they both dead?"

She said, "Yes."

Grabbing the gear they turned to the van, standing with the key in it as arranged. Chris took the wheel,

"Straight ahead." Peter shouted. Chris put the van in gear and drove straight at the vehicle approaching from the north. The driver was shocked as the van gained speed and drove directly at him head on. He lost his nerve and swerved to avoid the collision. The rear of his small truck clipped the rear of the van, ripping the bumper from the speeding vehicle. The unfortunate driver found himself heading for the steep slope down to the beach. He wrenched the wheel back toward the road. Combined with the impact from the escaping van, the small truck turned and rolled, spilling men and equipment across the path of the vehicle approaching from the other direction. That unfortunate driver ended up impaled on the steering column and consequently beyond punishment, having inadvertently prevented the capture of the female agent.

As she drove, Chris explained to Peter that the plan for the trio was to contact the local underground and set up an operation to unmask the spy in their organisation.

Caesar had been on the list, as had Monroe and Chris. "In these circumstances, everyone is suspect. Some a little more than others. So we were all aware of the outline. What we did not know was who the spy was.

"It seems that Caesar fooled us. We all thought it was Monroe. After the last operation he denied he had tried to surrender to the Germans. He said he had been held upright by Caesar, who had then made all three of us hit the water.

"Because of the doubts, this little sting was set-up to clear the matter up. The presence of the spy has cost us several cells and six agents over the past year."

"So, what do we do now?" Peter asked.

"We get rid of this gear and return to England. I'm heading for the rendezvous now."

"Where is that?"

"Just beyond Cap Gris-Nez. There is a way to the beach under the Cape itself. We leave the gear there with the van. They will lay on a pick-up for me—us, I suppose."

Peter looked at his watch. "If we can be at Wissant on the beach within two hours, the boat will pick us up tonight. At worst, arrange a later pick-up, if it is not possible for some reason at the time. The timing is critical because moonset will be then; dawn follows within forty minutes so we do not have a big window."

"We will be at Gris-Nez in twenty minutes or so. We have time." She sounded cheerful enough, but Peter felt there was something wrong.

"Pull over, please."

"Why? we must hurry. Time is getting on." Chris suddenly sounded tired."

Peter steered the wheel to the roadside, against her weakening grip.

"Where are you hurt?" He demanded.

She fell back from the wheel. Peter opened her coat. There was blood leaking through her clothes from a wound low just above her pelvis. "How did this happen?"

"Caesar fired as he dropped."

"You should have told me," Peter said. "Where is the first-aid kit?"

"Black bag," she gasped, now in serious pain.

Peter located the bag, and found a dressing pad which he pressed onto the wound. "Can you hold that in place?" He asked.

"I've got it," Chris said.

Peter found plasters and tape. Using another dressing pad on top of the first, he taped them into position. He then took the wheel and drove to Gris-Nez.

"Where?" He asked.

"The Tea Room," she gasped.

He found the shop down the track to the beach, stopped outside and met the occupants at the rear of the van.

"Hurry," he said. "My companion is wound-ed."

They quickly took the bags from the car. Peter slammed the doors and jumped back into the van. He reversed up the road to a point where he could turn and returned to the main road.

They arrived at Wissant with time in hand and Peter drove to the beach house off the main road. There was a German control box situated at the end of the road, with a red barrier.

The Feldwebel in charge was in a bad mood. He had been found out by the Oberleutenant, caught

making profit from the efforts of two local prosti-
tutes, hence the night duty at the barrier, and a promise of further action in future.

As the van drew up at the barrier he shouted at
the other man in the small office to get outside and
see who the devil was driving about at this time of
the night.

He lifted his head, noticing an officer getting
out of the van and approaching the guard. He sighed
in exasperation. Officers always wanted the senior
man to attend them.

Peter had leapt out of the car and approached
the single guard who had come out to the barrier.

The guard, seeing Peter's uniform in the semi-
dark of the dim light from the box and the van's
headlights, snapped to attention.

Peter shouted, "Vorsicht!" and pointed. The
guard swung his head around to see what Peter had
pointed at. The Fairburn knife was as deadly as it was
reputed to be. Peter grabbed the body and lowered it
to the ground.

He stepped into the control box where the
Feldwebel was still rising to his feet, he never made
it. The second victim of the Fairbairn died on his
feet.

Peter left the two bodies and raised the barrier.

Back in the van he drove down to one of the
empty beach houses. He dragged open the garage
doors on the furthest. Only then did he help Chris out
of the van and into the beach house. Leaving her on
the settee in the living room, he returned to the van
and reversed up to the barrier.

Dragging both men to the van he hauled them
in, then went and covered the blood on the ground
with sand. There was none in the office luckily, but
he took all the personal things he could see from the

office and both the men's weapons. Closing the barrier down and making sure it was locked, he rolled the van forward once more, scattering sand across the new tracks to make them look old. He arrived back at the garage. drove the van in and shut the doors. With luck, they might think the soldiers had deserted.

Looking at his watch, he decided he had ten minutes still before moonset.

Back with Chris, he could see she was not looking good. He hung her satchel bag around his neck and gathered her in his arms and set off down the beach.

***

Christine DeNeuve died on the way back to Portsmouth, despite all Dingle Bell could do.

"She had lost too much blood." He told Peter. She must have been shot before you left the landing place.

Caesar, Peter thought, won *in the end.*

***

The enquiry took time. Peter was there to give evidence, and attend the funeral. Chris was buried with honours.

His promotion to Lieutenant and the new command was a help in keeping his mind off his personal problems. The new boat was an improved version of number three.

She was a Type A Fairmile with extras. Her engines were an improved version giving her an extra 2 knots top speed. The engineer artificer he had been given reckoned that, with his personal delicate touch, he could probably get a little extra on top of that. The main armament was a three pounder gun, forward and two .303 machine guns mounted either side of the bridge. Aft there were two Oerlikons on individual mounts, as well as twin depth charge racks at the stern. The accommodation had been upgraded, as it was expected the crew would live aboard, where possible. Her electrics had been fitted to accept mains power in addition to battery power from an on-board generator. Her paintwork was a broken pattern of light and dark, designed to make her blend into the background.

The purpose of the Special Service flotilla was still not designated, though the training seemed to be directed at commando operations, rather than the regular donkey work of other ML flotillas.

Peter was allocated a Sub-Lieutenant, and a Midshipman plus fourteen specialists and Able seamen, with a PO Engineer and Chief Petty Officer Cox'n. The Leading Seaman Torpedo Gunner controlled the depth charges in action and supervised the gunners elsewhere on the boat.

Personally, Peter felt frozen inside. His life seemed to be on hold while he coped with the death of Chris. Just three weeks after taking command of his new boat, a familiar car drew up on the quay at the Poole yacht club, now the Special Services base. The Leading Wren driver drew the attention of all the male eyes present as she stepped out of the car with a package in her hand. She walked over to the nearest man and asked for Lieutenant Woods.

Charlie Procter, Leading Signaller on the number six boat, pointed to the gangway, "The Skipper is on board," he said with a smile. He was rewarded likewise, plus an elegant rear view as she stepped carefully down the gangway to the boat lying just below the level of the quay. Midshipman Colin Willis looked admiringly at the Wren standing in front of him. Amy repeated her request for Lieutenant Woods.

"Oh! I beg your pardon, Miss…Ah, this way, please."

Peter looked up as Willis stood in the door of his cabin. "What's up, Colin? You look as if you swallowed a frog?"

"Sorry, sir. There is this visitor, sir."

"Well, show him in."

"It's not a him, sir. It's a her."

"Midshipman Willis! Show the visitor in."

Turning, Colin beckoned Amy forward. "The Skipper will see you now, Miss."

He stood there for a moment. Then, realising it was not his place, he hurriedly left.

Amy stepped through the door and saluted, banging her elbow on the door. Peter looked at her and smiled. "And that, young lady, is why we do not salute below decks."

He stood and stepped round the small desk to face her. "How are you Amy. I have missed our trips to and from Portsmouth."

"Me too," she said. "And how are you. I heard the news, but there was no way at the time that I could contact you."

"There was nothing you could do really."

"I could have held your hand, just as you held mine."

He smiled. "Well, you are now."

Amy blushed and let go of Peter's hand. "Sorry, I didn't realise…"

"No need to apologise between friends. Sit and tell me what is happening with you these days?"

Amy sat on the bunk, the only other place to sit the small cabin. She placed the packet on the desk.

"Whoops, nearly forgot what I came for!" She pushed the package over the desk.

Peter looked at it. "What's this, then." There was an Admiralty seal on the flap, and a note 'to be signed for' by hand.

He signed the receipt and opened the flap breaking the seal. Inside there was a book and a letter with his name written by hand on the envelope.

Peter looked at Amy. She looked back suddenly concerned.

He opened the letter. A gold ring dropped out and rolled across the desk. Amy reached out, stopping it rolling off the desk and dropping to the deck.

Peter ignored the ring and read the letter.

> *Dear Peter,*
>
> *If you are reading this then I am no longer with you. In this job as you of all people know, there is never any doubt that death is a constant companion.*
>
> *I have written this letter to reassure you, that, in other circumstances, I would have been with you for the rest of my life. Since that can no longer happen I pray you will meet and marry in good time, and pass your grandmother's ring to your future wife.*
>
> *I love you,*
> *Chris*

Peter sat very still. Then he picked up the book. It was old and the cover had been worn by readers over the years. There was a small note tucked into the book. *'For Peter, love, Chris.'*

Peter looked at the book and read the note. He silently passed the book to Amy.

It was '*Sailing alone round the World*' by Captain Joshua Slocum. It was a first edition.

Peter stood and left the cabin. He stopped Amy from rising to come with him. Up on deck he stood allowing the breeze to ruffle his hair, and quietly, between himself and the elements, said goodbye to Chris.

He returned to his cabin below. Amy sat with tears in her eyes and Chris's letter in her hand. "Oh, Peter. I didn't know what was in the package. I'm so sorry."

Dry-eyed, he lifted her chin and looked at her. "I'm not. You are my friend. Perhaps someone realised that. I think. I know. I feel better, certainly, than I have been feeling for the past month. That is due to Chris's letter, and seeing you. I've missed our chats and the pub.

"I've got to go to London for a briefing with the other flotilla Skippers. It's a Monday morning do. Most of us will go up on Friday night. If you like, if you can wangle Friday evening or Saturday off, perhaps we could visit the pub, maybe go and see the boat?"

Amy dried her eyes and looked at him, considering. Then she said, "I'm owed a few favours. I can probably manage, but......?"

"There are no strings attached," Peter said. "I seem to feel that we've known each other for ages, though I know we haven't, in reality. I just would like to be normal for a while, with someone I know and like, who won't make demands on me. So what do you say?"

"Friday night, but we'll need transport. Saturday is not a problem. I have the weekend off." She smiled. "The pub is a bit far to walk!"

"I have that sorted out. Hector Stuart has asked me to look after his Morgan while he is on a course at Fort William. He is away for six weeks, so transport is not a problem. If we go to the boat, it might be an idea to bring overnight things. There is plenty of room, but just in case anyway? It's up to you. You can decide at the time." He looked at her waiting.

"We start with Friday night, 1900, outside the gate at the barracks."

"Thanks for coming," Peter said. "I really appreciate it."

***

As she drove back, Amy thought, *If he did but know how much arm twisting I had to do to be given the job of delivering that package, only to find that nobody else had wanted to take it, because they all knew it was bad news.*

Chapter eight

One day at a time

The Special Service flotilla sailed out of their base into the Channel. They collected the group of ships assembled in Weymouth Bay and, stationed around their convoy, they started out up-channel to hand the convoy over to another flotilla off Eastbourne, for the next part of its journey. The convoy's final destination was Tilbury. As they approached Eastbourne, flashes and sound of gunfire signalled an enemy attack on their relieving flotilla.

Lt Commander Danny Oliver signaled Peter and Adrian Quirk to join him with their boats, which left the convoy to the remaining three boats, while he investigated the situation up ahead.

As the three boats swept into view, flashes revealed the ML's having a face-off with three E boats, and a flak-ship. The flak-ship was armoured and the guns on the ML's was not really heavy enough to do more than dent it here and there. Meanwhile, it was doing damage with 40mm cannon, and a heavier gun which Peter thought might be an 88mm, perhaps one of the tank guns carried by the German Tiger tanks.

The three extra boats meant the enemy was outnumbered. All three of the newcomers concentrated on the flack-ship.

Peter called to the Chief, "We'll go for a depth charge drop."

"Aye, aye, Skipper."

He pressed the buzzer and spoke to the TGM at the Depth Charge rails. "Shallow setting, stand by to fire." The three pounder gun and the Oerlikons were hammering away at the gun positions on the flak-ship. As the flotilla leader swept past the bow, Peter closed on her stern and dropped his charges there. The explosion lifted the stern of the target to reveal the tangled remains of her twin screws, and a gaping hole in her hull.

The ship smashed down into the water once more. The power appeared to be cut off. The rate of fire slowed right down. The big gun, now pointing too high to affect the attacking boats, was silenced. The smaller shells from the three boats' main guns were now taking effect.

The flak-ship sank by the stern until she tipped-up. With bows raised to the sky she went under. The three boats turned to help with the E boats, who soon decided enough was enough. One was damaged so badly she could not make it away from the fight. The others left her to die alone, making their way off toward Belgium and their base at Ostend.

When the boats returned to base in Portsmouth. Peter looked longingly at Christchurch harbour as they passed.

***

Back at base with the boats tied up and repairs undertaken, Peter checked up on the Morgan. The little three-wheeler could get about in fine style. He looked forward to Friday and a chance to relax completely for a while. He wondered about Amy. Maybe he should not have asked her to keep him company. But he did not really want to be alone.

He shrugged So what? It will either be okay, or it won't. They were only friends after all. There was not the complication of past love at issue.

19:00 hours, on Friday, Peter parked to one side of the gate of the barracks, waiting for Amy. Ten minutes past and he was beginning to get anxious, thinking that something might have come up. He had not asked if she had a boyfriend. Perhaps she had and he had objected?

At 19:45 Amy finally appeared, trotting out of the gate, looking anxiously to see if he was there. He waved, struggling to get out of the car, but gave up when she noticed him.

She arrived, breathless. "I'm sorry. I was later back than I expected to be and everything went wrong. Where do I put my bag?"

Peter decided to struggle out of the seat, and showed her how to attach her bag to the rack behind the two seats.

When they had both piled into the car, Peter set off for the pub on the Ringwood road.

With the roar of the engine and the wind in their faces it was difficult to talk. So it wasn't until they were walking into the pub that they could hold a conversation.

The landlord's face lit up when he saw them. Though there were quite a few people in he took time to come over to greet them both. He was pleased to see them both smiling, after the gloom of their last visit.

"Well, how are you both? It's been some time since I've seen you." His friendly greeting got a smile and, "We're fine, thanks. How's business?"

from Peter; a shy smile from Amy, who whispered, "Thanks for last time."

Settled with their drinks, they chatted quietly. Just everyday matters, both of them a little shy and winding down from the pressure of work. It was an hour and a half later when the landlord came over to see if they would like something to eat.

Peter realised that he had forgotten to get provisions for the boat, so they elected to accept his offer of cold meat and bread with home-made chutney. It was late when they arrived at the boat. The landlord had let them have a small bottle of milk, so they could have a hot drink if they wanted when they arrived.

***

At the boat, the power had been switched on, and Peter found a note from the yard manager. There's milk in the fridge and fresh bread.

Amy laughed. "You do not know when you are well off," she said. "All these people look after you and you don't even realise it until afterwards."

Peter gave her a tour of the boat, allocating the fore-cabin for her use. He would use the stern cabin.

When they had unpacked, they sat together in the lounge with a drink, continuing their conversation from the pub.

Seated side by side, they watched the moonlight as it passed over the waters of the harbour. They were comfortable together. It was not long before Amy's head descended to rest on his shoulder. Peter suddenly realised how late it was. He carefully lifted her and carried her into the fore-cabin. As he laid her on the big bunk he found she had wound her arms around his neck. He was half kneeling on the mattress, in an awkward position. He heard her whisper,

"Don't leave me. Keep me company." He relaxed and slid down beside her, she turned and, still in the circle of his arms, kissed him gently on the lips.

He lay, watching her sleeping for just a few minutes before dropping off himself.

***

When he woke the following morning, his arm was numb and for a moment he wondered why. Then he opened his eyes and found himself looking into Amy's eyes. She was already awake.

She smiled, so did he. "I'll make some coffee and toast," he said.

"Sounds good to me." Amy said and kissed him. "Thank you for last night. I felt incredibly lonely for a while. When I woke and found you there beside me, I went back to sleep without a problem."

"All part of the service, madam." Peter said with a grin, working the blood back into his arm.

***

They spent a lazy morning pottering about the boat. Later they walked into Chichester to have lunch, and find something for supper. They had already decided to stay until Sunday.

As they walked back to the mooring Amy tripped and Peter grabbed her hand to stop her falling. Neither bothered to let go when she was steady again and they walked the rest of the way hand in hand. The weekend passed like that, both of them enjoyed the undemanding pleasure of each other's company.

***

Peter went to the London meeting to discover that the flotilla was being posted to the Mediterranean for unspecified special duties. He managed to let Amy know, but the hurried phone call was not really time to set anything up, apart from a promise to write.

Peter was left feeling uneasy. Amy was a good friend, and he did not like being parted from his friends. At least that was what he told himself at the time.

***

When the flotilla arrived in Gibraltar, they became aware of the way the Spanish government felt about the war.

At the docks, the boats were fitted with torpedo tubes. Each boat was armed with two of the weapons. This slowed things down a bit, but it did allow a stock of torpedoes to be delivered to Malta. The submarine base there was always short of supplies. Their contribution would make a difference.

While they were in Gibraltar, they learned about the Spanish allowing Italian spies to use an interned Italian ship at Algeciras, the other side of the bay from the Gibraltar Naval Base. Over a year ago, in September 1940, the ship had been used as a base to launch human torpedoes at British supply ships, moored and awaiting convoy. There were six ships seriously damaged. The response from the HD (harbour defence) force was sufficient to deter them from trying again, It did result in the authorities keeping an extra special eye on the so-called neutrals on the other side of the bay!

***

The flotilla accompanied a convoy to Malta, managing to arrive with all boats more or less intact. Adrian Quirk's number five boat had lost two men killed and received superficial damage to the super-structure, mainly the roof of the accommodation. The product of one of the Stuka dive bomber attacks the convoy had endured on the journey to Malta.

Peter's boat had been least affected as she had been stationed ahead of the main convoy on anti-submarine patrol, using the advanced asdic she had been fitted with. As the newest boat she had the most up-to-date fittings.

***

CPO Arthur Smith smiled grimly as the MLs entered Valetta Harbour. Luck was a fickle lady. He had not been too pleased when transferred to the new Number six in the flotilla. The skipper had done well since he arrived in Portsmouth, but he was the new boy. Arthur, having survived the loss of the last number six, had thought that a nice number in a ship, a cruiser, or even a destroyer might have come his way. "Ah, well," he opined, "It could be worse." He looked across at the other boats. Number five had a bent aerial and a row of holes across the cabin roof. He wondered if his mate CPO Grainger was okay. As he looked, Grainger came on the deck of the other boat and waved to him. So that was alright.

He watched the quay coming alongside and shouted for the fenders to be dropped into place along the rubbing strake. The two AB's on deck didn't need the prompt, but they acknowledged the order anyway. Once the mooring ropes were passed, Peter ordered the engines shut down. A cable, passed from the shore, was connected and the power switched on.

Peter stretched his shoulders, suddenly realis-ing how tensed up he had been after the continuous pressure of the voyage from Gibraltar. At least all the boats had made it.

He had been told to keep the torpedo tubes for the next few days, as there was a possible target the submarines might not be able to handle. The Boss's boat and No. 2 had also kept their tubes for the same reason. Peter was apprehensive. Although he had performed torpedo attacks in training. Having been assigned to ML's, he had never performed one in anger.

Ashore, he reported with the others to Admiralty house, which seemed to be part of the catacombs, based mainly in man-made caves. The set up was the same as it would be the world over. A big table, with the plot showing the movements of ships in the Mediterranean, dominated the largest room.

A harried-looking Lieutenant Commander hustled them into a briefing room. "Which amongst you command the boats with the fish still aboard?"

Danny Oliver, Adrian Quirk and Peter all raised their hands. "Right! Stand fast, you three. All the rest of you report to the Engineer Commander, for repairs and fuel. As the others filed out he turned to the three men remaining. "Your boats are being checked over now, fuel and ammo restocked. There is a flap on that the subs cannot handle because of time."

He put his file down on the table in the room and sat down on one of the kitchen chairs scattered around the table. "Sit for a minute or two." He waved vaguely at the three Skippers.

"The Italian fleet is out, and they have received a bashing from Admiral Cunningham, and his big guns, off Cape Matapan at the southern tip of Greece. A group of cruisers have been spotted heading Northwest from Gavdhos Island. We believe heading for

Brindisi. You have the range and the speed to ambush them if you set off from here pronto. They are all fast and our own ships are being outrun. You should be in position to give them a bellyache. You will not be alone. Our MGB's will be with you to run interference. They are fuelled up and ready to go."

He sorted through the documents in his file, produced three charts and passed them to the three skippers.

"That's it, chaps. There is nothing else I can tell you. Sorry it is such short notice. Any questions?"

Danny Oliver grinned ruefully. "Nothing different then. Just the usual panic. No .questions, sir. We'll be on our way."

***

All three had things to do on their boats, so they made their way back. The commander of the MGB flotilla was waiting for Danny on the quay. His boat was outboard of the No. 1 boat. Lt Cdr Basil Grant RNVR shook hands, "We will follow you out," he called. "We'll sort ourselves out on the way, if that's all right with you?"

"Good idea." Danny agreed, "Let's get the show on the road."

Basil Grant ran across Danny's boat and called, "Cast off!" as he hit the deck of his MGB.

Their destination was Otranto, on the heel of Italy; south down the coast from Brindisi. It was the best place to intercept the Italian cruisers, provided, that is, that Intelligence had it right. The long haul would run them short of fuel, so they were being followed by three ML's loaded with fuel in drums, hastily gathered, to be there for the returning boats.

The attack force was carrying one drum extra on the outward journey, the six hundred mile plus trip would take 36 hours at best. They should be in position in the late evening of next day.

The weather was not unkind. The overcast that persisted for most of the daylight hours was just that. It wasn't until evening that the rain came and made conditions unpleasant for the watch-keepers.

Peter managed to get some rest during the journey. He had a few hours during the first part of the trip, and made himself get his head down for two hours before they reached the vicinity of the ambush. Now on the bridge, he was aware of the smell of water, a hint of fuel, and the taste of salt from the spray on his lips. Sub Lieutenant Lawrence, his dark complexion and sharp-hooked nose giving him the nickname 'Arab', after D.E. Lawrence of Arabia, was on watch. "What is our location?"

The Sub said, "I've just been checking with the leader. We are in the zone. We three boats are to spread out across the line of track for the cruisers. The escorts are staging themselves to the east of south, down the track the cruisers seem to be following. I understand that they are shifting along at high speed. At the start they were making 32 knots, now they are down to 24. I think they must be running low on fuel. At high speed the fuel must run through the engines like diarrhoea."

"Thank you for that observation. Since you haven't eaten yet, take that thought with you." Peter smiled to himself. His number one loved using colourful language. Hopefully Aki Karim, the Indian deck hand was cooking tonight. He had a habit of producing ambitious curries which he swore his mother used to make. The main effect on the crew was a panic rush for the heads.

Chapter nine

Life on the edge

The escort flotilla was dispersed when the light on the lead boat began to flash.

Leading Signaller Tom Wells read off the message. "Escort report the southernmost boat has the sound of engines at speed, south-south-east."

"What's the leader got, bats ears?" The voice of the Cox'n could be heard drifting up from the wheelhouse.

Peter tapped the voice pipe. "Come on up, Chief. I'll need to control from up here. So I'll need you."

"Aye, aye sir. Hawkins, come and take over from me."

L/S Hawkins took the Chief's place in the wheelhouse when the Cox'n reported to the open bridge.

Colin Willis appeared, at the call to action stations. He took his position at the forward gun. L/S Pat Maxwell was already there. His ammo number feeding a shell into the breach was AB Paddy McGuire. The midshipman was nervous. This was their first torpedo attack and he was not really sure how he would handle it. He was desperately afraid of showing fear in front of the men.

Pat Maxwell looked at him, *Poor bastard, looks scared shitless.* He liked Willis so he made a point of commenting to Paddy, "This looks iffy, Paddy. Never done this before, have you?"

"Nah, how about you, Mr Willis? Have you done the torpedo bit before?"

Willis jerked back into the real world once more. "No, actually I haven't. But I'm told it can be exciting. I would think you'll be alright once the shooting starts."

In reassuring the Irishman, Colin Willis found he himself was not as scared as he thought he was.

On the bridge Peter had turned toward the increasing sound of the approaching ships. He caught a brief glimpse of the boat to his left, the flash of the white wake with the vague shape above. The boat was working up to full speed. The cruisers needed to be hit from ahead. Once they were past the ML's, with their speed they could not be caught. It was from ahead or nothing.

The leader was coming closer to port, as the boats converged. Adrian Quirk was on the other side of the leader's boat. The boats roared along through the darkness for several minutes before the leader signalled 'Enemy in sight.'

The cruisers were in line-ahead.

"Playing follow my leader," the Chief commented.

Peter shrugged. "We take number two, Helm, five degrees starboard wheel.

The boat started the curve away from the target before swinging in to attack. The guns on the cruisers opened fire and the water around the attacking boats became peppered with shrapnel from the shells and missiles from the smaller bore weapons. Peter heard the clunk of bullets hitting the boat. "Open fire when you are in range," he called to Willis on the foredeck. He used the loudhailer to issue the order. Willis waved acknowledgement and turned to Pat Maxwell. "Fire whenever you're ready, guns," He said tersely.

Strange, he thought, *I'm not scared any more.* Then he realised that he was still scared. It just did not seem so important now.

By now the 3 pounder was firing. Both Oerlikons were chattering away, with the thump, thump of the 20mm shells spitting fire at the approaching enemy cruiser.

On the boat, Torpedo Gunner's Mate, Will Farquhar, crouched over the sight which, though elementary, had been found to work pretty well.

Both tubes contained prepared torpedoes. The TGM held the trigger in his hand. The storm of fire from the cruiser increased if anything. Will Farquhar pressed the trigger and the two torpedoes leapt from their tubes, starting their final journey toward the advancing ship. Peter called, "Hard to starboard. Engines full speed ahead. As the boat swung round, all the guns were still firing at the charging cruiser. The boat received several hits from the light weapons on the cruiser, though luckily the heavier shells all missed. They drew out of range and circled round to see the effect of the attack.

They were rewarded with one explosion on their target. "One hit!" The Chief shouted, where the other torpedo went nobody knew. The racing cruiser slowed dramatically as the water ripped through the hole created by the blast, the speed nearly sinking the ship then and there. With speed reduced, the cruiser limped off into the darkness.

Danny Oliver managed a hit on his target. Adrian's target had increased speed as soon as the boats appeared and was overtaking Peter's target by the time Adrian was in position. He had released his fish but they fell short of the target.

With all their torpedoes expended there was no way the boats could hurt the cruisers. All the short-range weapons on the three big ships were actively working to keep the boats clear.

The lead boat signalled 'return to base', the three ML's and the MGB escorts turned and set course to rendezvous with the fuel supply.

Despite the fact that none of the cruisers had been sunk, the raid was considered a success. Once back in Valetta, patches applied and the boats ready to go once more, the discussion began. Where would they be sent next?

The torpedo tubes were removed from the mounting plates included, along with the pre-fitted gun mounts, on every Fairmile at the time of their construction. The system, part of every Fairmile model, meant that the boats had a versatility no others available could match, fitting as MGB's, ML's, or MTB's, Minelayers and Harbour launches.

***

The news from Greece was becoming more and more serious. Though it was rumoured that the boats would be sent on to Alexandria, the fact was that supply and reinforcement of the troops in Greece was becoming urgent. The Special Services flotilla was loaded with provisions and ammunition and, with rubberised blimps of extra fuel, sent off to Crete. Peter was not aware that the German armies in Greece were pushing south too fast for any proper defence to be set up. Since Rommel was pushing at the same time in North Africa there was no real chance of reinforcing the army in Greece in time. The MLs made their deliveries in Crete and, immediately, were sent to Piraeus in Greece to help with the evacuation of the remains of the expeditionary force. Getting in close to the beach was very difficult, with almost continuous attacks from the air.

The Oerlikons and the Browning turret had to conserve ammo until a direct attack was made. Collecting troops from the beaches and delivering them to the destroyers was tiring and hazardous. Tim Hammond in number three was hit, and his boat damaged by shrapnel from a bomb dropped on a destroyer, when he was delivering men. He spent the rest of the day with a bandage around his head, the boat being pumped for the first hour. Luckily a Royal Engineer found the hole and plugged it with his gas cape while he made an aluminium patch. Then, lining the patch with a piece of battledress, he hung upside-down over the side of the boat and slapped it on the outside of the hull, while his mate did the same inside. They screwed the two patches together and, job done, climbed aboard the next destroyer, while Tim carried on.

***

Peter's the day seemed endless, but in the Med the night starts at round about six in the evening. Darkness brought relief from the aircraft anyway. The evacuation continued until well into the night. The supply of men was thinning, and the bigger ships withdrew, hoping to get as far from the area as possible. They knew that they would be attacked as soon as it was light, but at least they would have room to manoeuvre. At midnight the order came to load all the men they could find and make for Crete. Peter managed to gather a platoon of Marines from the cruiser *HMS Ajax,* at least the survivors of the platoon. With seventeen men including a lieutenant, he set out for Iraklion. The Marines made themselves comfortable, but the two Bren guns they had were set-up ready for when dawn came. They were still travelling as the first air raid came.

Peter stopped engines before the planes came in sight hoping the lack of wash would cause the boat to be overlooked. They almost got away with it. The tail-end Charlie of one of the groups of aircraft, an ME 109, turned and came back to strafe the stationary boat. Realising what he was about to do, Peter started engines and waited. "Hard port rudder, engine full ahead." With a roar the boat almost stood on its head. The ploy worked and the ME 109 nearly finished up in the sea. It returned, to be met with a storm of fire from both Oerlikons, twin Browning's, and the pair of Bren guns operated by the marines.

Some of the plane's firing reached the boat, but the pilot jerked up out of his dive after sustaining hits which caused his engine to smoke. The Brownings stopped abruptly, the turret shattered and AB 'Spud' Murphy dead killed by 20mm cannon shell from the Messerschmitt's last attack. Peter throttled back the engines and surveyed the damage. He called the engine room. "How are things, chief?"

The scream of the engines at full throttle was still lingering in CPO Ben McLeish's ears, despite the fact that the noise was now down to a comparative mutter. The Chief was accustomed to the racket and guessing what the skipper needed to know he growled, "We're fine just now." He looked out through a new hole in the side of the boat. "Could have done without the new porthole. It's a wee bit draughty here now!"

Apart from Murphy, and a few cuts and bruises, the crew had got off lightly. One of the Bren gunners had gained a burn on one shoulder from a near miss, and a wound through the fleshy part of his thigh from a splinter of the armour-glass from the shattered Browning turret.

Tom Wells was working over him already with his first aid kit.

***

In the damaged aircraft, Leutnant Erich Strohm cursed as he struggled to keep his plane in the air. Reversing his course was difficult. Though the smoke from his engine was thinning, it was not going to run for much longer. The prop was off balance, causing the whole airframe to shake and the rudder seemed to have little effect. He tried his radio. Someone was shouting as he went in to attack one of the escaping ships, blocking the attack frequency. He switched to the emergency band. Someone was screaming in agony the garbled word "Feur!" again and again. Then silence, though the switch was still closed.

The radio cut out. The sea was getting nearer and Erich could do nothing about it. The engine coughed. It coughed again and stopped. The silence was only broken by the swish of the wind over the wings. The air flow swept the smoke away and Erich realised he was too low to jump.

With little control over it, he concentrated on all he could remember about ditching in the sea. He was in time to throw back the canopy, and yank back on the stick, causing the tail section to take the first impact on the water.

After that, all he recalled afterwards was the frantic struggle to unlock his straps and clamber out of the sinking aircraft. The dinghy deployed as he tumbled off the submerging wing. He pulled the loop on his lifejacket. It inflated to lift his head above the surface. The dinghy was floating beside him. He relaxed for a few minutes happy to be alive. None of his bones seemed to be broken, and he could see no blood, so that was alright.

He went through the drill he had learned at flight training school, for getting into a dinghy at sea. Using the memorised instructions, he raised his body to the surface as if lying in bed, and pulled the single man dinghy alongside. Then, holding the dinghy close, he rolled over. After the fourth attempt, he gave up and dragged the side of the dinghy forcibly under his bottom. Finally, he was out of the water and sat back with a sigh.

The mutter of an engine had been with him for some time without his realising what it meant. It was a shock, therefore, when the shadow of the boat he had been attacking fell across the dinghy he had struggled to get into.

"Up you come, chum. For you, ze war is over!" The voice of Pat Maynard shook him as a big hand grabbed him by his life-jacked and hauled him out of the dinghy.

"Can you stand?" The voice continued, as it removed the Luger from its leather holster buckled to his overalls.

"Of course," he replied, though with the movement of the boat and the shock, he was un-steady.

"Come along, now. We'll get your wet gear off, and, warm you up."

"Leutnant Erich Strohm," He replied to Peter's question. "I am from a base in Southern Greece. You are wasting time sailing to Crete. It will soon be in German hands and our positions will be reversed." He sat back puzzled. He knew the man in front of him from somewhere?

Peter said, "Your English is very good. Have you been to England?"

Erich remembered. "You are Peter Woods. I raced you in the 'Round the Island' in 1938. I was in *Valkyrie*. Your boat was new, *Salamander,* I think?"

"You nearly rammed us, if I recall?" Peter grinned. "You broke your mast. did you not, and withdrew from the series?"

"Our stupid Director, he always spoke of sportsmanship and honour on the face of things. But he liked raping Jewish girls for fun."

Peter thought for a few moments. "Albert Schiller? Is that right? I recall a tall man with a stiff neck, and eyes that wandered."

Erich nodded, "He has ended up there in the sty, with the other pigs!"

Peter looked at the prisoner in surprise. "In the sty?"

"Where else, the Gestapo!" Erich's face was grim. "I accept war as a fact of life. Right or wrong, it is inevitable. But murder and abuse of men and women, because they do not conform to the ideal image, is an offence against all humanity."

Peter looked at his prisoner, surprised that he did not conform to the newspaper's idea of the Hun.

"We will be at Iraklion shortly. I will have to pass you on to the POW people. Don't count of being released by your friends. It's not likely to happen."

***

They arrived in port, tied up alongside two other boats, and said "Cheerio" to the marines who filed ashore, taking their wounded man with them.

Peter reported to the headquarters, where he was told to fuel and report to Alexandria for the damaged turret to be replaced and holes patched. He was re-allocated the same party of marines for passage and entrusted with four QANC nurses under the command of a Sister, whose rank of Major made her, technically, the senior officer on the boat. The marine casualty, still with the platoon, was the subject of envy from the rest of the men on the boat as the nurses were all pretty, and the sister, who was probably at least thirty years old, was beautiful.

Like the others on the boat Peter was aware of the ladies, and particularly of Sister Paula Edwards. The fact that she was married was not really an issue, as there was no way that anyone was able to socialise on the journey across the Mediterranean.

The Special Service flotilla had been broken-up for the evacuation of Greece and the prospective evacuation of Crete in its turn. Peter, and Lt 'Snow' White of the No 4 boat, were in company with two MGB's under Lt Cdr Basil Grant. All were making the trip for different reasons, but the grouping was for mutual protection.

It was because of the attention the enemy were giving to the reduction of Crete that their voyage was not as taxing as it might have been. An attack made on the boats by German bombers was a hit-and-run badly executed, though it produced casualties on 'Snow' White's boat from splinters from a near miss. One of the aircraft lost an engine and limped off leaking smoke and fuel, ignored by the others.

Two nurses were transferred to attend the wounded, stepping from one boat to another with plenty of willing hands to assist. They returned from the disappointed No 4 boat that afternoon. Luckily none of the men had been badly wounded. The 430 mile trip took the best part of two days at the economical speed of 12 knots.

It was with a sigh of relief that Peter ordered 'finished with engines', at the Dockyard Quay. He watched the Marines going ashore, carrying their wounded man, with a nurse in attendance. Then he realised that the Sister was standing at the foot of the bridge stairs. "Permission to come up, sir?" she asked very properly.

"Of course. Please join me," he said. "I am sorry to see you all go. It has been a break for the men to have someone else to talk to these days."

"It doesn't do much for you though, does it?" Her voice was soft, something he had not realised.

"The loneliness of command can be a punishment at times, though in a boat like this it is not as bad as it could be."

They stood looking out over the busy harbour for a few minutes in companionable silence. Then Sister Paula Edwards turned to Peter. "You will be in Alexandria for several days, I believe. I understand you are a stranger to the place. If you are at a loose end and would like to chat, my telephone number and address are on this card. Feel free to contact me. I am usually at home or at the hospital. Thanks you for looking after us." Then she was gone.

Peter watched her walk up on to the quay, admiring the relaxed, controlled way she held herself and the feminine sway of hips as she walked.

He shook himself out of the daydream. "Not for you, idiot. She is out of your class." He went below to gather his personal gear together, prior to handing the boat over to the yard for repair and modification.

Chapter ten

Into the unknown

When Peter called upon Paula Edwards, he had no idea what her reaction would be face to face. He had phoned her at the hospital and she had answered briskly, and told him she would be home by 3.30. He looked at his watch as he waited. Then the door opened and an Egyptian servant took one look at him, then stood back. "The Madam is expecting you, sir."

Peter took off his hat and entered the cool interior of the traditional colonial style bungalow. The ceiling fans were stirring the air about but, to Peter, it was cool after the walk in the afternoon sun.

The man took his hat and led him through the house to the garden at the rear. There was a sunshade and chairs beside the swimming pool. As they came out, Paula rose from the pool dressed in a one piece bathing costume. It confirmed that Peter's observation had not been at fault. She took the robe handed her by the servant and sat down in one of the chairs, indicating the other to Peter.

"I apologise for not being ready, but I have just returned from work and I find the swim helps me relax.

The servant returned from the interior of the house with a jug of lemonade tinkling with ice cubes. The glasses on the tray were misty cold from the refrigerator. Paula poured lemonade for them both.

"What would you like to see first?" Paula asked.

Peter sipped his drink and said, "I am in your hands, I'm afraid. I really know nothing of Alexandria."

"Good! In that case we can relax for a while today. Later, I'll show you the night life of the place. I am free tomorrow. If you wish, we can take in the museums and high spots of the city. How about that?"

"Sounds great to me. But what about your husband? Will he be agreeable?"

Sorry. I thought you might have discovered. The rings are a defence mechanism. They belonged to my mother who died some years ago. In my job I found I was having to fight off the advances of doctors and consultants. Wearing the rings put off the pushy types. If there was somebody I felt like getting to know, I simply told them the reason for wearing the rings. They then had the option, if they were also interested, to approach me.

Peter took another drink of lemonade to cover his interest in her explanation.

"There is a costume in the summer house if you would like to swim," Paula said casually. "And plenty of towels and things."

"That sounds like a great idea, if you don't mind."

Paula opened her robe to show her swimsuit. "Why would I mind?" She said with a smile.

Peter found the costume and a robe and rejoined Paula, a little embarrassed at the pattern of tanning his body displayed. His lower arms were brown, his upper arms and chest were pale, apart from the vee of brown at his neck where his open-neck shirt had allowed the sun to do its work. His legs were also pale, though the beginning of a tan was appearing around his knees.

Paula didn't appear to notice. When Peter mentioned it, she said, "I was the same when I arrived, I soon got over it. With the private pool, I send the servants out and bathe in the nude. Now I'm tanned all over.

Peter hurriedly dived into the pool to hide his embarrassment, enjoying the feel of the water on his hot skin. As he turned to swim back he found Paula had joined him in the water. She was treading water. "I sent Youssef off for the rest of the day, so you need not feel awkward about getting a tan. It allows me the freedom to swim without the costume as well, much more liberating!" She turned and started swimming back down the pool. Peter realised that she had shed her costume. She was quite naked in the pool.

He shrugged. Rather than embarrass his hostess he slipped his costume off and put it on the edge of the pool. Then he swam down the pool to join her.

***

Peter was briefed to set up a base on one of the small Greek islands south of the mainland of Greece.

"Theo Parker will be your guide and help you get set up. He has a base in mind which the Germans and Italians are unlikely to bother with. It's a small uninhabited island, with a grotto his family found on holiday one year. Most of your work will be collecting and returning agents and saboteurs, and possibly the odd escapee. I understand you have been involved in operations in France, and you have received commando training?"

Peter nodded. "I was trained at Hamworthy by the Royal Marines in unarmed combat and small arms."

The Commander nodded thoughtfully. You may be called upon to help out if anything goes wrong. But we'll face that when we come to it.

He stood up. Commander Roger Lancaster was Peter's height and walked with a slight limp. He had been a lecturer in History at the University in Athens. His limp had been acquired during the past six months.

"Theo Parker is Greek-speaking, the son of a Greek father and an English mother. He lived in Crete until the Germans moved in."

Peter looked up sharply. The Commander nodded soberly. "Crete fell yesterday. They have been moving people out for that past four days. It will be announced officially today."

He continued, "Theo is a Sergeant in the Engineers. His speciality is explosives. He was recruited direct from his civilian post and given the rank of Sergeant. His civilian job was demolition. He knows Crete well and has climbed and walked the mountains since he was a boy. He went to Harrow, and left to work on a building site. His interest in explosives started then, and he has studied the subject over the years since then."

He looked keenly at Peter. "You will need to go in under cover of darkness. And leave and return each time in the dark. The island is known to be uninhabited. You cannot afford to be seen. If there is nothing else, I understand your boat is loaded and ready to go. The tanker has already delivered to the island and it will be returning there in two days' time. Goodbye and good luck." He held his hand out and shook Peter's.

The evening was fading into night as Peter swept the horizon for what seemed like the thousandth time. All around the boat watchers were alert. It was the most dangerous time, with light playing tricks on tired eyes. On the rim of the world ahead the shadow of their island destination had just begun to appear, before it was lost in the swiftly falling night.

With a relieved sigh, Peter allowed the binoculars to hang from their strap and turned to Jerry Lawrence standing beside him, "Well, can we see our destination in your magic box?" He referred to the radar set, fitted during their refit in Alexandria.

Sub Lieutenant Lawrence, hot and bothered from peering at the radar screen under a black cowl to prevent the light from the screen giving the location of the boat away. "It's there, clear and easy to see. I can also see what looks like the fishing fleet."

Peter said quietly, "The Island we are headed for is unoccupied. We have to enter the cove from the north side. Our contact should be there waiting for us, we need to show a red light, if all is clear he will show a green. The cave, or grotto if you will, is situated on the west side of the cove and it will entail a 90 degree turn to enter."

Jerry had been reading up the brief. "There will be room to swing around within the grotto, which by the way, has a depth of water in excess of 5 fathoms."

Peter peered at his number one with the suspicion of a smile on his face. "Why do I think you are making a point?"

"Me, sir? Not me, sir. I spent most of my time in the base at Alexandaria swotting up on out orders and the locations for our next tour of duty, sir. As I was ordered, sir. Unlike some others I know who appeared to have insufficient time between visits to a lady's house where it appears a golden tan has been acquired, sir."

"Ah! I understand. You are not yet aware of the need for your seniors and betters to relax when time allows. It is part of a lad's training to learn the ins and outs of his chosen profession and then, and only then, gather the fruits of this knowledge when he reaches the dizzy heights of command. There, the need for his full attention to guide and instruct his juniors, entails the need for the relaxation earlier referred to."

He turned to the signals rating on the bridge and said, "See if you can rustle up a brew, Horrocks. I believe number one is in sore need of liquid after his session with the radar."

AB Horrocks grinned "Right away, sir. a brew all round, sir."

He disappeared below in search of the brew, leaving the two officers together. Peter called for an increase in speed now that it was full dark. Turning to Lawrence he said, "Let us get the radar man up here now. We are getting into bandit country. You take your action station aft. I'll send a brew down when it appears."

Lawrence disappeared aft, leaving Peter alone on the bridge. The night was warm and his mind drifted back to the few days spent in Alexandria. Having been comparatively inexperienced when he met Paula, his education advanced considerably. By the time he returned to duty, he has acquired the promised body tan and an appreciation of the human form that he had never imagined.

He turned with a small sigh as Horrocks arrived with the brew, tea for a change. The radar operator turned to and filled the mugs from the dixie, the

AB then went off to look after the other watch-keepers with the tea.

***

They arrived at the island at 0200hrs. and safely negotiated the right-angle turn into the grotto. There was a small jetty, apparently a survival from the family holidays of Theo and his parents. The only real addition was a screen covering the entrance, to prevent the lights inside from giving the location away. Peter was intrigued to discover that the closing of the screen switched the lights on. Opening shut the lights off as soon as the opening sequence began.

In an alcove behind the jetty was a large fuel tank, and stacked drums of fuel were arrayed along the ledge that extended into the grotto. On the far side was another ledge with supplies and cages of ammunition and weapons. There was a cabin which was used as accommodation by the people staying on the island. Last, but not least, was an Greek island fishing boat, previously used by Theo to get about.

***

Theo Parker was stocky and fit-looking. He greeted Peter and Jerry with a beaming smile. "You are just in time to eat. We eat late here for obvious reasons. So come and join us in a traditional Greek meal." His companions were Kat and Nick. Kat was small, dark and stunning. Nick was big, dark and menacing. Both were old friends of their host, having known him since they were all kids.

The meal was goat, but in the stew it was very tasty and a change from the bully beef hash from the boat. "Did you cook?" Jerry asked Kat. Kat grinned and pointed to Nick. "He cook. I blow up buildings!"

After they had eaten Theo showed them his map of the region. It was a Michelin road map, so Jerry brought out a chart for the area, and they compared the information, transferring it to the chart.

"What have you got in mind for the first operation?" Peter asked.

"You are scheduled to do a pick-up of four soldiers from here." He indicated a bay on the north corner of the island of Crete. You should be there tomorrow night. I got the message before you arrived. It will be two flashes with a white light. The shore line there is beach, you will need to use the dinghy to collect them. They are armed and they will have their equipment with them."

"That won't be a problem as the dinghy is plenty big enough. How about German troops?"

"That, we don't know yet. They are still securing the place. The only thing going for us at the moment is that the place is remote, with no houses or farms there. It's pretty barren in that part of the island, so there is no real reason for them to look."

"Let us hope you are right. We would be pretty exposed if they were in place there."

Jerry asked a question that he knew Peter was interested in. "What sort of work would we be involved in otherwise? Our boat is pretty big to hide and, though we are quite fast, we cannot compete with E boats or the Italian MAS boats for speed.

"What I had in mind was the landing and retrieval of sabotage teams and specific operation personnel. Because of our current shortage of bodies it might entail you," he indicated Peter, "Stepping in to see agents ashore and in safe hands before returning to the boat. That involves extra risk. As soon as extra staff can be located, you will, of course, be backed up and, on other occasions, replaced in that task."

Peter nodded thoughtfully. "Let's get this pick-up out of the way and we'll take it from there."

***

After the meeting they took a walk around the base, which had been set up over the past two months. "This seems to imply that you were expecting the Germans to take over Greece and Crete."

Theo smiled grimly. "Some of us did. I am afraid not all, but enough people to swing the establishment of this base and two others elsewhere in the Med. It is not enough, but it's a start. His smile broadened," We have been thinking up some nasty surprises for the Germans. Obviously we were working on targets a little further north than today's. Transferring the action to closer targets will not be such a difficult task."

Kat spoke for the first time on the subject. "You will recall the special target you agreed when I joined the group?"

"I have not forgotten."

Later that evening Peter asked Theo what target was promised.

"Kat was on her way to her home when the Germans moved in. You recall the Italians were having no success in their invasion of Greece. Well, the Germans stepped in. All the places which had resisted the Italians were destroyed. Kat's mother, father and brother were shot out of hand. Her sixteen year old sister was taken for the soldier's brothel.

"Kat arrived as the soldiers were leaving. She found her parents and her brother, who was dying. He managed to tell her about her sister before he died.

"Life expectancy is not good in the brothels. The women are used and discarded, and, if they get rough treatment, so what! The girl lasted two weeks. She was discarded and left to die. Kat found her, but could not save her. The Grenadier Company who performed the massacre is currently on the mainland at the eastern end of the Corinth Canal, possibly one of the most heavily defended places in Greece, because of the canal."

Peter smiled. "That need not be too much of an obstacle. Find out exactly where the troops are billeted. I have an idea that just might work. By the way, have we a German speaker? I'm thinking fluent enough to pass for German?"

"I think I can help there. I certainly know one, a lady of character and nerve," Theo volunteered. Let me know when and I'll arrange a meeting."

***

The ML was using the exhaust suppressors and was silently drifting under very low throttle into the bay at the north end of the Isle of Crete. From the shore at intervals a white light blipped twice and stopped. Now they were in the shadow of the headland. Horrocks blipped his light twice in the green.

The white light acknowledged and the dinghy was launched with Jerry Lawrence and CPO Smith. AB Paddy McGuinn worked a paddle.

The soldiers came aboard the ML wearily, with their kitbags, rifles, and a Thompson sub-machine gun. All three men looked exhausted, but the Sergeant stood erect and saluted Peter, "Sergeant Harry Mitchell, Green Howards, L/Corp. Bill Hardy. KRR's sir. Pvt Colin Wallace KRR's".

Peter accepted their salutes, turned to Jerry Lawrence. "Get them below. Get them fed and let them get their heads down, Chief! Let's get the show on the road. We might need to use this place again, so I would rather we did not hang about too long."

***

Three hours later the ML slipped into the bay and quietly disappeared into the grotto. Peter turned the boat round facing the entrance to the grotto, and they tied up to the jetty. He then called to finish with engines.

Theo joined him in the cabin producing a bottle of ouzo. Peter leaned back wearily. In his opinion, the sort of pick-up just performed was probably the most exhausting task of all.

Sipping his drink, he grimaced as it passed his tongue, but enjoyed the warmth it produced in his stomach.

Theo started talking, explaining his reasons for the next operation. "I mention it because Kat is a very useful explosives hand. If we can keep her happy she will be a serious asset to our team."

Peter said nothing, just took a second sip of his drink. He decided that it was not as nasty as the first sip.

Theo carried on with his theme. "You mentioned there was a reason why it was not impossible." He sat back and sank his glass of ouzo.

Peter ran his hands through his hair and sat up. "Right. This is what I can offer. When I was sailing in the Med in 1938, we tied up to a private quay near Kechries, south of Corinth. As you possibly are aware, the canal passed through two cliffs. The owner of the quay was a Greek millionaire who stumbled on the crack in the southern, seaward side of the massif. It is impossible to spot if you do not know of the key points on the rock-face. The owner was crewing on my boat, despite the fact that he had one of his own. On his own boat he never made mistakes. On mine, I swore at him for mistakes, just as I swore at the others. He always said he sailed with me because I treated him like a member of the crew. His own people could never forget he was the boss.

"He is dead now and his boat lost. He was using it in the evacuation when the Italians first started their attempt at invasion. He and his boat were lost at sea during an air attack on a small boat convoy at the end of 1940 by Italian aircraft. Stavros was buried on his estate in Crete. I was informed but I could not attend, of course. I am sure he destroyed the records of his hidden quay, because he stressed that, if the invasion succeeded, it was a way-in that no one was likely to find without help. The quay in the area to the south of the Canal would give us a base to work from."

Peter pulled out the chart for the area. He pointed to the land between Paleo Kalamaki and Kechries. "The entrance is in this area. Plan from there. Now I am going get my head down." He rose to his feet and walked over to the ML and down to his cabin, hung his hat on a peg and lay down, already asleep before his head hit the pillow.

***

He found Kat awaiting him when he got up. She served him figs and yoghurt, and a cup of strong coffee. The sounds of the various tasks being undertaken on the boat were a reminder that he had probably overslept.

While he was finishing his coffee Kat came in and sat down facing him. "I will need four hours ashore, and two men to carry my gear."

"You will also need an escort and a diversion. I presume you have the destruction of the barracks, with the men inside, in mind?"

She nodded slowly.

"Leave it with me until tonight. We will talk again." He held his hand up. "Wait! The two men to carry; Greeks, I presume?"

She nodded.

He nodded back. "Tonight!" As he watched her leave his eyes followed her through the window, as she walked along the quay to the store rooms.

Chapter eleven

Plans

He was still at the table in the main cabin when the Sergeant found him.

"Hullo. Sergeant Mitchell, isn't it?"

"Yes sir. Can I have a word with you?"

"Sit down. Take your hat off, and tell me how you got to the bitter end of Crete where we picked you up. By the way, I was told there would be four of you? "

"Paddy Martin, Corporal, Irish Dragoon Guards, Special Operations, left us to look at something on our way as we passed the airfield. He missed the rendezvous. We waited an extra day. Then we had to come on, or miss the boat."

"Right. So carry on. How did you manage to escape?"

"My company were in the retreat down Greece, fighting alongside the most vicious bastards I've ever met. But they could fight. God help any German or Italian they captured though. Their presence in Greece was a personal insult to each one of them. Their problem was they only had rifles, against machine guns, tanks and APC's. The Greeks hardly had any trucks. Their tanks were a joke, and the machine guns had mostly been sold on the black market to supplement the wages they seldom received. But they fought anyway. I was scouting one of the passes in the mountains, two men with me. The rest of the company and my officers were trying to organize the

Greek company with us into some sort of order, when German mountain troops appeared out of no-where. They were all armed with MP40's, you know, that Schmeisser sub-machine gun. They came from all sides, lower down the slopes than the three of us. They slaughtered both companies. There was no cov-er and those who got shots off were shooting uphill. It was a prepared ambush. One of the local Greeks had informed them where the assembly point was. My two wanted to mix it. I could see there was no way we could make a difference. We would have been just three more corpses. We watched those troops go through the dead and wounded, killing all the survivors systematically. Finding our way through the hills we made it to the coastal plain to find everybody on the run. We joined the rush and managed to get on to one of the boats going to Crete. There we were attached to a composite company and told to hold an airfield. Both the men who escaped from Greece with me, died when German paratroops dropped on the airfield. Christ, there were hundreds of them. We held them for a while, but we ran out of ammo, and they didn't. It was a simple as that. The two lads, Hardy and Wallace, were part of the made-up company, Wallace was carrying the radio. When the others were being rounded up, we decided to make a run for it. That's how we ended up with you. I've talked it over with the lads, and we agreed we would like to get our own back. So if you'll have us, we would like to join your group. Bill, Cpl Hardy and Wallace are both marksmen, and I can shoot pretty well too. We have all been under fire….." He trailed off, there was nothing else for him to say.

Peter looked at him. "You would be in plain clothes and could be shot as spies."

"We thought of that. We can be shot anyway. We'd be just as dead either way."

"Torture?"

"Are you trying to scare us? We take our chances just like you and the others."

"Very good, Sergeant. I'll check with HQ. If it's ok with them, it's ok with me. Good enough?"

"Thank you, sir. I'll tell the lads."

***

That evening Kat appeared trailing two Greeks. Both men stank. Both had ragged moustaches, and both looked as if they could stand in for Atlas in his world-carrying duties.

"Anthony and Aristotle are brothers from the island of Adamantas, on their way home from working as stone masons in Alexandria. They now know that their home has been taken by the Italians. They are to act as my carriers. How about you?"

"Three British soldiers and me, will that do?"

Kat looked at him eyebrow raised?

Peter turned so that she could see the dagger emblem received from the Royal Marines on his left sleeve. "I have been on night operations in occupied France. I was trained in combat, unarmed and armed, despite being in the navy."

He rose from the table. "I would like to get my men sorted out with equipment. We will need civilian clothes, I presume?"

Kat said something to the two men. They shrugged and went off down the quay. Kat accompanied Peter to the weapons store. Peter carried his gunbelt with him, slinging it round his waist and settling it where he could get hold of it without any problem.

The three soldiers were there already, studying the selection of weapons.

Peter selected a box of 9mm for his handgun, and an MP40 with spare magazines. Sgt Mitchell took an MP40. He looked at the Luger pistols and picked one up. Peter said, "Unless you are accustomed to using a handgun, forget it."

Harry Mitchell looked at the holstered pistol at Peter's hip.

"Have you used a pistol before?" Peter asked.

"No, I just fancied the idea."

"Bring it down to the range. See what it is like."

At the end of the quay there was a natural passageway, at the far end there was a light and a man-target. There were positions marked, at ten and twenty yards. There were also sheets of cork along the walls to deaden the noise. Peter took the Luger and loaded the magazine. He then cocked the weapon, removed the magazine and ejected the cartridge in the breech. He replaced it in the magazine and handed gun and magazine to Harry Mitchell.

Harry loaded the magazine and duplicated Peter's action, cocking the Luger and setting the catch.

"Now, walk down to the ten yard line." Peter accompanied him, followed by Kat and the other two soldiers.

"Watch what I do, then relax and try it for yourself." Peter drew the Browning, cocked it, raised it in his right hand and fired, all in one smooth movement. He fired twice more, then returned the gun to his holster. The bullet holes were in a small triangle.

"Don't worry about where my bullets went. Concentrate on lifting the gun and shooting at the target. Harry stood as Peter had, moved the catch on the Luger lifted it and fired, three times. One of the bullets hit the target, the other two missed completely.

"How was that?" Peter asked.

"Bloody hell! What did I do wrong?"

"Most things. Would you depend on a handgun in battle conditions?"

"I don't think so." Harry handed the gun to Peter.

"If you want to learn when we have time, it's there for you."

"I'll stick to the MP40 for this occasion, I think!"

***

The fishing boat puttered along through the night. Their purpose was to locate the private quay suggested by Peter. They had collected the boat at Milos, and were now approaching the mainland, just one among the gathering of other fishing boats. The fleet had carried on working, as if there had been no invasion. How long that would be allowed was a moot question.

As the coast loomed ahead they dropped further and further back, until the group of boats disappeared into the pre-dawn darkness.

The engine stopped and the boat drifted close to the face of the cliff. Peter slid over the side and swam to the small beach. Then, using a shaded torch, he made his way along the beach to a point where it disappeared and a stretch of dark water met the foot of the cliff. Peter stepped into the water, and finding no bottom, swam slowly along the face of the cliff.

The entrance was there. He had found it. He flashed his torch twice to Theo on the boat, and swam into the concealed channel. The 30 metre swim up the channel seemed endless in the darkness. At last he bumped into the stern of a small boat. Hauling himself aboard, he sat dripping water and gasping for breath. The torch shone over the quay, a big power-boat sat on a lift above the waterline. The remainder of the quay was empty, where the racing yacht had once been moored. There were stacks of anonymous materials against the back wall and it looked like there was storage or accommodation at the far end.

Peter found oars and untied the dinghy, and rowed back down to the entry. Sitting in the gap, he shone the torch, signalling Theo to come in.

He heard the engine start and shortly the boat loomed out of the darkness. As it came level with the entrance, he reached up and gripped the fender hanging down to protect the hull.

Then, shining the torch into the entrance, Theo was able to nose the boat in and, taking care not to squash Peter against the wall, allowed the boat to putter forward into the cavern.

Back on the boat Peter changed into dry clothes, and then joined Theo on the quay.

"There is a generator in here," Theo thrust open a door and indicated the motor squatting in the middle of the room. "There is fuel in the tank and it looks ok. Shall we try?"

Peter said "What about the noise?

"The room is insulated." He pointed at the wall. "You mentioned that your friend was paranoid about secrecy."

While Theo primed the engine and checked the levels, Peter explored by torchlight. He found the accommodation. It was basic but clean and tidy, as if the owner had left yesterday. The atmosphere was fresh, meaning that there was air circulation from somewhere. From along the quay he heard Theo curse. Then a clanking noise, whirr. The lights flickered and came on, all along the quay. The muted noise of the generator could be heard through the open door of the room. Theo emerged with a beaming smile on his face. When he closed the door the sound disappeared.

"Your friend left everything ready to turn on." Theo volunteered with a smile. If this base is as secure as you suggest, we will be using it regularly."

Peter turned toward the accommodation. "I saw the way out through here," He led the way through the sleeping area, and the kitchen, to a glass-panelled door. There was a key hanging on the wall, taking it he opened the door, revealing a passage cut through the rock. The natural tunnel had been enlarged, the face of the stone marked by the chisel used, curving to the right, then curving again to the left. The tunnel roof was about three feet above their heads. It was uneven and there was a string of lights pinned to the upper wall illuminating the way. The floor of the tunnel rose steadily as they followed the lights to a second door. There was a switch beside the door and Peter guessed it was for the tunnel lights, to be used before opening the door.

He pressed the switch. The lights went out, then he opened the door. He stepped into complete blackness. He chanced a glimmer from the shaded light of the torch to see they were in what was apparently a light lock. With the torch he identified the control for the outer door. With the inner door closed the outer door responded to pressure on the handle.

The sky above was visible from within the cleft on the ground. Using the shaded torch once more, he located the outside door control, by comparing the inner handle with the exterior. A lump in the rock face disguising the entrance had to be lifted, and turned to operate the lock. The door when closed, formed part of the rock forming the cleft. A fold in the ground above shielded the cleft from casual view on the ground. Even from the air it would be just a cleft in the ground, one of nature's anomalies, 80 feet from the cliff-edge, completely divorced from the concealed grotto below the ground. The farm buildings on the other side of the field were dark.

As they stood, Peter was suddenly aware that they were not alone. Theo also reacted. Both stood tense with their guns in hand.

"Mr Stavros?" It was the voice of a boy. "Are you there, Mr Stavros?"

Theo spoke. "Who are you?"

"I am Panides. I watch the door, for Mr Stavros. You are not he. So who are you?"

"I am Peter Woods. Mr Stavros used to sail on my boat...."

"Ah, Mr Woods. Yes. You are welcome. I remember. Mr Stavros bring you here before. 'Bloody Stavros,' he said. You called him 'Bloody Stavros.' He said you were the only one who dared. Welcome. Please come and meet my father. He has been waiting for someone to come."

In the farmhouse the father of the boy appeared, dressed in a dressing gown. He was followed by a woman also in a dressing gown, who immediately stirred up the fire and pushed a pot on a moving arm over to the heat.

The man, having been introduced to Peter by his son, grunted and walked over to the dresser where he retrieved an envelope from a false flap in the woodwork.

In English and Greek, it was addressed to Peter or whoever comes to the quay.

If you are reading this I am unable to join you, or I am dead.

I trust you are an ally and I hope you are Peter, my good friend. First: the use of the quay is in your hands. There is fuel power and food, mostly dried and tinned, and the fridge will need to be turned on. The boat I left in there is still there to use if you need it. When this war is over it goes to Giorgio and his family. They should be able to hire it out for an income, or sell it at least. There are facilities to use and Giorgio will keep an eye open above, to warn you if things go wrong. He will show you where the alarm is situated near the landside door.

Good luck, and win.

Regards, Stavros.
(Bloody Stavros)

Peter folded it and returned it to the envelope. "In case we get lost, please replace it," he nodded at the dresser. Giorgio took it and put it back into the concealed compartment.

Chapter twelve

The silent assault

Back in the grotto, the three sat around the table discussing the plans. Nick was away with a group in Crete gathering more of the soldiers still surviving in the mountains.

"For this operation, we cannot take the big boat all the way, it is not suitable. Here we need to go softy, softy. It means leaving the boat or perhaps, towing the fishing boat as far as we can in the hours of darkness, say as far as Milos. It can hide through the day like last time, and run back here the next night. From Milos we go as before to the 'quay'. By the way, we need to call the place something other than the quay. It could be confusing, How about 'Ritz'? That's comfortable and well-fitted. No locations, so no mistakes. Nobody outside this room must know it exists."

"What about Nick? Kat said.

"Does he need to know?" Peter asked.

Kat shook her head slowly. "No. I see what you mean, just we three."

"The soldiers and your two men will have some idea, but even they will not know where it is exactly." Peter added. "The explosives and weapons are all stacked ready and, just for the record, whilst I understand your feelings about the Grenadiers, the reason for their positioning is the communications base they are guarding. The base controls radio traffic for the whole of the Eastern Mediterranean Area, and that includes the North African area where Rommel is creating havoc. If we get rid of the comm centre, we shut down all the established lines of communication between Germany and its Mediterranean and North African forces. I am aware that they will be replaced by other stations but that all takes time.

"That is what we are aiming to destroy. Removing most, if not all, of the Grenadier battalion is an added bonus. Are we all clear with our objectives? The radio station is priority!"

Theo nodded and, after a few seconds, so did Kat.

***

The MAS boat motored importantly over to the dirty, Greek fishing boat. Theo stood at the helm with a pipe in his mouth. Kat's two Greeks were playing with the nets on deck.

The dapper officer on the Italian motor launch used his microphone to amplify his orders to stop in broken Greek.

Theo leaned forward and pulled the throttle back. The noisy engine slowed, the noise reduced to a low mutter.

"Who are you and where are you going?" The Italian called.

Theo shrugged, pointed to his ears and threw his hands wide in a gesture of misunderstanding. Slowly, the Italian repeated his request for information. The crew of the launch were lounging about. The man at the machine gun mount was picking his teeth. Theo launched into a diatribe explaining that he was just a poor fisherman trying to make an honest living with this b..... war interfering. Below, Peter and the three soldiers were preparing their

MP40's in case they were needed. Kat, dressed in loose blouse and shorts poked her head out of the cabin, and, seeing the big power boat alongside, loosed a stream of Greek at Theo. Her blouse made the most of her bosom, a fact the Italian officer immediately noticed, distracting him even more from the answers Theo was giving.

A German officer appeared on the bridge of the launch, shouting at the Italian in Italian. Theo translated for the benefit of the men below. "He is telling the man to get on and check the boat and stop pissing about. It looks as though we are to searched. All set below?"

Kat smiled at the Italian who was looking uncomfortably at the German. He shouted to his men to get alongside and start a search. Kat ducked into the cabin and picked up her MP40. Cocking it raised her head once more. Theo had a grenade in his hand ready to toss into the radio compartment of the launch. The Greeks on deck had their guns under the nets. As the ropes were tossed over to keep the two boats together, each threw a double loop and hitch over a cleat, then collected their guns and opened fire on the German and Italian officers. Both were gunned down and Theo threw his grenade. The machine gunner woke with a start and started to bring his gun into line. Kat shot him with a quick burst from her MP40.

There were shouts from below as the grenade went off. The radio went up in smoke. Another grenade tumbled in, and exploded and a fire started. Kat reached into the cabin of the fishing boat. "Cut free she shouted in Greek. The two Greeks on deck slashed the ropes keeping the boats together. As the launch drifted away, Kat threw a satchel into the companion-way down to the cabin of the MAS boat.

The explosion that followed, muffled to start with, was followed by a second turning the smart craft into a shower of debris.

Theo had the throttle wide open and the fishing boat was moving at a speed which would have shocked the Italian had he been alive to see it.

Some of the debris reached them, but most hit the water and the burning pieces were rapidly extinguished by the blue Mediterranean waters.

***

They reached the mainland as darkness overtook them and cautiously slid into the concealed quay. They were joined at the quay by Giorgio who produced a sketch plan of the weapons and ammunition dump. The barracks of the troops guarding the facilities were arranged on three sides of the compound enclosing the establishment. The fourth side of the square was the wall of the comm station itself. The courtyard enclosed by the buildings was used for drill, and vehicle parking for the trucks used to distribute materials from the depot.

The sentry sequencing was critical, and timing vital. They chose the widest time gaps between sentries passing, and decided on going in immediately following a sentry changeover. They packed their explosives into bags for easy carrying out of the Ritz to the transport which would take them to the site. Theo and Peter would create the gap in the fence, and see the raiding party through, Kat and her two Greeks would start placing charges around the barracks, and insert incendiaries in any handy trucks parked in the courtyard. The other charges were to be laid by Theo and Peter while the three soldiers kept watch over them. Wallace had retained his rifle which had a telescopic sight. They had identified a place where he could watch the entrance to the guard room. There was a light over the doorway to provide a point of focus. That was all he would need.

The planning done they all went to bed. The plans were for the next night. Until then they were left to wait and wonder.

Peter found that waiting was the hardest thing to do in these circumstances. He thought of Amy and the pub, wondering how she was getting on. Her last letter had been still quite cheerful and she did not seem concerned about finding another boyfriend. Too busy to do other than sleep, eat, and work these days, was the way she put it.

***

He woke with a start several hours later. Late afternoon already, he stirred himself out of the bunk and out to the quay where the shower and toilets were situated. Others were stirring and he found something to eat, then went through to the outer door and took a look at the weather. He did not know whether it was fear or nervousness, he just wished it was all over. Keeping below the horizon he sat for a while in the evening sunshine, fighting his nerves. He was joined by Kat as the sun disappeared, and darkness descended. She came and sat silently beside him. He was surprised when she spoke, her low soft voice asking what his wife would say about his work here.

"No wife, I'm afraid," he smiled. "One day perhaps."

Kat looked at him. "Tonight you may die. I may die. You like to make sex?"

"What? Here? Now?"

"Here. In bed. What difference does it make? It's still good. It's still better than being dead."

Peter grinned. She had a point. She was good-looking too. He made one last try, "What about your husband?"

"He is not here, now. He is in the Troodos Mountains in Cyprus, probably having sex with some partisan woman. Come." She took Peter's hand and walked out of the rocky cleft into the grassy area of the surrounding field. "Here is good." She said and pulled her blouse over her head. It was dark. Only the stars gave a little light. Peter shrugged and undid his shirt.

She was warm and entered into things with enthusiasm. Before it got serious, she said, "This is between you and me. Not serious. Just friends together. Yes?"

Peter agreed. No strings. Just friends. "Yes!"

***

Two hours later they boarded the truck and set off for the camp and the target. Peter was quite calm and relaxed now the action had begun. He thought about the early evening with Kat. That had done him no harm, nor her it seemed.

They bumped and clattered through the darkness until the truck stopped. The party dismounted and collected their gear.

They split into their sections. Peter and Theo set out for their place at the fence to the enclosure, which now loomed up ahead of them. Before leaving they checked watches at 0200. "We leave by 0300," Theo made the point, then turned and departed with Peter in tow. They approached the barbed wire fence and located an upright pole that braced and secured the fence in place. Checking that the wire was not electrified, Theo produced tape and bound the wire firmly to the pole at every point where wire and pole met. Then from his pocket he produced metal hooks with a loop at the shank end. As he cut each wire he left it to Peter to pass the cut wire through the loop and twist it tight. The wire could be now hooked back in place to appear complete. The others now joined them and all the inside party passed through. Wallace took up his place on the slope and checked his lines-of-sight. Peter hooked the fence in place, and joined Theo, Sergeant Mitchell and Corporal Hardy, poised awaiting the sentries.

Though Peter was tense, he was also prepared. When the sentries appeared he stepped forward, knife in hand and despatched him without a sound. Theo managed his own in similar silent fashion. The two men then departed to lay the charges at the comm building, shadowed by their cover party of the two soldiers.

Theo nudged Peter to get his attention. The doorway next to the comm building doors was marked. Peter looked at Theo unable to make out the sign and not understanding. Theo grinned in the reflected light of the small gaps in the blackout. Then he made the sign of a big explosion, and tapped the sign on the door.

Peter realised that the sign was a warning emblem with a picture of an exploding bomb. Understanding dawned and he grinned in turn. They made sure the charges they laid included the part of the building that included the magazine.

All went well for Kat until the last minute. Having placed the charges without being discovered, they made their way back to the fence, just within the time limit set by Theo.

As Kat approached the wire, a light shone and highlighted them. A sentry appeared and called them to halt. His MP40 was cocked and covered them.

They were on the inside of the fence under the light, and there was no place to run.

She shrugged and signed for her two men to lay down their guns.

The sentry approached, avoiding the beam of light from the lamp trained on them. Peter and Theo had returned just before the light burst into life exposing Kat and her two men. Theo stepped over to the origin of the light, while Peter closed the gap to the sentry holding them. The scene was frozen when the crack of a rifle coincided with the disappearance of the beam of light. Peter stepped forward and grabbed the front lip of the German soldier's helmet and yanked it back. The crack of the man's neck, as it broke, was clearly heard by the small group.

Theo joined the party. "Go now!" Kat and the two Greeks picked up their weapons and ran to the break of the fence. Peter opened it, and then took the time to close it once more. Wallace's rifle spoke again, once twice and then a third time. Then he joined the party for the return to the truck. They started to hear the explosions as they boarded the truck. Several smaller bangs. Followed by a big bang that just seemed to grow and grow.

The group looked at each other and Peter grinned. Sgt Harry Mitchell laughed aloud. Kat smiled and nodded her head, and the others joined in to celebrate the success of their mission.

***

Back at Ritz Giorgio had produced half a sheep. His wife had been cooking it all day at the farm. When they returned with the good news, the meat was brought to the Ritz and the entire party had a celebratory feast. They did not drop their guard. The watch on the farm spotted the slow approach of a truck from the direction of the town. Giorgio and his wife made it home in time to get up out of bed in a bad temper to receive the intruders. The Italian troops searched the house, and finding nothing carried on along the road to continue their search of the area. It appeared that the explosions had devastated the area in the vicinity of the communication centre and the barracks. It had also created havoc at the tank farm, where the fuel storage tanks had been punctured by flying debris. Most of the stored fuel had been lost in the fires that resulted. The Italian searchers, showed little concern for the casualties received by their German allies and, according to Giorgio, they had been roped in to do the present duty because of the high casualty rate among the Grenadiers caught by the explosion and collapse of their barracks.

That night, Kat joined Peter in his bed. Her whispered excuse was, "We survived, didn't we?"

The following day Peter went over the Stavros cruiser, checking engines and all the other equipment, before starting them up and running them to test that they ran smoothly. Then he topped up everything against the possibility of the boat being needed during the next few months. The radio-coded call to 'Arab' Lawrence, confirmed the appointment for pick up from Milos.

Three nights later they left the Ritz in the charge of Giorgio and his family, for the return to the Grotto. The three-day journey failed to excite, since it passed without incident, to the considerable relief of the group. Reaction had set in, and all were feeling the let-down after the excitement of the raid. Sub Lieutenant Lawrence was waiting in the ML as arranged, and brought the party back to their Grotto sanctuary.

Chapter thirteen

A flying visit

The atmosphere in the grotto was subdued. Peter felt, as did the others, the reaction from the up close and personal killing, which he accepted was necessary. But it still made it difficult to sleep.

It showed in his manner, which tended to become impatient and irritable for no apparent reason.

The others had problems as well. After action like that, there was always a bill to pay, fear catching up with apprehension about what comes next. Everyone was jumpy. It was with relief they received the news of their next project.

Theo spent time in the communications area decoding a recent batch of signals. So it was with some concern Peter, Kat and Harry Mitchell met in the main cabin of the ML, to discuss their next assignment.

"The island of Crete is now in the hands of the occupying forces!"

The other three looked at Theo surprised. They were all aware of this, weren't they?

Theo expanded on his opening statement. "The occupation is in fact not quite as complete as the Germans would have us believe, and it is now evident that even after the most brutal attempts to subjugate the population, the occupying forces are expending troops and resources on keeping islanders quiet. Troops have to move in numbers for protection from ambushes and snipers. There is no such thing as a safe place, except for within heavily guarded areas.

"These Partisans need supplies and we need to keep the Germans jumpy. One of the occupation forces' main assets is the Luftwaffe. To the Partisans that means two things, the Fieseler-Storch spotter plane, and the JU 87, the Stuka dive bomber. The Storch can almost hover. It is ideal for spotting and is becoming a serious threat. It makes communications in the mountains difficult, and means the partisans are spending more time keeping out of sight and less time panicking the Germans.

"Our job is to rendezvous with two fishing boats offshore with supplies. Then five of us will be dropped off at Iraklion. Our job is to wreck as many aircraft as possible and—where possible—blow up their fuel supply." He paused and rolled out a chart.

Peter commented, "Iraklion is the biggest town on the island. Surely it will be well defended?"

Theo smiled nastily. "You are right. But it is the most difficult to approach for the partisans in the mountains. The town itself seems to be just carrying on, the people keeping their heads down with all the troops about. Also, there are probably more collaborators in the town than in the rest of the island put together. I expect the airfield guard to be less jumpy than in the other airfields closer to country areas and more accessible to partisan attacks."

He pointed to the map. "We land here and cross to the main road. We have a cart to carry the explosives, and tools for runway repairs. I have been promised that a raid will happen causing holes in the runway. It is risky, but we all knew that."

Kat said, "How about me?"

"You are our secret weapon. While we argue our way in you arrive in a car with a chauffeur. If we don't talk our way in, we remove the guards and drive inside in the car. Towing our gear. We blow the guard house once we are well inside the base. Hopefully, they will believe we are trying to get in, or just being destructive."

"How about the car?"

"It is arranged already."

Peter looked sharply at Theo. "Arranged already? How long has this been planned."

Theo smiled again. "Several plans have been ongoing since Crete was taken. This is one that has been anticipated for some time. I supported it because we have the right people and the resources to carry it off. Your boat was the deciding factor. The fishing boat might have worked. But now they are all logged in and out. So, instead of a quiet entry through the harbour, we use a secret landing on the coast. It will mean a long walk out for recovery. I estimate 35 miles to a place called Plaka on the shores of Mirabello Bay. Because of the distance, I have arranged for a truck to take us at least part of the way there." He looked around the group his face absolutely impassive, "Any questions?"

Kat said, "If the truck is left in town, we must each know where to find it, have you town maps for us all?"

Theo said, "In each pack, along with clothes and weapons."

Peter said, "Weapons? Why do we need weapons?"

Theo said, "If you are caught, you must have German or recovered British guns only. They must think we are guerrillas from the Island, not raiders from elsewhere."

Peter nodded slowly, he could see the point.

Theo looked around once more. When there was no more questions, he added, "Your part in the raid is in the pack. Read it and absorb the information, then bring up any problem you see. We leave 15:00 hours tomorrow. Operation starts 03:00 hours.

***

Peter was in his cabin when a knock came at his door.

"Come in!" He called his back to the door. He turned as he heard the door shut and the lock click. He found himself facing Kat. She looked at him defiantly. "I am scared. I have been given these things, and no gun." She spilled sexy underwear and a small dress, high heel shoes. "I must dress like a tart, but cannot defend myself."

She stepped forward and Peter held his arms out and hugged her. "You'll be alright. We will be there."

"Oh, Peter. I do not like this. Can I stay tonight?"

***

The ML crept slowly, closing the shore until it came to a halt. The dinghies were pulled alongside. Theo, Peter, and Kat boarded the first with one of the Greeks. Sgt Mitchell, Wallace and Hardy boarded the other with the second Greek. The dinghies were joined by a rope with the second on a rope from the ML being paid-out until the boats reached the shore. After the boats had been emptied of all their gear, the line was jerked The crew of the ML hauled the dinghies back and they were brought inboard and stowed. The shore party moved off together, Kat carrying her high heeled shoes, clad temporarily in overalls and boots.

They walked along the foreshore until they reached the slipway of a boatyard Theo led the way to a shed where the push cart was located. He and Peter unpacked it checking the contents carefully. When they were satisfied they replaced the tools on the top and signalled the others to begin their part of the operation.

Kat and one of the Greeks went off with Wallace to collect the car. Peter and Theo waited for the promised air raid. Sgt Mitchell, Hardy and the other Greek left the shed to find locations near enough to the main gate to give support if the gate needed to be blown.

***

The drone of aircraft, followed by the wail of sirens, warned then that zero hour was almost there. The crump of AA fire could be heard as the aircraft approached and the noise became louder. Finally, the roar of engines swept over their shed as the bombers came to perform their part of the operation.

The two men struggled to get the cart onto the road, finally managing it with difficulty. Having got it moving, they made their way toward the airfield. The attacking aircraft had now gone and there was a pall of smoke hanging over the field.

At the gate there were several people hanging around, pushing and shoving, being thrust away by the sentries. Theo pushed through and spoke to the sentry, Peter watched as he spoke vociferously, pointing to the tools on the barrow and the airfield, where the smoke was still boiling skywards. The sentry was shrugging his shoulders when the car arrived, with Kat seated in the rear.

The confusion increased as she and her Greek joined the growing turmoil around the gates. Other

guards came out of the guard room to assist their colleague with the crowd. Peter dropped the satchel
charge he carried, and stepped into the guard room in
time to see the guard commander, an Unteroffizer,
reaching for the telephone. He looked up as Peter
came in. Peter pointed to the phone and shook his
head. The German reached to rotate the call handle.
Peter's knife flew. The phone dropped to the desk.
The soldier grabbed desperately at the knife that pro-
truded from his chest. His hands fell and he collapsed
to the desk. Peter replaced the telephone and withdrew his knife from the corpse. Collecting an MP40
from the chair at the side of the desk, he removed a
Walther P38 from its holster and thrust it in his
waistband. Through the window he could see Theo,
now struggling with a guard who was trying to bring
his gun to bear on the group of people. Waiting for a
moment, Peter set the fuse on the satchel charge he
had left outside the door. He stepped through the
door and fired a burst from the MP40 he carried. The
civilians in the group ran, leaving the four guards the
car, and Theo and his cart. With the weapon pointing
at the guards he beckoned them forward to disarm
them, wondering what he could do with them at that
juncture.

His problem was solved. The man, who had
been struggling with Theo, lifted his gun to shoot at
Peter. Peter beat him to the shot. As he fell the others
tried their luck. Theo shot two and Peter killed the
last one.

Theo threw the gate open and the car rolled
through. Tossing a second satchel charge into the
gates, Peter joined the others in the car, they rolled
into the growing cloud of smoke covering most of the
airfield. They were nearly at the first flight line when
the first of the charges blew. The second went off as

Peter, followed by one of the Greeks, hung his next charge on aircraft number three. There were only four Fieseler Storch planes in the open. If there were more on the airfield they had to be in the hangers.

Harry Mitchell took Hardy and Wallace with him around the revetments, where aircraft were held safely from air attack. Theo, who was busy attending to the Stukas along with Kat, was still working, so Peter and his man went toward the area where all the airfield people seemed to have gathered. Through the smoke there he made out the figures of people rushing back and forth, with hoses operating on a stack of cases which looked familiar. He suddenly realised what the panic was. The cases contained canisters of fuel for flame throwers. Beyond the stack was the shadowy outline of a Junkers JU52 cargo plane, the corrugated skin highlight by the flickering flames from two burning ME 109f aircraft. Peter sent his man back to the cart for more charges. When the man returned he had six. "All gone now."

With them in hand they circled around until he reached the other side of the Junkers aircraft. The pilots were standing in front of the aircraft, waiting while a big tractor, with a blade mounted in front, pushed burning wreckage from the path needed to extract the cargo aircraft. Peter fused and tossed one of the charges through the door of the aircraft then he rolled under the fuselage and put a fused satchel in the stack of boxes of flame-thrower fuel. Withdrawing from the scene, they made their way to the two hangers. Both just walked, each carrying two satchels over their shoulders and ignoring the people rushing past in both directions.

Nobody challenged them as they strode, as if they belonged, straight to the first hanger. Peter poked his head around the door. There were people running back and forth, around and among several single-engine aircraft. Peter was not concerned that they were one thing or another. His main concern at that moment was to cause as much mayhem as he could. He walked into the hanger, unslinging one of his satchel charges. Breaking the three-minute fuse he hung the charge on the pitot tube of the nearest aircraft, depending on the scatter of explosive and incendiary, to cause the maximum damage.

In the second hanger there were supplies, mainly clothing and stacks of parts, with some boxes of weapons off to one side. Peter looked into the boxes and found MP40's. Another contained magazines. He noticed the topmost magazines were loaded and picked one up to examine it. He unloaded the magazine into his other hand. There were fifteen bullets, so the mag was loaded without stress on the spring, He loaded the bullets into another of the magazines filling it and seating the loaded magazine into one of the new MP40's. He passed it to his companion, who received it with a grin. At the back of the hanger they found a pick-up truck. The keys were in a box on the wall marked Auto-schlussel. There was only one set of keys. There was only one truck. Peter shrugged thinking he was sick of walking anyway.

He climbed in and started the engine. It started with no hesitation, He indicated the guns and magazines. They loaded them. They also found ammunition. One box of ammunition and an assortment of uniforms went into the truck. Peter then drove out of the hanger into bedlam. In the back of his mind he had been registering explosions. Outside there seemed to be fires everywhere, and explosions still carrying on. He drove toward the place where the car had been left. At the side of the road Theo, Kat and the other Greek sat, hands on heads, with two armed guards covering them. Peter pulled up beside the soldiers, the Greek got out, stepped round the truck and shot the two men as they turned to speak to Peter.

As the men dropped, Peter called to the three seated prisoners, "Shall we go then?"

Theo looked up. There was a bruise on his face. He saw Peter and grinned. Wincing as he did so. Kat looked and leaped to her feet to help the Greek, who, Peter now saw, had been hurt. They all piled into the bed of the truck and Peter set off once more.

A small tank pulled into the road in front of them, as they came through the smoke toward the rendezvous with the car. It had a 20mm cannon in its turret it opened fire as soon as they came into view. Peter shouted, "We've been spotted!" He swerved off the road, onto the landing field itself. There was still plenty of smoke about but it was thinning already. "That tank is moving pretty fast," Peter shouted above the noise of the engine and the roar of the flames.

Kat said, "Turn left here, quickly!"

Peter swung the wheel and the truck skidded round to the left, round a thick cloud of smoke.

The tank swung early, to cut them off by going through the smoke cloud. Then Peter realised there was a burning aircraft in the smoke, as a gust cleared the smoke for a moment.

The tank must have realised too. It swerved abruptly to avoid a collision with the burning plane. The tank missed the aircraft, but the turn was too sharp and it tipped over with a crash. The fuel tank must have fractured, because there was a whoosh and the wrecked vehicle was suddenly enveloped in flame.

From behind them came an almighty explosion of flame and noise, as the fuel for the flame throwers went up. The eruption of superheated air dragged the smoke clear of the field for a few moments and the entire field was visible. The car stood waiting perhaps two hundred yards away. There were burning aircraft all over the near side of the field. Individual fires burned in the revetments along the far side of the hangers. The near hanger was burning. The supply hanger seemed to bulge as they watched.

"I think it's time we left," said Peter quietly. "We have probably upset a lot of people with our game this evening."

He reached the car and shouted to Sgt Mitchell, who was at the car already, to follow the truck. Because of the extra gear they had brought he decided to take both vehicles. Peter thought they could leave the guns and ammo for the Partisans in Crete, if they could actually locate some before they left the island.

Getting through the outer area on the opposite side of the airfield from Iraklion was likely to be a little difficult, as the turmoil at the airfield had attracted a certain amount of attention. People stood on the roads, slow to move for the two vehicles. Once they were through the immediate crowds, they thinned rapidly as they moved east. Unfortunately luck only went so far. As they progressed they realised that roadblocks had been set up on the road ahead of them. There was a queue already formed as they rounded a bend. Peter, who was driving the first vehicle just had time to swing off to the right before he became part of the line of waiting traffic.

Chapter fourteen

A Nest of Hornets.

Peter had turned into a gated road leading in toward the centre of the island. The road was lined with trees and he was aware that they were concealed from the main road and the roadblock. Despite their dimmed lights, the avenue was, because of the straight road that rose and dipped over the rolling ground without deviating, easy to follow.

At the end of the drive, because that was the nature of the road, they came to a house surrounded by dimly-sensed gardens. Gravel on the drive was apparent as the building loomed up out of the night.

The headlights lit a parked car at the door of the house. As Peter stopped the truck the front door opened. A figure came out with a lantern which illuminated the truck. The flood of Greek altered to broken German. Peter realised she was telling him to get the hell off the property.

Without thinking, Peter, who had his gun in hand at this point, spoke in English. "I beg your pardon, Madam, but the main road was rather busy. I took a wrong turning by mistake."

"You are English?" The voice was low and throaty.

"Yes, I am. I'm afraid there are German soldiers out looking for us. We rather spoilt their airfield."

"Well, come in. You can tell me all about it in comfort. Put the truck and the car behind the house.

There are stables there." Kat had come out of the truck. The lady saw her and took her arm. "Come in with me, my dear. The men can deal with the transport. By the way you can put the gun away, young man. You are among friends here."

Embarrassed, Peter did as he was told, and re-mounted the cab of the truck to drive off around the house and find the stable buildings. Having parked the two vehicles they found the rear door of the house opened. The entire party trooped in.

With the door closed, the lights were switched on to reveal a big kitchen with a wood stove giving off heat and a big pot bubbling quietly on top.

The lady, who had met them at the front door, was revealed as an elegant woman, perhaps thirty five-forty, with green eyes and a handsome face. When Peter walked in she turned to him, and held out her hand. "I am Countess Madeline Gruber." She raised her hand to forestall comment. "I am Austrian. My mother and father came from Watford. I am a widow, and my husband, the Count, hated the Nazi's passionately. We moved here in 1934, as he foresaw the Anschluss.

"The local occupation forces have merely as-sumed that I am a sympathiser, and they have left me alone so far.

"There is soup in the pot, and dishes in the cupboard there. Monika will be here in a few mo-ments to help with the serving." As she spoke the door opened, and a slim Greek woman entered, looked around and then opened the cupboard and handed out dishes.

The Countess looked at Peter and indicated that he should accompany her through to another room, where he found Kat ensconced in front of a big fire with a glass in her hand. Their hostess indicated the bottle on a tray with glasses. Peter poured drinks for Madeline and himself.

All practicality, the Countess said, "You cannot stay here, unfortunately. Somebody will have seen the truck and car come here. There is a track across the fields behind the house which will take you to Agriana. From there it must be a cautious run on back roads to the coast between Sarantaris and the point at Hersonissos. There are beaches there. They are patrolled but, if you can be picked up, with the present panic you may find the patrols have been reduced because they think you are within their cordon."

"We are placing you in danger while we are here. We should leave quickly." Kat said.

"You are right. I think if you could tie us both up, we can take a hour to get free and call for help. It should allow you to cover over twenty miles on your way. I do not wish to know where you are headed. What I do not know I cannot reveal."

Peter looked at her keenly. "Would you like to come along with us?"

She smiled. "My husband is buried here. This has been our home for the past six years. We came here to grow old together. If I survive I may yet be of use to you or others like you. In that case, if you contact me by telephone, use the word Medilan for my name. My answer will be 'My name is Madeline', it will signal all is well. If I do not answer, or a man, answers? It is not! If you approach the house without prior notice, seek for Monika, or myself. If there are others, it may not be safe. There is a stone in the sundial column where we keep a spare house key. It is immediately beneath the table top containing the dial itself. Feel around and it will move. A message can be left there if you wish. It is checked every day."

***

The two vehicles growled up the rise and the sound of the sea was suddenly there. It had taken two hours to cover the thirty miles from the Countess's home, but they had taken no chances.

Pick-up could not be until tomorrow night, but he had realised that. There was a cave in the cliffs below them. But, more importantly, a contact had been made with three troopers from the Greek cavalry who had gone to ground as soon as the parachutes started to fall. Their Sergeant had decided that their best tactic was to provide information and hurt the occupying forces. They had encountered Peter on that last stretch of road before reaching the cliffs.

The Sergeant had been informed that the party was on its way by the priest in a village where they stopped to check their directions. Though the questions were all asked by the Greeks in the party, the priest guessed and spoke to Peter in English. A message was sent to the Sergeant, by the radio kept in the Priest's house.

Though the Sergeant had collected some arms and ammunition from the troops leaving the island, the guns and ammunition provided by the raiding party was a welcome addition. The explosives remaining would also be left.

As a result of the meeting they did not use the cave after all. They stayed at a hideout the Sergeant had found in the hill slope behind the small group of houses at the beach. Both vehicles were disposed of, the car being taken to a garage on the south of the island to be re-sprayed, the truck to a barn in the centre of the island.

For Peter there would be no rest until they had made it back to the grotto at least. He was worried about the Countess, especially if the Germans suspected she had helped them?

They did not get off the island on this occasion without some serious opposition. In the village down the coast, the hairdresser had been told that there was activity on the sea shore where the party were relaxing in the sea, swimming. Someone heard English spoken by some of the swimmers. The wrong person overheard the conversation. He passed it to a contact in the Italian occupation troops at Agios Nicolaos. By the time troops arrived to investigate, the swimmers had gone. When the pick-up time arrived, they found soldiers along the cliffs above the foreshore they would use for the embarkation.

Both sides opened fire as the raiders moved down to the beach. Two machine guns opened fire from the cliffs, but were at a disadvantage firing downhill. Peter blasted off two magazines of 9mm ammunition from his MP40, which caused them to become even more erratic. The ML opened up with the three-pounder and caused the cliff to crumble beneath one of the machine guns. When they turned the gun to fire at the other emplacement, the machine gunner gave up.

Peter turned in time to see Theo fall back from the dinghy into the water. He instinctively dived after him and caught the weakly struggling man, dragging him to the surface. He was bleeding from a wound in his upper chest. Hands reached down and hauled him into the boat. Peter hung on to the grab rope while they pulled rapidly to the ML.

Tom Wells took charge of Theo, while the others concentrated on getting dry and finding the food laid out for them. Peter spoke briefly to Lawrence on the bridge then retired to his cabin to change and get started on the necessary reports.

***

The arrival at the grotto was anti-climatic after the excitement of the past few days. After the initial euphoria of success and survival, the downside was just a natural reaction. The fact that Theo had been injured at the last moment was an additional source of worry for the group. He would need serious medical attention.

Rendezvous was arranged with a Walrus aircraft, despatched from a convoy en-route to Alexandria, meeting the ML at the location of Strabo Trench south of the islands. The ML stood by while the crew refuelled the Walrus from a rubber blimp using a pump driven from the engine. The blimp, once emptied, was transferred to the ML for disposal, while the bandaged and sedated Theo was passed over to the amphibian with a packet of documents and reports for Peter's boss in Alexandria.

The entire operation was a nerve-racking exercise for both boat and aircraft. The sea was calm enough, but the Walrus was still tossing about alarmingly as far as Peter was concerned. Discussing it later, Jerry Lawrence mentioned that, watching the antics of the ML on what they regarded as pretty calm sea, could be equally alarming.

The rubber fuel container completely emptied was put into store for use by the ML and/ or the fishing boat. It could increase the range of either craft with minimum disruption. When carrying the equivalent supply of fuel in cans, it entailed endless cans to be stacked on deck, with the consequent increase of risk in action.

***

The arrival of Captain Phillip Poppadopolis, recently transferred from Popski's Private Army, was intended to reinforce the unit and replace Theo. Phillipo, as he liked to be called, had been trained in most aspects of the violent arts of guerrilla warfare. Having taken part in three separate raids behind enemy lines, and participating in the destruction of three separate fuel dumps, he had earned his spurs with the eccentric Colonel in command.

His attitude, when he arrived in the Grotto, was signalled by the way he looked once at Kat, and decided she would be his.

Peter, who met the Captain after his initial discussion with Kat, looked with some amusement at the burgeoning black eye and the scratch which made the basically handsome face look a little lop-sided.

Peter had been courteously interested upon their introduction. "Have you met Kat by any chance? She is a very important member of the team here."

Phillipo smiled grimly. "A magnificent woman," he acknowledged admiringly "I am sure we will be able to work together."

"Currently, we have a problem. On the face of it, just a simple pick-up from Agios Pathos, scheduled for tomorrow night at 2200. Among the documents you brought with you there are things to be done. The first is not quite as straightforward as it appeared. The Castle at Agios Pathos is the rendezvous, and though it is not too far from the beach, there is a road that takes a similar time to drive. The road is a good alternative if we had transport. If we are on foot the enemy could chase in their vehicles and that would be a problem."

Phillipo said, "What about a diversion to keep the area clear?"

"Sounds good. I presume we would need to do something about the soldiers stationed in Yeraki. It

could be useful. We need uniforms! If we could release the prisoners in the prison there, it should distract the troops from chasing us?"

Phillipo had been thinking meanwhile. "I have
a friend." He shrugged. "Maybe acquaintance, at
Agrila. It is further down the coast from the Castle. I
would need to go there one day before the pick-up.
Kranko is a crook. He is bound to have a vehicle."

"How well do you know him? Is he trustworthy?"

Phillipo looked at Peter in astonishment.
"Good God! No! He is a thief and, I believe, a mur-
derer, but he loves money and I will appeal to his
patriotism." He smiled as he said this. "He will not
betray us, do not worry."

Peter made the decision. "Right, Phillipo. Take
the two Greeks and the fishing boat. If you go now,
you will be there in the darkness tonight. "He looked
at his watch. "Maybe four hours for the boat to get
there from here. I cannot spare the fuel to do the two
trips needed in the ML. Collect as many Italian/
German uniforms as you can. We will need them for
future operations."

At Phillipo's raised eyebrow, Peter said, "We
also need a MAS boat, if you happen to come across
one."

"I'll keep it in mind," Phillipo said drily. "I
should be on my way if I am to get to Agios Pathos
on time. I will make the distraction and be at the
pick-up point by 2200, probably with transport. " He
turned and made off in search of the Greeks.

***

The dinghy retreated back to the fishing boat as
Junos, the boatman, drew it in by its attached rope.
Once it was close to the boat, he tied off the rope and

started the engine. The fishing boat disappeared into the night on its way back to the Grotto.

***

On Agios Pathos, Phillipo hitched the MP40 onto his shoulder and followed, by the brothers, set off up to the road that ran parallel to the beach. They approached the darkened house with caution. Phillipo made his way to the door and knocked. After a pause the door opened and a figure appeared wrapped in a sheet.

"I am Poppadopolis, here to see Kranko."

The girl stood aside to let him in. Phillipo lifted his gun and pointed to the sheet.

The girl shrugged and removed it, and turned around to show that she was entirely naked. Phillipo, pink-faced, gestured for her to replace the sheet and entered the room beyond. The girl went through a side door and, still in his view, got into a single bed. The room was otherwise empty. In the main room Kranko sat at the table. He did not look as if he had been in bed and Phillipo guessed that he had not.

"So it is you," Kranko said. "Leave my daughter alone!"

Phillipo shrugged. "Of course! I see you are still in business, as am I. I need transport and assistance. I have people to collect and a diversion to arrange. I have the feeling that any help you give will earn rewards after the war is over."

"And when will that be? I am quite happy with things the way they are. Why should I help you?"

"Perhaps I will let slip that I was informed by Kranko, directed even, to shoot a few soldiers."

Kranko thought for a few minutes. Then, "I have a truck. Where do you need to go?"

"I need a diversion. What is in Yeraki?"

"There is a small barracks and a prison there, not much else." Kranko was sounding cagey.

"Presuming you will come and help, you can wear a mask. They won't recognise you."

Again the shrug. "Maria, feed us. Where are your men?"

"Just the two outside."

"Call them. We can eat, then we go tomorrow evening. There is time."

The pretty girl, dressed now, passed Phillipo at the door as he went to call the brothers. They were there immediately, and came in to be introduced.

***

Phillipo took the opportunity to sleep through the day. The brothers played cards and flirted with Maria, finally dozing, in turn. Until nightfall.

As soon as darkness fell Kranko got the battered pick-up from behind his house and they set off up the road. Plans had been made and they now were ready to carry out the raid on the prison in Yeraki.

***

At the prison, the Italian Sergeant, dealt the cards to the Corporal, seated opposite. The guards at the gate were yawning already. One idly strolled down the road to investigate a noise, out of sheer boredom. The other heard his colleague returning and lit a cigarette shielded from the barracks by the gate post.

He started to turn to speak to his colleague, only to find himself facing a big Greek with a wooden club in his hands. Anthony clouted the hapless sentry with it. The sparks from the cigarette scattered as the glowing tip hit the ground. The sentry was caught as he fell by Anthony, who was joined by his brother dragging the other sentry. Both men worked to strip the guards removing their uniforms. They signalled the others. The truck rolled down the road engine off, coming to a halt beside the prison gates.

The two unfortunate guards were gagged and bound, and thrown in the back with their uniforms.

Inside the office the card game was well in progress. The two NCOs were joined by the jailor who entered rubbing his hands together and grinning.

"What is so funny?" The Sergeant asked.

"All those women in there. I have been watching them. Some of them are 'whoee'." He made a sign with his hands. "I could do them a lot of good."

The Sergeant grinned savagely. "They are for our lords and masters. You touch them before they get their hands on them, they will cut your jewels adrift and feed them to the dogs." He laughed. "Mind you, from what I saw in the latrine last night, they probably wouldn't notice that you had been there." He laughed coarsely at his own humour.

"Where is everybody tonight?" The jailor asked.

"They sent the Lieutenant down to Lakos, with a squad to escort the special prisoner for interrogation by the Gestapo pigs."

"Shit! She was the best looking of them all."

"Nothing but the best for the Gestapo," the Corporal commented. "So, with Mario and Paulo on the gate, we are rather short-handed, you stay here tonight. No slipping off to see Angela."

Grumbling, the jailor left the office to make up a bed in one of the empty cells. He preferred the soft bed and the soft arms of Angela. She was not the best looking woman in town, but she was friendly and accommodating, and it was a long way from Brindisi. He wondered sometimes, as he worked, if his wife had a friendly lover in his absence. The shrug that followed the thought was expressive. *What happens in Agios Pathos, stays in Agios Pathos!*

***

Phillipo and the two brothers entered the office armed with their MP40's. Kranko, now hooded, followed. Aristotle went through to the jail while Phillipo supervised the stripping of the two NCO's.

"Where are the other members of the platoon stationed here?" He asked in good Italian.

The Sergeant considered a moment, before deciding to tell the truth. "They escorted the woman spy to Lakos. They will be back soon."

Phillipo considered for a moment. "Good. Put the prisoners in the gatehouse cells. We'll blow up the prison when we leave. That should get the attention of the island population.

Aristotle came through from the prison followed by a string of women.

"What the devil is this?" Phillipo asked.

Aristotle said. "The prison is being used to hold the women until they can be deployed to the brothels for the German army."

One of the women stepped forward, eyes flashing and fists clenched. "My husband is a partisan. I am at home alone when the bastards come and grab me as brothel bait. I am a respectable married woman." She waved her hands at the others. "Here are girls of sixteen/ and others, like myself, married women, to be given to these animals to play with." She spat at the Sergeant standing in his underwear.

He shook his head, "Not us, madam. It is the Germans."

The unfortunate Italian received a slap across the face from the irate lady. "It's the Italians rounding us up for the Germans to use. That is worse."

Phillipo looked at Aristotle.

Aristotle shrugged. "Seventeen women. Ten will join the partisans in the hills. The others have no relatives here."

Phillipo made the decision. "Send the ten home to collect their things and go off to join the partisans. They must hurry, so get them away. The others stay with us." He turned to the Sergeant once more. "How many men are with the lieutenant?"

"Six, sir. The others of the platoon are detached to aid in the search for partisans in the north of the island.

The sound of an approaching vehicle began to filter through the night.

"You two get into uniform and on the gate." Phillipo turned to the remaining women. "Back into the prison while I deal with this matter."

He grabbed the uniform of the corporal and slipped the tunic on. His trousers were the same colour and they would pass in the semi-darkness outside the front door.

To the brothers he said, "Take out the last two, then follow the others in." They nodded, and went out to the gate to take up their posts as sentries.

He took up his MP40 and hung it from his shoulder by the strap. The handguns, taken from the two NCO's, he slipped into the drawer of the desk.

He stepped over to the door in time to meet the young lieutenant, who ignored him and walked into the office removing his gloves. The men with him followed to the door and stood awaiting their orders.

Phillipo lifted the MP40. "Place your pistol on the desk and stand facing the wall."

"How dare you, corporal. I will do no such thing…."

A burst of fire splintered the floor in front of the young man causing him to jump back in shock.

"I will not say it again!" Phillipo said.

The lieutenant drew out his Beretta and laid in on the desk. He then turned and faced the wall.

The men outside the door stepped into the room with their hands up. Between them, the raiders disarmed them, then supervised their stripping to collect their uniforms.

The entire contingent of soldiers was crammed into the holding cell located behind the office.

Phillipo went through to the prison building, located on the other side of a courtyard behind the office building. The explosives were in small packets, each with a separate timer. He strung four around each of the supporting pillars within the old building.

Using the Army truck, they piled the women in and set off for the rendezvous at the castle. Kranko followed in the pick-up.

As they cleared the small town, the satisfying roar of an explosion signalled the end of that part of the mission. Phillipo looked through the window to the rear of the truck. The women were all chatting among themselves. He wondered what Peter would have to say about this.

Chapter fifteen

Rescue and retribution

Samantha Brown approached the rendezvous carefully. Her partner, Emma Kovak, had been captured this afternoon. Sam had got away because it seemed that the searching troops had only been told of one agent.

She was upset, but she knew that Emma would not give anything away. She had a pill if they started to use torture.

Ahead, she saw the truck beside the road. She had ducked down when she saw the outline on the skyline. Now she saw the flicker of moonlight glint from the windscreen.

A voice in her ear scared the life out of her. "You must be either Samantha or Emma?"

The man in the British army uniform had Sergeant's stripes on his sleeve, "Hullo, I'm Harry Mitchell. Which one are you?"

"I'm Samantha. Call me Sam."

They walked together to the truck.

Peter saw her and turned to the others. "Right Mount up. We'll be on our way."

Turning to Sam, he said, "I'm Peter Woods, the boat driver. Where is your friend?"

"She was taken today. Down to the prison in Yeraki, I believe. I saw her taken off. There was nothing I could do."

Phillipo said, "She is the one the Italians took to Lakos to meet the Gestapo. Kranko, over here! What is the set up at Lakos?"

Kranko thought for a moment. "They have a jeep! But they are short staffed. Like here, they send their men to search the hills. There will be about twelve men, plus the Gestapo man when he returns."

Peter looked at Kranko, eyebrow raised. Kranko looked back unfazed. "With a shrug he explained. "I supply all the local garrisons with little extra's, so they all know me and they talk. I speak Italian and I lived in Austria for two years. I have good ears. I am a businessman, so I have customers on both sides of the line. Money is international," he said, with a defiant grin.

Phillipo and Peter exchanged looks. "How long will it take to get there?" Peter asked.

"Using the coast road, about forty minutes." Kranko said promptly.

Peter looked at the men gathered there, Two Greeks still in Italian uniform and Phillipo also in uniform, plus his own landing group, which included Sergeant Mitchell, Private Hardy and Private Wallace.

He turned to CPO Smith. "Take the ladies to the boat and wait, while we pop along and see if we can liberate Emma."

The cool voice of Sam interrupted the proceedings. "I will come with you, sir. Emma will not know you and she will suspect a trick. She came from Yugoslavia where things are a little different. If I am there, she knows she can trust me. So I am coming with you."

Peter nodded. "Okay. Mount up. Check your weapons, but no shooting until I order it."

They piled aboard the truck. Leaning out, Peter spoke to the CPO. "Wait out of sight until 0300. If we are not back by then, go back to base and call back tomorrow night. I'll contact you with the small radio."

***

At the army base at Lakos, (it was actually the police station), Scharfuhrer Helmut Schmidt stretched his back and yawned. It was boring just sitting waiting for the Gestapo man to arrive. As the senior rank in the base at present, the Wehrmacht Major, Hans Vogel, who commanded the base was in the hills with his men. Schmidt was here for the benefit of the Gestapo. He considered the woman brought in by the Italians. *Better than average, not Greek, south Europe*, he guessed. He sighed; he would not have kicked her out of bed, that was for sure. Mind you, when that little shit of a Gestapo Oberst had finished with her, she would be of no use to anybody.

He heard the sound of the army truck outside, and the sound of the sentries snapping to attention. Lazily, he rose to his feet. After all he was in the Major's chair. A woman with a Walther automatic was a surprise. The man in Naval Officer's uniform was another. He was British. The officer reached across and took the Luger from the holster on Schmidt's hip.

The realisation that this was a rescue party sank in.

"Where is the woman prisoner?" Peter said in passable German.

The denial came almost to his lips, until common sense was re-established. He said weakly, "Cell three."

"Uniform off." The order, accompanied by the lifted gun, encouraged him to strip off his tunic and pants, and finally his beloved boots.

He found himself thrust in with the other men in their underwear.

The jeep and truck drove away from the base, carrying the raiding party, and the contents of the armoury.

***

The rendezvous was made in time and, having transferred the passengers, the truck and the jeep made their way back to Kranko's village. The jeep was driven by one of the rescued women whose husband was a partisan, She was already considering how to get the weapons to them. Kranko was grateful for the new truck, and the jeep. He was resigned to the fact that he would be used by Phillipo while the war was on. It was odd. For the first time he began to think about the occupation in terms of people rather than profit.

***

Dawn was breaking as the ML finally tied up in the grotto. Kat took the two agents and the rescued ladies along to the section already annexed for the females of the group. Peter and Phillipo went through to the room used as an office. Nick, who had been monitoring the radio while they were away, greeted them with a bunch of signals in his hand. "Did it all go well?"

Peter shrugged. "As well as can be expected, I suppose. What have you got for us?"

Nick passed over the messages, stacked in order. "Basically more of the same. Get hold of a MAS boat to use as cover for general operations. There is also a priority target, which will be easier to plan for, when we actually own a MAS boat. The rest is general admin stuff."

Peter nodded looking at the priority target. "Anafi? What is there, to make it a priority target."

Nick answered, "They are building an airfield there. They will be able to control the airspace all around the Med, and raid Alexandria from there."

Peter nodded slowly. "I see. Well, you had better get together all the information on the place that you can. We will take a look in the morning."

Both Peter and Phillipo headed for their bunks. Neither had slept for the past twenty-four hours. When Peter's head hit the pillow, he was asleep instantly.

***

When he wakened, to accept a priority message nine hours later, he felt better. The message was a general fleet address from the Admiral to all unit commanders, thanking them for their contribution to maintaining Malta and the Egyptian bases for the past year.

It was only then Peter realised that Christmas was coming.

There was also a letter from Amy. As he opened it in the privacy of his cabin, he wondered at the anticipation he felt whenever he received one of her letters. It still struck him as strange the way they had immediately become friends from their first meeting on the car journey to Hamworthy.

As usual the letter was full of the general chat which he had learned to enjoy about her life in general. There was no mention of a boyfriend or sign that she was seeking one, she asked how he was enjoying life in the sun. He looked around, and grinned.

He was under a canopy of rock, generally only going out at night. Though he conceded they did see the sun when they needed to travel in daylight.

He finished the letter noting the simple. 'Yours, Amy' at the end. He thought briefly about the pleasure her letters brought. He wondered for a few moments more. Then the interruptions began. He set aside the letter and started dealing with the next objective scheduled.

***

A meeting, following the rescue, sorted out the distribution of the ladies from the prison. Four of them elected to accompany Emma Kovak to Alexandria where they would be looked after by the staff. Samantha was scheduled to stay at the grotto for an unspecified period. Her task had been to bring Emma out. Her knowledge of the islands could be useful to the raiders. The other two volunteered to look after the people in the grotto, to stay near their families at least.

It was Samantha who mentioned it. "On Agios Pathos, at the village of Zante in the north, there is a battered MAS boat, anchored out of the way. It's waiting until someone could be spared to fix it or sink it. Furthermore, at Chalki off the west coast of Rhodes, there is a MAS boat moored for most nights. The officer in charge is sleeping with the Mayor's wife.

"Emma recovered a stack of information from his briefcase and pockets. He is supposed to be there for the foreseeable future. If we hauled the damaged boat to a point offshore from Chalki, and stole the boat from the harbour, the damaged boat could be blown-up in sight of the shore, to make the enemy to think the stolen boat was destroyed. We would then have a boat we could use to deceive the enemy, which they would not know we had." She stopped and took a breath, "What do you think?"

"I think you will fit in here very well, Sam." Peter turned to Phillipo and Kat, "How does it sound to you two?"

Kat nodded. "Sounds good to me."

Phillipo also agreed. "If I take the fishing boat, I could tow it to Rhodes. We could probably make up a convincing order on paper for me to do the towing job, if I am stopped."

Chapter sixteen

A gift horse

The two women stood in the wind on the bridge of the ML, both gripping the grab-bar firmly as the boat crashed and smashed through the three foot waves. It was an exciting place to be, but debilitating as well. Eventually, Samantha elected to go down to the saloon to lie down and relax for a while, leaving Kat and Peter alone on the bridge.

The starboard machine gunner spoke up. "Boat approaching, sir. Correction. Two, maybe three boats starboard bow. Coming up fast. My guess would be 'eytie' MAS boats."

Peter brought the boat round to a course parallel to the approaching boats, and gradually increased speed until, by the time they were abreast of the ML, he was ready to shadow them.

They were three boats, the two leading boats ignoring the third, which seemed to have trouble keeping up. It was nearly 100 metres behind them as they dashed across the waters through the darkness. Their location perfectly clear from the wash of white water they were creating. Peter dropped back to the third boat and instructed the Chief to get fenders out on the port side, and muster a boarding party,

The Chief reported all was ready. Peter called Jerry Lawrence forward to take over control of the ML. Then, on his order, the boat drew alongside the MAS boat. The helmsman seemed to think the ML was one of his colleagues. The boarders slung loops of rope round the deck rails, and leapt aboard. The gunner standing behind the bridge jerked upright, too late to do anything, collapsing from the blow from the CPO. The boarders swiftly took control of the boat, the engine controls accessed and shut down gradually. The bulk of the Italian crew were taken in their berths or in the mess room. A German Naval Lieutenant drew his pistol, but only managed to shoot his foot as Peter hit him with a roundhouse swing, the nine millimetre automatic gripped in his hand, causing the man to spit out two teeth as he collapsed to the deck. Peter took the gun from the man's hand and pointed to the blood, now visible, coming from the wounded foot. The Italian medic checking his fellow crewmen shrugged and reached for the first aid kit.

Within five minutes the boat was secure, and the crew penned into the mess. All ten Italians, plus the German officer, packed into the main cabin under the watchful eyes of Anthony and Aristotle.

Peter, Jerry, and Arthur Smith quickly worked out the control set-up. With Jerry Lawrence now at the controls, the MAS boat was sent back to the grotto to be refuelled, with strict instructions to keep the prisoners unaware of where they were. They would be transferred to Alexandria when Peter went for the brief on the next assignment.

The ML rendezvoused with the fishing boat as arranged and the decoy boat diverted to a cove on the island of Manos, for possible use in the future.

***

Back in the grotto the two boats were re-fuelled and the Italian boat checked over for problems. Peter questioned the Italian Lieutenant, Bonetti, who had commanded the captured boat. He seemed quite pleased to be out of the war and, when it was put to him, he grinned. He indicated the German lying in the cot at the other end of the room used as their cell. "'Herr Schicklegruber' there is an arrogant son-of-a-bitch. He threw his weight about with the full co-operation of my exalted leader, Contramiraglio (Commodore) De Lazio. I preferred to keep him up-set and annoyed, in ways he could not challenge. He is trained to drive a battleship and knows little about MAS boats. So I make sure that he spends most of his time grinding his teeth in frustration. There is nothing wrong with my beautiful boat. She is the fastest in the flotilla, just cannot perform for Leutnant Wagner there."

Bonetti's speech was delivered 'sotto voce', entirely in New Jersey-accented English, a result of the three years spent with his uncle in Newark, USA.

Peter looked keenly at the Italian Lieutenant. "I take it you are not impressed by your German allies."

"That specimen is typical of the people they have sent to us. He is an inexperienced, arrogant prig who treats us like serfs. Our senior officers put up with it, because they treat us like serfs also. My di-rect commanding officer, who is the hands-on leader of the boats, is one of us, but his commanding officer is a career Captain who has only been to sea as a pas-senger. Never had a seagoing command, but gives his orders for us to obey, regardless of the consequences. The German people are there to stiffen out back-bones." The grin re-appeared. "You should have shot him somewhere more final, I think!"

Peter smiled, "Did you not know? He shot himself by mistake!"

Bonetti looked astonished. "He shot himself?"

Peter nodded.

"He has been telling us that he is the only one in the crew to be wounded by fighting back against the enemy. We thought he had been wounded by your men."

Peter smiled. "I wounded him. I hit him round the ear with my Browning 9mm. He lost two teeth. That was when he shot himself."

Before Peter departed for Alexandria he spoke to Phillipo, Kat and Nick about Bonetti's revelations regarding the Germans posted to the Italian units. "We must keep it in mind. There may be ways we can exploit the differences, to our advantage."

***

Peter left with Kat and the prisoners in the ML the following evening. A rendezvous had been arranged with a patrolling destroyer, fifty miles south of Agios Pathos Island.

Signals exchanged, the two craft lined up and the destroyer dropped its motor launch into the sea. The transfer was made in two rapid trips.

Leaving Jerry Lawrence in command of the ML to return to the grotto, Peter, Kat, and the prisoners were deposited at Alexandria 18 hours later.

Commander Marker greeted then coolly. "The briefing is in the CO.'s office. Get yourselves some lunch and be back here at 14;00. Oh, by the way, promotion has come through for your number one, Lawrence. To Lieutenant, with immediate effect. So, with your recommendation, he will be due a command."

Peter looked at Marker, restraining his anger at the dismissive attitude. He nodded "Thank you. I'll let him know."

Peter and Kat bumped into Commander Lancaster as they left the office.

"Here already, are you?" Roger Lancaster said. Let's go and have lunch. Turning promptly, he led them off to the jeep parked beside the road. "You drive, Peter, will you? I still get twinges from my leg, and it gives me a chance to canoodle with the lady." His grin removed any offence from the comment.

***

They ate in the officer's mess on the base and Roger used the moment to get a progress report from Peter.

At the table he took the time to give them an outline of the projected raid. "Basically the raid is to stop the construction of the airfield on the island of Anafi.

When they returned from lunch, there was no sign of Commander Marker. Instead a willowy Wren second officer, named Marion Wotherspoon, was waiting. In her briefcase were several personnel files. Commander Lancaster smiled when he saw her, "I'll leave you two to chat," he said, and taking Kat's arm he steered her into his office, calling over his shoulder. "Use the other office. Marker is away for the afternoon."

Marion Wotherspoon led the way into the other office and sat down behind the desk. She opened her brief case and said brightly. "We have several matters to discuss."

Peter sat in the other chair waiting for her to begin, wondering if perhaps Commander Lancaster was well acquainted with the lady.

"First, I must congratulate you on your promotion to Acting Lieutenant Commander with effect from the first of this month." She produced two epaulette loops with the two and a half rings of his new rank attached. She picked up the telephone, speaking briskly and requesting the tailor to attend the office forthwith.

The knock at the door testified that there had been arrangements made in advance. The tailor entered and removed Peter's jacket with the murmured assurance that it would be returned immediately. He left equally swiftly.

"Now, I have here the formal promotion notice for Sub Lieutenant Lawrence. G. RNVR, promoted to Lieutenant with effect from today.

"Finally, I have documents for the crew for what I believe is called a MAS boat, or torpedo boat. It is now designated ML2 on the official records of the Special Operations flotilla, under your overall command, individually commanded by Mr. Lawrence."

She passed over a stack of personal records and then announced the promotion of Midshipman Willis C RNVR to Sub Lieutenant with immediate effect, and the appointment of Sub-Lieutenant Andrew Porter RNR, Midshipman William Haggard RNVR, Midshipman Harry Brown RNVR and ten other ranks, to bring both boat crews up to strength.

"The actual appointments between the two boats under your command will be up to you, sir."

Peter nodded thoughtfully. He fully understood the reason for the situation. With his small command the personalities of the people concerned was something to be sorted out on the spot.

A knock on the door announced the return of the tailor with the uniform rank amended by the addition of the half ring. "Thank you," Peter said, as the tailor helped him back into his jacket. "What do I owe you?"

The tailor shook his head. "Nothing, sir. I am the base tailor."

Peter pressed a pound note into the man's hand. "Well, thank you, anyway."

Peter turned back to Marion Wotherspoon, who was gathering her things to leave.

"Would you like to wet my stripe?" Peter asked.

"I think there will be plenty of others to do that," the Wren suggested. I am sorry it would have been fine on another occasion. As it is I am committed tonight. If things don't work out I'll see you in the hotel bar with the others."

She left, leaving a hint of perfume in her wake.

Peter left the office carrying the files, to be met by the Commander and Kat. Both were in the outer office.

"Mission briefing tomorrow morning. There is a passing Catalina which will drop you off at your rendezvous tomorrow night. Meanwhile we will adjourn to the hotel to get together with the others."

Mystified, Peter passed over the files to be placed in the safe. Then joined them in the jeep once more.

***

"The acquisition of the MAS boat has been a real feather in our cap. It will allow us to use the boat for undercover operations. The first will be the island of Anafi." Commander Lancaster produced a map of the island situated between the Grotto and Santorini. "There is construction work being undertaken, which we now know to be an airstrip. The problem is that, if it is brought into operation, Cyprus will be within range of their bombers, as will Alexandria. Although Iraklion has the range and is even nearer, we can reach Iraklion with our own aircraft. We cannot, at the moment reach Anafi without getting heavy bombers brought in. Frankly, they cannot be spared from the European theatre as yet."

He paused and looked directly at Peter, picked up his pipe from the ashtray on his desk and carefully lit it. Then he continued from with the cloud of aromatic smoke.

"The fact is that the Germans are building in the only practical place on the island. Because of the urgency of their need for this airstrip, they have ignored the drawback to the site. It's a flaw that could ruin their whole operation for several months, and that we will be trying to exploit." He pointed to the map. "There is, as you can see, a cliff face extending 600 metres along the length of the runway. In the 1937 survey of the island the geologist discovered a fault in the cliff, sufficient to prevent the authorities from putting in an airstrip at that time. The need to drop the cliff face to remove the threat to the runway below meant an expense that the Government at the time was not prepared to fund. The whole idea was dropped. It is possible that either the Germans don't know, or they are ignoring it deliberately, so that they can get the airstrip in operation swiftly."

He paused again to relight his pipe.

"Anyway, they have put in an Italian engineer, a Brigadier Cominetti, who is charged with constructing the airstrip. He has some heavy equipment and a lot of labour, scoured from Athens without regard for their suitability for the task. They have swept in six scientists from the Government Research Establishment. All were on the run, and caught in a random sweep by the Italian army. Regardless, they were brought to the island to swing a pick and shovel. Thus far they have not been discovered. We believe they soon will be, when their records catch up with them.

"Your task is two-fold. Wreck the project, and collect the scientists.

"The supply of explosives at the grotto has been expanded. I understand that Kat here is an expert in their use, as is also your deputy, Captain Poppadopolis.

"A platoon of Royal Marines will be available for you to collect at the rendezvous. So it will be necessary for you to use both boats on this operation. The Marines will act as security for your demolition party, and as back-up for the collection of the scientists.

"The photographs and details of the scientists are in the pack that comes with this particular operation. The scientists are very important in this case, and, in the case of a choice between the two parts of the operation, the scientists take precedence.

"The fly in the ointment is that the security on the island is in the hands of the SS, just one platoon, plus a company of Italian Alpine troops. We are therefore committed to a quiet infiltration, hopefully without an alarm being given. With their overwhelming numbers your small party would have no hope, so secrecy is the key."

Peter stirred in his seat. "Have they any naval assets, guard boats etcetera?"

"Only the odd visit from passing boats. The whole exercise is low key from their point of view, so they are trying to avoid drawing attention to themselves.

"One final point." He passed over a photograph. "This is Yasmin O'Hara. She is one of us. Please do whatever she asks, if it is within your power. bring her back if she is ready to return."

Chapter seventeen

An ounce of prevention.

Brigadier Alonzo Cominetti was no fool. He was, in addition to being an army General, an engineer with architect qualifications, and he was stuck on this bloody island to build an airstrip, with the sword of Damocles hanging over the construction. The cliff face that he was being careful to avoid was probably secure if undisturbed. But all it needed was some ham-handed machine operator to ram it in a vulnerable spot, to bring the whole lot down.

Now, just to add to his problems, the shot firer had investigated the fault area in the cliff face. On a hunch Cominetti had told him to take a look to see if pouring concrete could act as a stopper and consolidate the whole mass of rock. It seems someone, in 1937, had expected to bring the cliff down. It also seemed that whoever it was, having started the preparations had been interrupted. Cominetti's engineer had found a stack of boxes of dynamite, weeping quietly in the fissure.

He refused to touch it because it was so unstable. The nitro had leaked and formed pools in the recessed places in the floor of the crevice. He was considering placing a fence across the entrance to prevent anyone wandering in and disturbing the unstable explosives. They would need specialists to come in to remove the threat.

He sighed. He had told them they would have to remove the cliff face before any other work, but a

German engineer had come, taken one look through his binoculars, studied the 1937 report and decided the risk was negligible. Cominetti knew that meant if things went wrong it would be his fault. He shrugged. Nothing changed. At that point soft fingers slid round his neck and stroked his ear. The perfume used only by Yasmin, his mistress, became part of the air around him and he relaxed back into the soft welcoming embrace of the lovely Egyptian woman.

"You wicked woman," he said quietly. "You know I am at work and you should not disturb me here."

"Do I disturb you, cara mia! Would you like me to leave, perhaps to return to my stinking homeland?"

"I suppose I must consider it. You should not be here."

"There are other women here. Why not me?"

"They are part of the workforce. you are not."

She stroked his cheek. "Do I not work for my living then? Am I not good at my job?"

Cominetti had to admit she was the best 'worker' he had ever employed in his bed. His wife, back in Naples, regarded the sex act as a breeding exercise to be endured to ensure an heir was in place to carry on the family name. The need for more than one, as with fine china, was accepted in case of breakages. Once that matter had been dealt with there was little need to carry on with the beastly business, which had required the Brigadier to seek solace elsewhere.

He had since found out that his frigid wife had discovered, in his absence, the advantages and pleasure to be gained by the attention of a succession of young men who made it their business to attend to the needs of the wealthy, both male and female. Even as he enjoyed the attentions of Yasmin, his not so frigid wife, was relaxing in Naples with her lover and his girlfriend in the Brigadier's enormous bed.

Yasmin played with Alonzo's hair and studied the papers on his desk, memorising as much as she could while she was there.

***

For Alonzo, having Yasmin in his lap was an increasingly obvious distraction that meant he was unaware of her interest in anything but his increasing tension. A matter that the skilled hands of his mistress quickly took care of.

Her departure was hastened by the approaching presence of Captain Keller SS, who commanded the troops on the island and showed a lack of respect for the authority of the Brigadier bordering on insolence.

As Yasmin disappeared through the door to Cominetti's private quarters, a rap on the office door was followed almost immediately by the appearance of Oberleutenant Keller, his uniform immaculate, his boots polished and his face shining from his close shave. The scar on his cheek did nothing to enhance the sullen face which was all planes and angles. His salute was the Nazi lift of the flat right hand. In this case the brief flap of his hand was an insult in itself, which Cominetti resented. His answer was "What is it this time?"

"I am disturbed by the number of men lounging about on the building site. Surely it would make sense to employ the men not on duty with some occupation to keep them away from the site itself. They are a distraction and look untidy."

"I presume these are the Italian troops you are referring to?"

"They are!"

"As I have told you before Oberleutenant, if you have a complaint about the troops on site call on Major Pitti.He commands the troops."

"Major Pitti refuses to deal with me. He claims that, since he commands the island garrison, it is not my place to interfere with the way the garrison is run."

"There is nothing I can add to that, Oberleutenant. If Major Pitti approves that is the end of the matter. Carry on!"

"But, sir, I wish to report to my superiors. This is intolerable!"

Brigadier Cominetti rose to his full height. "How dare you speak to me in that tone of voice? I not only outrank you. I command on this island by the authority of your masters. You will apologise immediately, Oberleutenant Keller!"

Shocked and dazed by the outburst, the Oberleutenant apologised, saluted properly and about-turned, leaving the office, wondering if he had ruined his career.

Cominetti sat down in his chair shocked at his reaction to that little turd. He realised he could have strangled the man. He really had to rein himself in. Up to now he had managed but as the job was winding down so did the enthusiasm. He was sick of being pushed around by pipsqueaks like Keller. He was a Brigadier General after all.

Yasmin came in and cowered in front of him. "Oh, master. You are so dominant. take me and beat me if you must. I am proud that you threw that Hun out."

"You must be careful what you say, Yasmin. The Oberleutenant is our ally."

"He looks through my clothes and gropes me whenever he gets close enough. He makes my flesh creep." She took Cominetti's hand and dragged him through the door into his private quarters. "Come, let us play a little. We'll take the thought of that pig away and replace him with happy memories."

***

At 22:00 hours, the two launches entered the waters around Anafi with suppressed exhausts. The sound of the slow-running engines could hardly be heard over the sounds of the sea. The MAS boat slid into the spot where the visiting boats normally moored. The ML moored further along the trot, as the MAS boat put a dinghy into the water. Four men boarded it and rowed ashore. They were met by two soldiers, who noted their Italian uniforms and accepted that they were legitimate. They were disarmed and put into the now empty dinghy which was swiftly withdrawn to the moored boat. Two of the boat's passengers took over the rifles of the hapless guards and started to walk the beach. They assisted the dinghy from the ML, which arrived as they trudged along. The six Royal Marines dressed in black, with balaclava helmets and blackened faces, melted into the darkness. Armed with silenced pistols and their knives, they had come to pave the way. As the replacement sentries patrolled the beach, the dinghies moved back and forth, dropping the other marines and the demolition party under Phillipo. Kat landed with the snatch group led by Peter. All wore black with blacked faces. All carried silenced guns and knives.

Peter and Kat, with their small party, made directly for the buildings where the labour force was billeted. There were three guards who never saw them coming. All were Italian, and all were rendered unconscious before they knew what was happening.

Inside the first hut the occupants were mostly awake. Kat called out names and three of the scientists answered. They found the rest in the other hut, and bundled them down to the beach. Yasmin was waiting with the contents of the Brigadier's briefcase. She had contemplated slitting his throat, but decided there were others more deserving of her knife. When watching for the arrival of the raiders, she had paid a visit to the communications room as soon as she saw the first dinghy approach. The duty operator had not believed her when she had suggested she would cut his throat if he did not disable the radio. As it was, she had relented and belted him with the pickaxe handle, then smashed the equipment with the same weapon.,

While they were being transported to the boat off-shore, the fire-fight started. The entire platoon of the marines was now ashore. Kat, with her two Greeks and Peter, had joined the main party. Armed with additional explosives, they were engaged in destroying the heavy machinery, so essential for construction jobs like the airfield. The warehouse was on a sentry path, but not specifically guarded. The alarm had been raised when the sentry heard noises in the barn. He had poked his head inside to see what was happening. Peter shot on the turn, hitting him silently enough, but his rifle had been cocked. When it fell, it went off and the bullet smashed a window in the barrack area. The troops who poured out were the SS platoon, looking for trouble.

The alarm raised, Peter lifted the MP40 they all had strapped on, and opened fire on the SS men bringing down three with his first burst. The others joined in, while Kat found the rear door to the barn. She had laid her charges, and the timers were running. All three of the boat party, plus three marines, gave the SS men a good hose down with their weapons and then dashed to the back door of the barn. They passed through and slammed it shut, throwing the bar across.

The group ran away fast but they all hit the ground when the barn blew. the walls bulged and the roof rose in the air. Seven of the unfortunate SS men died inside. Combined with those wounded in the first skirmish, half their strength was lost. The rest split up searching for the intruders.

Peter and his group contacted the party accompanying Phillipo on their way back to the beach. His group had been forced to remove six guards. It was the seventh who raised the alarm and the balloon had gone up pretty fast.

"What about the big bang?" Peter asked.

Phillipo looked at his watch, in the light of his small penlight. He said "I suggest we all hit the deck now!" He dropped flat, followed by the other twelve in the party. The world exploded. The entire cliff face and more, lifted away from the cliff and deposited itself across the area already graded for the airstrip. It was now a huge mound of rock and rubble. The heavy equipment was still burning.

"Time to go." Peter said and hauled himself to his feet. The blast had flattened all the buildings in the area, "How did that happen? We surely didn't have that much explosive."

Phillipo said, "There was stuff already in place. I only used one of our small packets. I expected it to trigger the whole lot.

A scatter of shots came from behind the ruins of one of the huts. Three of the marines returned fire as the entire party retreated. Both boats' dinghies were waiting. The landing party piled aboard, and the power boats moved off, towing the dinghies away from danger, hauling them in at the same time. The remaining SS men all came to fire on the retreating dinghies, only to receive a welcome from the machine guns from both of the motor launches.

Brigadier Cominetti was upset, not about the raid, but about the missing Yasmin. He had yet to discover the loss of his briefcase.

Captain Keller smiled quietly to himself. The disaster would fix the Brigadier. That was the good news. It was possible he might even gain out of this, since he was in effect under house arrest at the time.

His next meeting with the Brigadier was not the triumph he had anticipated. The Brigadier encountered Keller and informed him that there would be an enquiry into the failure to identify the spy in their midst! He would be the subject of the enquiry.

***

Yasmin O'Hara enjoyed the journey back to the grotto. She had boarded the stolen MAS boat commanded by the nice-looking young man named Lawrence, Jerry Lawrence. Her thoughts lingered about the name. He was a personable and young, near her own age at a guess. Her early life in the brothel with her mother had prepared her well for the career her mother had planned for her. Courtesan was the name her mother always used. Prostitute was the more common name. Her introduction into the arts of the profession had been careful and she had been taught the many ways there were to keep men at bay as well as bring them to heel. She spent time maintaining her body and appearance and was well aware of the effect she had on most men.

On the bridge of the boat with the wind playing with her hair, and her make-up washed off for once, she was not unaware of the impression she was making on the crew around her.

She had been eighteen when the war caught up with her mother. Then ensconced as the mistress of the Italian attaché, the war had caused her rapid eviction and resettlement in a less salubrious house in a more colourful part of Cairo.

Yasmin, having been well tutored in the art of separating her real life from the acting part played in her working life, had already decided that selling her body was not a career she envisaged following. Her studies, not discouraged by her mother, had meant she was now not only skilled in shorthand and typing, but also language skills which had surprised the academic tutors, instructing her in the grammatical construction of German, French, and Italian. It had not occurred to her or her mother that her speed at learning was anything but normal. The fact that her instant recall of everything she had ever read, meant more than a parlour trick, might have passed her by, had it not been spotted by the man who had recruited her.

Her appointment as secretary to Commander Lancaster, had been prior to his enlistment into the ranks of Special Operations. The attraction of the job had been based on his archaeological qualifications, a popular occupation in the Egypt of her time.

For the Commander the discovery that his extremely talented secretary was, in his opinion, a genius was only surpassed by the shock of discovering that she was also, to put it genteelly, a fully-qualified courtesan.

This latter information had only been gleaned after the archaeologist had become the Commander.

When he had questioned Yasmin on the subject, she held nothing back. Rightly, her upbringing had been the result of her mother's care and she felt no guilt or even embarrassment in discussing her past.

The indiscretions of the attaché, who had been Yasmin's mother's protector, rebounded upon him and sadly her. She was found murdered in her house having been tortured savagely, presumably for information. The murderers left a note pinned to her body, referring to her as a spy

The episode with the Brigadier had been as a result of a certain amount of panic, combined with Yasmin's willingness to repay the Axis nations for the murder of her mother. Her beauty and expertise had assured her easy insertion into the life of the Brigadier, nearly seamlessly.

It was, as far as she was concerned, a one and only operation. Her contribution would be whatever the country demanded, apart from sex. The feeling of relief following her return from Anafi had been the final straw. Her first act on boarding the boat had been to wash off the make-up, brush out her hair and don shirt and slacks under the bridge coat. The courtesan was out of business.

***

The arrival of the boats at the grotto was the excuse for a party. Two of the marines had been injured, not seriously. They were both attended by the doctor who had then allowed them to participate.

Jerry Lawrence was intrigued by the dark-haired beauty who had returned with his boat from Anafi. He had noticed her then and at the party, though he had stayed in the background. She had sought him out, she said, to thank him for bringing her back safely.

"I don't believe you." Jerry said. "You were just overcome by my dashing good looks and the fact that I drive the Ferrari of speedboats."

"Damn it. You have seen through my subterfuge. I will have to invent another ploy."

Peter came over and joined the laughing couple, curious to find out what caused the hilarity.

He never found out, but was happy to see Jerry looking so relaxed. He was only too aware how stressful it could be commanding your own boat for the first time. The waters of this part of the Mediterranean were not regarded as the restful sailing area they had once been.

Peter introduced the pair to each other by name and left them to their own company.

***

The following night, both boats, loaded with the marines and Yasmin with the six recovered scientists, departed from the grotto to meet the gunboat flotilla from Alexandria. They had been making a sweep for maiale (mini-subs), one of their regular activities since the sinking of an 8000 ton tanker and battleships HMS Valiant, and HMS Queen Elizabeth, in December 1941.

They met Lt Commander Basil Grant RNVR at the rendezvous. The motor gunboat flotilla had assembled in loose formation so the two boats from the grotto moved from boat to boat dropping their passengers throughout the flotilla. On the MAS boat Lieutenant Lawrence finally dropped Yasmin off with Basil Grant. The parting was with sorrow, but they would keep in contact. Both were sure of that.

The two boats finally turned with a flourish of foam and returned to the grotto.

Chapter eighteen

Greek Odyssey

The Island of Crete had been in the hands of the Germans now since April 1941, apart from the first raid on Iraklion. Both Peter and Commander Lancaster agreed it was time for a revisit. Despite the risks involved they agreed that the airfield was still the best place to attack. It would cause the maximum disruption. The movement of shipping in the sea area north of Crete had been inhibited by the actions of Allied submarines and aircraft. It meant that much of enemy essential supplies had to come by air.

On the negative side, having been raided once already, the defences would be prepared. Both agreed the time lapse would probably have made the guards slacken off a bit and give the raiders bit of an edge.

Based on their current situation, there were Peter, Phillipo, Kat and Nick, the three soldiers, and the two Greeks. Samantha had elected to return to the field in Greece and she was already on the way to the area of the Gulf of Lakonia, on the mainland of Greece. She had contacts in Athens and also in the south-western Peninsula forming the western side of the Gulf.

It was difficult to deviate from the idea of a direct attack on the airfield. They were still faced with the problem of gaining entrance, and, once there, selecting the best targets. There was no doubt the reaction time would be shorter and they would encounter a more intense search thereafter.

With the assistance of partisans on the island, Peter decided there would be a good chance of success for the current proposed mission. Preparations for the raid consisted of the assembly of as much in the way of munitions as they could carry. The contacts with Crete had been well established by Alexandria. Using people who had been suggested by them, Peter had been arranging for a place where the ML could be concealed, and had settled on the village of Plaka, facing across the channel between Spinaloga and the main island. The long, fishing boat repair and building shed, still standing though in need of repair, was big enough to accommodate the boat. It had direct access to the open sea. The partisans would keep watch. Because the second boat would not be required, the other crew was available. Peter decided to take CPO Smith with Farquhar, Martin and Wright from his own crew as members of the raiding party. All had been involved in raids before and the extra men could make a difference.

Over two more days the preparations were made, waiting for the dark of the moon. On the third night, contact was made with the Partisans who confirmed that all was clear and that they were ready.

There was no question of laying on an air-raid. The battle in North Africa was at its height. Nothing could be spared. There was a silent crowd on the ML that night. As soon as it was dark they boarded and departed for Crete.

***

The darkened ML crept into the zone where the island of Spinaloga loomed off the shore of the big island. The village appeared out of the darkness. A signal light flashed to indicate the doors of the big shed.

With the engines muttering through the exhaust suppressors the boat drifted through the doors and was pulled alongside, using the ropes thrown to the willing hands on the quay.

Snugged and secure, the doors now closed, the group stepped ashore and commenced unloading the supplies for the partisans.

Once the supplies had been unloaded, the materials for the raid were brought out and checked. They were stacked within one of the enclosures within the shed, and the big dust sheet was drawn over the ML.

The entire raiding party was bedded down for the day. The time for the night raid would come soon enough.

Thankfully, there were no alarms and excursions to disturb the people throughout the day, so that, by the following evening, the party was ready, impatient to get going.

***

The truck had a closed back and was driven by a man in Italian uniform. The logos on the truck identified it as part of the maintenance battalion stationed on the island.

They moved off on the road to Aitania to visit the Countess if it was safe to do so. In the interest of secrecy they stopped well back from the house. Peter, Kat and Sergeant Mitchell scouted the house carefully. A black car outside was not a good sign. The driver, lounging smoking, was German. While they watched he dropped ash on his black coat. "Scheiss!" Was the word he used instinctively. Kat walked out and approached him quite openly. Peter and Harry Mitchell went around behind the car and, using it for cover, managed to approach close from behind to back up Kat.

"Who the hell are you?" Kat said in Italian.

"I am the driver for Colonel Holtz. Who are you?"

She could not resist it, seeing Peter poised to club the man from behind. "I am your worst nightmare!"

The man laughed and reached out to grab her.

Peter brought the club down on his head with considerable force. He dropped as if the stuffing had been removed from him. Peter did not wait. He made for the house, gun in hand fearing the worst.

In the front hall Monika was struggling with a man in a black leather coat, Peter did not hesitate, with his gun he clouted the man on the back if his head, knocking him to the ground with a cracked skull. Leaving Monika to Kat, Harry and Peter ran upstairs, where voices could be heard.

In the upstairs drawing room a light shone through the slightly-open door. Peering through the gap, Peter saw the man he presumed was the Colonel standing over the Countess. He had a riding crop in his hand. The Countess was on her knees in front of him, and there was blood on her dress. A second man stood behind her, holding what appeared to be a leash with a collar attached.

Peter looked at Harry. Harry was shocked at the fury in Peter's eyes. Peter whispered, "Two men, with the Countess. You take the right hand man. I'll take the left!"

Harry nodded and gripped his MP40.

Peter flung the door open and stepped into the room. He had his automatic lined up and pointing at the head of the man on the left. Harry ran straight at the man on the right and rammed the MP40 into the man's abdomen. The man doubled up, dropping the leash and grabbing his middle. He fell to the floor with a groan. Harry stood over him gun ready.

The man covered by Peter was pale with reddish hair, thinning on top. His long black leather coat was standard dress for Gestapo. The crop in his hand dropped as he looked down the barrel of the automatic. Kat came into the room with Monika. Both ran to the Countess and helped her to her feet. The weal on her face had not broken the skin, but her mouth was swollen and the blood had come from there.

Peter looked at her and swung round to the Colonel, his gun-filled hand smashed him round his face, and the white skin reddened immediately and blood sprang from his mashed lips.

"Enjoy that, did you?" Peter spoke in German, his voice quiet and full of menace.

The man staggered and nearly fell, grabbing the back of the chair beside him.

Peter turned to the Countess, "Are you all right?"

She nodded and said in a slightly slurred voice, "He had just started, I believe. At least that was what he implied. I confess I was not looking forward to it."

The two women took the countess through to the bathroom to attend to her wounds.

Peter looked at the Colonel. "Why are you here?"

The Colonel sneered, "The English bitch was laughing at us. Countess whatever she called herself. She is a spy and my job is to catch spies. Despite your uniform you are also a spy, and I will get you and all your friends."

Peter looked at him searchingly, then he dropped the automatic into his holster. He turned and spoke to Harry. He saw Harry's eyes widen and spun round lifting the gun as he turned. The Gestapo

Colonel had his gun in his hand, when Peter's first bullet took him in the centre of his chest. The second was between the eyes. The Colonel's gun had not fired once.

With Harry's attention on the Colonel, the fallen man behind Harry half rose, pulling his gun. But Peter's spin continued after shooting the Colonel. The gun pointed directly at the second man. He went white, and dropped his gun. Suddenly there was the scent of urine as he wet himself.

Peter did not fire. "Tie him up. We'll take him with us. I have no doubt he will have something to say."

The three women returned, as Harry was tying the live Gestapo man with the cord from the curtains.

The Countess was looking a little better, though her face was still swollen.

"You will have to leave here now!" Peter said. "This will be a recorded visit. Others are bound to follow."

Madeline nodded thoughtfully. "You are right of course. Monika and I could probably make it to the coast in the car, while you do what you came to do."

Kat smiled. "You know you are dying to come along with us, and see just what we are up to. So this is what is going to happen. We will go ahead together, sabotage our target, and only then race across country to our boat. Then it's off on the ocean waves, possibly direct to Alexandria, where we will deliver you in safe secure surroundings to the authorities. You can come back here when the island is free once more."

The Countess smiled. "You make it all so simple. It is much more complicated than that, I assure you. I have commitments that I cannot just cast aside."

"Madeline, this house is no longer safe, your role on the island is over."

"I am responsible to all the people who come here, making sure that they are fed and watered. there is no one else that is in a position to do such things"

"After the war, madam. After the war."

"Right. Let's get the show on the road. Harry take the car here. You others follow me back to the truck.

It all went off rather well. Under the eye of the Countess they all changed into black coveralls. Each now had a hood and a face-mask covering their features except for the eyes. Also painted black, the mask gave them a sinister look, adding to the effect and made them difficult to see in the dark. On the way the car was left concealed in a copse of trees where it could be retrieved by partisans later. Harry joined them in the truck and donned his overalls.

They drove to the airfield and pulled off into the area behind the wire. Despite the fact that the trees had been cut back, there were still areas where vehicles parked. So they drew up in a designated place. The official nature of the truck and the Italian driver created no problem. In fact the Italian staff at the depot, hardly looked at the truck. The gate man waved it in, still talking to his companion. They parked the truck. Everyone except the driver, the Countess and Monika, slipped out of the back and made their way to the fence where they cut a way through.

On the other side of the road opposite the vehicle park, the fence around the airfield was broken by a building providing an alternative entrance to the perimeter track within the field itself. There was a barrier and gate within the building, though the real use of the area had been an alternative entrance for the aircrews. On the other side of the official car park was a gutted building which had once accommodated aircrew and senior staff for the airfield. It had been an early target for the Partisans, and had fallen out of use. The building and gate had become the site of a local black market operation for the occupying forces. In the courtyard provided by the building and it's outbuildings, a regular market was staged for those in the know. The official guards were all looked after, and the place was a popular duty among Wehrmacht troops assigned to perimeter security duties.

The arrival of the raiders was a rude shock to both official guards and the black-marketeers. The people, there to buy and sell, were rounded up in a group and imprisoned in one of the outbuildings, after they had been relieved of briefcases and documents. Four of those present were recognised, and secured separately for transmission to Alexandria along with their papers.

Once the way was secure, Harry returned to the parked truck through the gap in the fence. The driver moved off to leave the parking area. Once again the gate control on the official vehicle park ignored the truck, which moved down to the airport access area and parked among the vehicles brought by the black market people.

Having secured their retreat, they unloaded their gear from the truck, and passed through the gate in the building. They deposited the prisoners and the documents in the truck, and left them under the eyes of the driver, the Countess and Monika. It would only be necessary to evade the patrols rather than anything more complicated. Their first, most important task was to traverse the airfield unseen and start their sabotage on the other side. The truck would await them this side for 90 minutes.

***

The raiders moved through the airfield, and set off across the broad expanse of grass. Phillipo was tail-end security. He caught up before they dropped to the ground so as not to alert the patrol passing, though it was well behind them.

Approaching the hanger complex from the other side, they were able to see things hidden from the main road running along the south side, where they had entered. The store constructed there had been made from concrete blocks. The door was metal with two lever locks, all of massive construction. Phillipo took a look and said, "This will take some time to open, I'm afraid. Perhaps the bazooka might do it?".

A guard appeared at the corner of the hanger 30 yards away, so they melted back into the darkness. When the guard had passed, Peter said to Phillipo, "I would like to know what it hides. But, just in case it happens to be poison gas, we'll leave it until the wind comes from the south." The close proximity of the sea at the northern boundary made that suggestion feasible. "On a night like tonight, with no real wind, definitely not."

Phillipo shrugged, and they carried on to the first of the hangars. Inside, a huge Focke-Wulf Condor filled the space. The bomb bay was open and there were racks being fitted. Peter looked at them. There was something familiar about them. Then it hit him. They are mine racks. "This plane is being fitted to drop mines. The concrete store next door, mines perhaps?"

They placed explosives around the building. Hearing voices outside they slipped out through the side door and made for the next hanger. A group of mechanics entered the main door of the hanger with the Condor. Phillipo passed a bar through the link holes used to secure the hanger doors, effectively locking them. The side door he left unlocked as there was no way of securing it from the outside.

Kat and Harry, with the two Greeks, had assembled a bunch of six prisoners in the next hanger. The other soldiers, Hardy and Wallace, were prowling the darkness between the other two hangers. Neither could fire their guns before the alarm sounded, but they could still find targets, and plant explosives. All the aircraft on the apron had charges awaiting a spark. Six men were out of the proceedings, unconscious, in a row and helpless to interfere with the activities around them.

They had set charges and, using grenades, booby-trapped several doors just to make things difficult. So far they had either captured or evaded anyone who might raise the alarm. But it was going to be tricky from now on. There was a shift change happening. Several trucks were arriving at the hangers with the next shift. Peter looked at Phillipo and shrugged, He turned back to the plunger for the charges within the hanger. Pressing it, he heard the first bang and started to run as the explosions occurred one after the other in the building with the Condor. Then the fuel tanks blew, and the building went in all directions. Kat and Harry ran from the second hanger. The entire group ran to the third where the Greeks had opened the ball with a handful of grenades and four magazines from their MP40's There were eighteen bodies, four light aircraft and a half-track inside.

Out on the apron the linked explosives blew as one, distributing the aircraft there all over the hard standing. A captured DC3, repainted in German livery and fitted for executive use, awaiting the return of the Luftwaffe General, here on an inspection visit. It seemed to jump in time with the explosions around it, miraculously surviving apparently untouched. Provided the General took off within the next two hours an unpleasant surprise awaited him. Otherwise, just the DC3 would suffer from a timed bomb fitted here in the airfield.

Outside the fourth hanger Hardy and Wallace were engaged in picking off the new arrivals who had just turned up in a truck. the crack of the Lee Enfields distinctive even against the screams and the roar of the flames. The two Greeks were now grinning as they chased down two fleeing naval ratings. Toward the distant gate flashing blue lamps signalled that it was time to leave. Calling the people together, the group made their way as prearranged to behind the hangers, all heading to the fence on the south side, to meeting place already arranged. The truck was there complete with the prisoners, the Countess and Monika. They all piled in and settled down for the journey back to the boat. They did not call at the countess's home, nor anyone else's either. The truck wended its way across the island unhurriedly, the driver stopping twice to enquire of passing vehicles, what all the fuss was about.

They walked the last mile through fields grey and cold, the darkness making it difficult to see exactly where they were going. When they finally reached the boat the entire party collapsed, exhausted more from the tension than from any exertion. It was the reaction to the zigzag progress dodging between searching patrols.

For Peter being back on his own boat was far better that all the sub-rosa activities of the past days.

However needs must, he thought, *and we did give them a bloody nose again.*

***

They settled down for the day, once more visited by the partisan chief who was there to wish farewell to the countess and to congratulate Peter on the raid. Both were aware of the repercussions of acts of sabotage. But they were also conscious that they gave the people of Crete faith that they were still making a contribution towards reclaiming their land from the invaders. The countess and both Kat and Monika spent the day relaxing and or sleeping after the trauma of the previous night. The arrival of the Gestapo Colonel had been a shock for the countess, but not a surprise. She had been shaken because he had come without warning. She had expected a visit ever since the Gestapo came to the island. Her husband had been outspoken about the Blackshirts and the Brownshirts. She had not expected their successors to forget. But she had hoped to be warned by one of her friends in the HQ in Iraklion.

They had not been able to warn her because the Colonel had not informed anyone of his actions. There was the strong possibility that, since the scene had been sanitised by the partisans and the Colonel's car had been concealed elsewhere on the island, her disappearance, mysterious though it may be, would not have been associated with the disappearance of the colonel.

***

On the journey back to the grotto Peter spent the entire time on the bridge. It gave him time to think. He found himself going over the last letter he had received from Amy. Receiving mail was depend-

ant on visiting, or visitors from Alexandria or, sometimes a rendezvous with a MGB for special drop off
or pick-up

There had still been no mention of any other
man in her life, and he could not help feeling happy
about the fact. This was one of the matters that he
needed to think about. Despite the fact that both had
steered clear of any suggestion of romance in their
exchange of letters, Peter could not help the increasing warmth he felt when her letters arrived, nor how
much he looked forward to receiving them. He had
the suspicion that Amy felt the same. It was the lack
of certainty that kept him from mentioning anything
in his letters to her.

He was joined on the bridge by the Countess
wrapped in a shawl against the cool night air. "Peter,
if I may, I would like to thank you for your timely
arrival, saving me from the attentions of the horrible
man. I confess I had dropped my guard to some extent due to the friendliness of the other enemy officers I encountered. My experience of the Gestapo was
entirely second hand as it were. my husband had expressed himself on the subject often enough, but that
had seemed to be then, and in Europe, not here and
now.

"I see now I should have accepted your suggestion in the first place and returned with you then.
Now men have been killed because of me directly. I
know they were evil men, but I still feel guilty."

"Madeline, the men you are talking about were
bound to be killed. The way they lived made sure of
that. They took pleasure in what they did. Hurting
people was fun. Please do not waste pity on them.
Your wounds were the beginning. They would have
continued until you begged to die to stop the torture.
We have seen it here already. The Germans and Ital-

ians both in their own way have shown their worst side, the Italians in Abyssinia, and the Germans to the Poles and Jews. Save your pity for the victims of this war.

"Tell me. Have you any friends in Alexandria or Cairo, or perhaps in England?"

Madeline shook her head. "None living, sadly. All are now gone, one way or the other."

"I have been requested to take you to Alexandria personally, so there will be someone you know with you when you arrive. I am sure there will also be things you can do until you return to Crete."

"Thank you, Peter. You have been most kind. Monika has asked to stay with me. So if you do not mind, both of us will be travelling to Alexandria with you."

Phillipo came when Madeline left. "I understand there has been a message from Samantha?"

Peter looked at the Greek officer warily, wondering if the dashing Poppadopolis had been spreading his net once more. There was no indication of any but academic interest.

"It seems she has sorted out something for us to do on the mainland. I'll not know about it until I have been briefed by Roger Lancaster."

"Good. I enjoyed out little excursion on Crete, but I am Greek., I look forward to returning to my homeland and killing Germans. Your team know their business. Popski would be happy to use them." Having delivered what for him, was the highest accolade he could bestow, he returned below to continue his campaign with Kat.

Peter was astonished at the praise, and at Phillipo's single minded concentration on his pursuit of Kat. For the remainder of the trip he was left with his own thoughts, as the others relaxed below deck.

Chapter nineteen

What goes around

Peter's departure to the Mediterranean had been unsettling for Amy. After the letter from Graham she had felt really bad, and Peter had been so kind. She finally admitted that they had become real friends over the past months. She also realised that she had been merely passing time, driving people about when there were better things for her to do. It was time she put some effort into doing them. Her application for a course in communications and cyphers went in the following day. To her surprise, within three weeks she was posted to Portsmouth and in training in radio and signals, The three month course was followed by the special course in cyphers, and her success in the two courses saw her promoted to Petty Officer.

Her new uniforms collected and her new posting secured, she stripped and had a bath before donning her new uniform for the first time. As she dried off in front of the mirror she looked at herself wondering what Peter would think of her. A blush turned her white body pink. She shook her head impatiently. What was she thinking? He had never said anything to make her think…..She got dressed swiftly dismissing the thought.

***

The room in the base was warm. The people sitting around the table were discussing the news received from Samantha via her contacts in Greece. Peter, Cdr Marker RN, Cdr Lancaster, and an unnamed member of Naval Intelligence, were dressed in white shirt shorts and long socks. All the others were in summer uniform. The man from ONI was speaking in hushed tones. "What we have here is a base for the maiale, the Italian mini-subs which caused mayhem in Alexandria, sinking the Queen Elizabeth and the Valiant.

"A man named Frascati, Contramiraglio Arturo Frascati, commands the base. He is a submariner of some notoriety having been linked with several of the famous beauties of the thirties, and, incidentally, operated a bathysphere on several of the deepest dives made while he was at it.

"The base has been established out of the way so that trainees can learn without pressure. His second-in-command is Kaptainleutnant Albert Schiller of the German Navy. He was wounded apparently in an action off Eastbourne in 1940. The E-boat he was passenger on was sunk by ML's on convoy escort." He turned to Peter. "I believe you were involved in that action?"

"Very possibly, I did take part in sinking two out of three E-boats at about that time."

Tell me. Schiller. Was he the man who managed the German sailing team in '38?"

"He was. Did you know him?"

"Knew of him. Not a nice man apparently. Enjoyed raping captive women as I heard it. I recall he withdrew the German team when their boat's mast was broken."

"That's the man. He now has a wooden foot, and is in place to take over the base from the Italians when they change sides. Since his injury he has been almost exclusively been engaged in espionage."

"What sort of people do you need to carry out a raid?" Roger Lancaster wanted to know more about this set-up.

The ONI man said, "We stopped a tramp carrying four of the mini-subs en-route to the base. It was escorted by a destroyer. We need to get moving pretty quick to take advantage of it as a way-in. Unfortunately we have lost the destroyer. The nearest one of a design that could pass as Italian is the other end of the Med"

Peter said, "We can get over that problem. Where is the tramp steamer?"

"It is here in Alexandria, rather, just outside of Alexandria, under wraps. It has been screened off since it arrived by the destroyer which captured it and brought it in. If we are to use it we will have to send it out attached to its destroyer and only light the boiler when it's out of sight of land. Otherwise it will be obvious and might give the game away."

"Good, get it underway now. We need to make up time. If your destroyer can get it past Manos, I can take over from there, escorting it with our MAS boat. Now what do I need to spoil Schiller's sleep?"

The Intelligence man studied the papers in front of him. Roger rang for a messenger. When the man came he passed him a sealed note for his aide, Theo, Peter's former partner in the grotto.

Roger said, "I have just ordered the move. The destroyer is on standby, so it should be on the way promptly."

"Good!" The Intelligence man started to list the assets gathered at the enemy base. "In the surrounding area there are roadblocks and roving patrols, two platoons on rotation, German SS and Alpine Italians.

"There is a cliff wall around the cove where the base is located, and we have discovered what are believed to be two .88 anti-tank guns covering the entrance to the cove. There are also two quad-Vierling AA guns, which can be depressed to cover the quay below and the beach where the maiale are laid in a row. On the quay is a long building containing a workshop and quarters for the senior staff. The junior staff and crews occupy a converted shed further down the quay. I have a map of the layout here." He passed Peter and Roger copies of the map. Marker had already got a copy with what looked like a file similar to the ONI man.

"You have an envelope of six days to arrive and enter the cove. Samantha Brown is in the location with the partisans in the area. They have already agreed to attack the gun-positions, and distract the roving patrols. The tramp has been wired up to the explosives with the cargo of mini subs, hopefully to block the entrance to the cove. The Italian skipper will cooperate with the help of the Royal Marines on board, to get the ship into position. It would be handy if we could get some munitions into the cove before the ship sinks."

"Perhaps I should fire my torpedoes." Peter said with a smile.

"There is a beach where the maiale are laid out, and the quay, both good targets?"

"Will they work?" Peter said doubtfully.

Roger said, "Why not? As long as they hit something they should go off."

"Right. In that case it's time I got moving. I have things to arrange and places to go. Can the pilot take me to the rendezvous?"

***

Back at the grotto Peter got straight down to planning the operation in detail. Phillipo went off to Ritz on the mainland of Greece immediately taking the fishing boat, and the brothers, Anthony and Aristotle. The boat was still run by Junos. Beneath the layer of oil and grease, he was apparently British, though he spoke and swore in colloquial Greek with an Athens accent. Whenever he travelled in the boat, he was always accompanied by a long case containing a Browning .5 calibre, machine gun. The box of belted ammunition and a selection of magazines were now located under the seat in the cabin of the fishing boat, where he had taken up permanent residence.

Noticing the additional fitting of an upright tube clamped solidly on both sides of the boat just aft of the cabin bulkhead, Phillipo asked Junos what they were. "Mounts for the gun," in a cockney accent, was the terse reply. Nothing else seemed to be forthcoming, so Phillipo let the matter drop. On the way to Milos, with the sea deserted all around them, Junos threw two oil cans over the side and produced his machine gun which slotted satisfactorily into the portside pipe fitting. He clapped on a short belt of ammunition and opened fire with single shots at the floating cans.

To Phillipo's surprise, two following bursts of three shots disposed of both cans. At that point the gun was whipped off the mount and across the boat to the other mount. There, slotted in and ready, the boat swung round. Junos sighted briefly and blew the remains of both cans out of the water. Junos removed the weapon from the mount and laid it carefully on the engine box. The barrel was hardly warm. The boat now back on course, he removed the cleaning kit from the weapon, extended and locked the cleaning rod. Whistling softly between his teeth, he ran the cleaner through the opened barrel and cleaned the chamber before re-stowing the Browning.

***

At Ritz Peter was discussing with Jerry and Kat the arrangements for the MAS boat. Each torpedo had to be withdrawn and serviced ready for use, and the guns checked. The engines were running perfectly according to the Artificer PO. Italian uniforms for the crew and a German uniform for Peter.

Gathered around the table for the final briefing, Peter detailed the tasks. "Samantha and Phillipo have the partisans organised to keep the patrols at arm's length. Phillipo has explosives to take out the guns. They will not be blown until the steamer hits the entrance to the cove.

"The MAS boat will be inside by then and, hopefully, will have torpedoed the mini-subs. On our way out, we will drop depth charges under the steamer and sink her in the entrance."

He looked around at the others. "Has anyone anything to add?"

"Crew of the steamer: who's doing it, and how do they get off the boat?"

"Italian Skipper, with Royal Marines for the crew. They will have a dinghy ready alongside to get away in. Last man out will pull the plug just in case the depth charges don't work.

"The steamer is set up to self-destruct just in case."

He looked around once more. "One last thing. The MAS boat will return to Ritz after the action, picking up the marines on the way. It should be fully dark by that time and the boat can fit in easily. I need to get there to make sure the rest of the team have a place to come to. Neither Phillipo nor Samantha know where Ritz is. Junos does. If that's all," he rose to his feet.

Jerry left to oversee the work on the MAS boat.

Kat lingered, "Will Phillipo be okay. do you think?"

Peter nearly smiled. "He is a pretty level-headed man, accustomed to playing spy games. I think he will be alright. Are you worried about him?"

"Oh, he is a member of the team. I worry about them all." She spoke casually, almost offhand, and she walked out of the room.

Peter shrugged. 'Well-well'. Perhaps Phillipo's plan of action is working out for him." He decided to keep an eye on things. It could get interesting.

He sat down to go over everything once more, just in case there was anything he had missed. His eye caught the glint of the thin wavy gold ring on his cuff, tucked between the two wider rings. He sighed 1943 already. It seemed that he had been on the run ever since he stepped onto the deck of that first ML number three in 1940. He recalled the way his C.O Paul Evans had quietly died on the bridge of that same boat. Nearly three years seemed to have passed without him realising it.

"If they had but known?" He murmured to himself.

***

The MAS boat rode over the low swell at 22 knots heading for the rendezvous. Peter was below in the cabin leaving the bridge to her skipper, Jerry Lawrence. Kat sat chatting to Sergeant Harry Mitchell. Private Wallace sat in the corner of the cabin cleaning his sniper rifle with a soft cloth. He took each cartridge out of the box and wiped it down, feeling for any slight irregularities in the bullet or catches on the casing. There were three discarded bullets in the lid of the box already. Those he selected were being loaded into the magazine one by one. Lance Corporal Hardy was asleep. The three soldiers rescued from Cyprus at the beginning of Peter's tour in the Mediterranean area, had fitted into the team without causing a ripple. They had settled in and undertaken every job which had come their way regardless of the odds. They were accepted and valued members of the team.

Peter had accepted the offer of Jerry's cabin and was doing his best to make up on his sleep. The problem was that there were plenty of things to keep his mind active. So far they had been incredibly lucky. Apart from the injuries received by Theo, they had only suffered minor casualties in the team. The operation they were engaged with this time was much more up front with a real risk of injuries.

He did manage to get some sleep, but was awake once more by the time he heard the call that there was a ship in sight. He joined Jerry on the bridge and received the news that contact had been made with *HMS Legion* and she had cast the tramp adrift.

The destroyer raced past as they approached the tramp that wallowing in the swell over the Cretan Trough, the smoke from her funnel sending a dark stain into the night sky. With the brief signal, "She is all yours, and you are welcome to her. Good luck!" The destroyer raced off back to her regular duties.

The tramp got under way and the two craft made best speed for the Greek mainland, through the channel between the island of Kithira and Elafos into the Gulf of Lakonia.

With the steamer now working up to her full speed the MAS boat was logging 10 knots.

The Captain of the tramp called the base at his destination. His message was rehearsed and given under the knife of the Marine Major, "Just in case," he said.

The Italian Captain was terrified of the major. It was difficult to envisage him doing anything but whatever he was told by his escort. His ETA, being established for dusk the next day, appeared to be within the timetable expected. The report that the destroyer had been forced to return to base and had been replaced by a MAS boat did not go down too well. But after all, what could they do about it?

**

Contramiraglio Frascati was not happy. That little shit Schiller was no more a naval officer than Maria, his mistress. In fact she had more ability as a sailor, despite his credentials pre-war managing the German sailing team.

This latest business was really upsetting. Three of his best officers were under suspicion of betraying secrets, as a result of Schiller's prying. There was absolutely no way any of the pilots could communicate with the outside world without getting control of the radio. Also since the arrival of the base security section, run by Capitano di Fregate (Commander) Montego, he had found no evidence to implicate the three officers concerned.

He suspected that Schiller had been planted on him ostensibly to support him. But, in fact, it was really to assume command if there was any suggestion of deviation from the program of training or action undertaken. He also suspected that, if no evidence was forthcoming some would be fabricated, because that was the real reason Schiller was here.

He walked along the quay to the accommodation building. His aide, Tenente di Vascello (Lieutenant) Alberni came running along from the comms room, stopping breathless to present a message to Frascati.

"Slow down, Toni. You will give yourself a heart attack." Frascati liked the young officer. Son of an old friend, he had actually known him since he was a baby.

He opened the message and saw it was from the steamer bringing the modified maiale. It looked like they would be arriving tomorrow, escorted by a MAS boat?

"Thank you Tonio, carry on."

Tonio saluted and returned to the comms room at a more sedate pace. Frascati resumed his walk.

He was not surprised when he was joined by Schiller. The Kaptainleutnant (Lieutenant) was immaculately turned out, and deferential as usual. "Have we any news of the shipment, sir?"

"As you may have observed, Schiller. I have just received a communication, and it concerned that very matter."

"May I ask if there is anything new happening?" Schiller spoke through gritted teeth, still polite but hating the need for it.

Frascati stopped and looked at his German deputy. "The ship will arrive tomorrow night. In view of the secrecy of our operation I am happy it will be so. The destroyer has been replaced by a MAS boat."

Schiller looked upset. "Why have I not been informed of this change in arrangement?"

"I have just informed you, Herr Schiller!"

"I should have been informed immediately this information was made available!"

"May I remind you once again, Kapteinleutnant Schiller, I command here. You are my deputy, and as such you take your orders from me! Is that quite clear?"

"I am subject to the orders of the German High Command. I am not part of the command structure of the Italian Navy!"

"Then, sir, what are you doing here? While you are here on my base, you are subject to my orders. Having addressed me in a disrespectful manner, you will go immediately to your quarters and remain there for the next two days, appearing only for meals. Have I made myself clear?"

Schiller opened his mouth and abruptly closed it when he saw the look on Frascati's face. "Perfectly, sir." He saluted and made off to his quarters in the accommodation building. Despite his acquiescence, he was fuming inside. *How dare he talk like that to a German officer of the Kriegsmarine? Bloody Italian poseur, all pretty uniform and no guts, just like his ridiculous Il Duce, Benito Mussolini.*

Frascati continued his walk. he had surprised himself. He meant every word he had said. He made a note to tell the security man, Montego, that if Schiller appeared before the time was up, to arrest him and place him in the lock-up.

The remainder of the day passed quietly. The trainees spent time in the water with the training boat. Schiller stayed in his quarters and fumed.

***

Late the following afternoon, the Capo (Petty Officer) in command of the docking team came out onto the quay as darkness was falling. His team of ratings were scattered along the quay, prepared to accept the ropes of the ship when she finally entered harbour. The lights of the tramp and her escort appeared off the harbour entrance. The two lamps lighting the jaws of the entrance, were lit.

The roar of the engines of the MAS boat rose to a crescendo as she accelerated through the harbour mouth. Frascati was not quite sure but he could have sworn that the boat had fired her torpedoes

The shattering explosion smashing huge lumps of concrete from the quay, verified his impression. From above, one of the Vierlings started to stutter and other explosions shook the air, which was suddenly filled with debris and bits of gun from the mounts on the cliff above.

The Vierling was trying to follow the MAS boat, now leaving the harbour at high speed. The steamer meanwhile was coming into the harbour entrance, smoke from her funnel billowing as the engine thundered at full throttle for the gap. As it passed the steamer the MAS boat slowed then increased speed as it roared out of the harbour just as the steamer crossed the bar. Suddenly the waters erupted in a huge explosion. The stern of the steamer rose in the air and crashed back into the roiled waters. The ship stopped immediately, sinking fast by the stern, settling and blocking most of the harbour entrance. Two men ran from the deck house aft of the bridge and flung themselves into the sea.

The MAS boat was standing-by just outside the harbour entrance, the deck machine guns firing streams of lead at the still firing Vierling on the cliff top. The other torpedo, fired at the beached maiale, had impacted the cliff face beyond the row of mini-subs, having slithered up the sandy beach. The explosion brought the cliff down on the beach smashing the equipment and the mini-subs, and dumping the foundations of the .88 guns on top of the mess. The

Vierling, mounted on the cliff above the quay, finally toppled onto the accommodation building at the end of the quay.

Schiller had, of course, come out as soon as the first shots were fired. He reeled at the impact of the torpedo on the quay. The structure shook and he was flung down scraping his face on the rough surface. He staggered to his feet blood streaming. He was hurting in several parts of his body, gaze darting everywhere, searching for shelter or a way of escape. The path along the cliff face was gone and there were no boats alongside any more. Those which had been tied up were completely smashed by the impact of the torpedo.

Contramiraglio Frascati appeared from his office along the undamaged section of the quay. He looked unhurt and Schiller suddenly stopped looking for a way out, his hatred for the man all he could think of. He dragged out his pistol and started along the shattered concrete towards the Italian.

Frascati saw the bloody figure staggering toward him, gun in hand. His Beretta came out smoothly. He chambered a round and stood gun in hand pointed at the ground. As Schiller neared his pistol fired, the bullet flying off into the night.

Frascati shrugged, now convinced that Schiller was trying to kill him. He lifted the Beretta and shot Schiller in the leg.

The German office dropped to the concrete. His gun fell from his hand and lay inches from his side. Frascati stepped toward him. Schiller grabbed his pistol and lifted it to shoot. Frascati kicked it out of his hand. It fell into the water off the quay edge. He leaned down close to the ravaged face of the German. "I am unhappy to lose my command like this. You were never of any use here and your purpose was obviously to take over from me. I happily hand over my command to you. Since I cannot stand you—crawling, traitorous, piece of garbage—I am going to save you the trouble of explaining your failure to your bosses."

He lifted the Beretta and shot Schiller through the temple, watching the eruption of bloody matter from the other side of his head. He then stood up, holstered his weapon, then bent and heaved the corpse in front of him into the water.

***

On the cliff top Phillipo saw the whole thing. He refrained from shooting the Italian officer. He shouted to his party of partisans, "Time to go boys. The roving patrol will be with us otherwise."

Samantha Brown appeared by his side. "My lads are already on their way, so I'll say goodbye. It's been a pleasure working with you." She turned and ran over to the Volkswagen standing awaiting her. It roared off as the truck for Phillipo's men appeared.

He boarded the truck after the two wounded and the three dead men had been loaded and prepared to leave, back to Giorgio's farm.

His people had done well. The men killed had been because of over-enthusiasm. Their leader had confirmed bitterly that they had always been the impatient ones. Otherwise they had quietly placed their explosives and sat back awaiting the arrival of the ships. The three dead had seen the ships and opened fire with their light machine gun at the Vierling site. With their bullets striking the armour plate, the quad mounting had rotated and replied with devastating effect, three dead and the other wounded from the spray of fire the Vierling gunners expended. They had been unable to get to the charge placed at the site of the Vierling, men detailed for the job being those wounded and with the gunners warned and alert it was not possible to get to the trigger. He looked at his watch. The Vierling had fallen with the cliff that gave way, but the explosive had not yet gone off. The fail-safe should trigger itself any second. The explosion took out six of the men searching for survivors on the heap of rubble where the accommodation block had stood.

He waved the driver off with a grin. The driver grinned back at him and put the truck in gear.

Chapter twenty

The Waiting Game

On the MAS boat there was some damage mainly caused by the Vierling quad. There were three wounded and Peter had several pieces of glass in his arms from the shattered windscreen. He also had a cut on his cheek, which he had not even been aware of until Kat had wiped the blood off and taped it up.

They had looped around as they left the harbour, picking up the two men left on the steamer to set off the scuttling charges. The depth charges had been to make sure it stopped in the correct place. The scuttling charges had not gone off, making the movement of the wreck a hazardous operation at best and pointless since the secrecy of the harbour was compromised and the quay destroyed.

Having collected the two men from the water they made off back to the grotto. The temporary repairs effected by the medic and Kat on board, were placed in the hands of the doctor, who treated them all professionally. He decided that Peter and a bullet-wound in another of the men should be taken to Alexandria for more specialised treatment. Thus with both arms bandaged and his cut cheek re-taped, Peter and the wounded rating were collected by Catalina from the rendezvous.

After an accelerated de-brief at Peter's insistence, Peter was sent to hospital in Cairo for specialist attention.

His face was the least of his problems. The stitching, was in the words of the specialist, the best bit of sewing he had performed this year. He had been left with, what was described as, an interesting scar. The arms required more attention and he had been admitted into the hospital because of the danger of infection.

***

He awakened after his surgery, to find the anxious eyes of Amy looking at him. Disregarding his bandages he reached out, drew her face to his and kissed her. Happily she responded wholeheartedly, with relief that she had not misread the situation between them.

"What...How did you get here?" Peter asked.

"I decided to go for promotion and I am now a Petty Officer in communications. I applied for a Middle-East posting and here I am, rather I am in Alexandria, 100 miles down the road.

"You said nothing about it in your letters?"

"I did not want to tell you until I had completed my courses, and then I was posted here. So I left it until I arrived, and could tell you in person." She laughed, "I really had no idea they would send me here."

"How did you wangle the trip to Cairo?"

"I'm afraid told them I was your fiancée. So they gave me the weekend off to come and see you." She blushed, "I'm sorry if I have embarrassed you but there was no other way I could get the time off."

Peter took her hand. "Fiancée sounds good to me. But what about a ring?" He reached over to the cabinet by the bed and opened the drawer. He rummaged about then came up with the ring he had shown her in England, his grandmother's ring. He took her hand and slipped it on her finger. "There that should do the trick. If you change your mind you can always return it, otherwise you'll have to wait until I am back on my feet to take you to buy a proper engagement ring."

"But I didn't mean….."

"Don't you want to be engaged to me then?"

"Yes. Of course I do. But I didn't mean to…..You mean you want to make it official?" She was really blushing now.

Peter looked at her searchingly. "Yes, of course, unless you had other plans. I would like to marry you and therefore I would prefer ……."

The kiss was enough to stop him talking. They were occupied in murmuring together when the sister put her head around the door.

She decided not to bother them and put the 'do not disturb' sign on the door handle.

***

Peter was in hospital for two weeks before they would allow him to return to Alexandria, and, once there, he had leave if he wanted to take it. He opted to report to the office and spent the time there working up plans for the beginning of the way back across the Mediterranean. It entailed selecting places for raids on the Italian coast. The North African campaign was rapidly drawing to a close. The retreat of the German army from El Alamein was well under way and, with the American army approaching from the west, the replacement of Rommel seemed to underline the defeat the Axis were experiencing in Africa.

Already plans were in process of preparation for the invasion of Europe.

Among the members of the Special Operations team the opinion was either Sicily or mainland Italy, perhaps one following the other.

As the year ended Peter and Amy found the ring to confirm their engagement and were able to spend time together that neither had expected.

The New Year saw Peter back at the grotto organizing raids once more with the emphasis on Italy rather than Greece.

Preparations to move the base to a more appropriate site were well advanced. The distances involved made access to the Adriatic unrealistic. The campaign on the Greek peninsula would continue based on Ritz. Phillipo would take over command of the Greek zone of operations.

Peter was scheduled to move operations to the recently liberated Tripoli or Tunis. In the meantime the attacks on the outposts of the Axis influence were producing results, in forcing both abandonment of some bases and the reinforcement of others. The attachment of elements of marines and/ or local units of Greek irregulars drawn from island partisans, enabled the Special Ops groups to make a significant impact on the occupation forces.

***

It was returning from a raid on Santorini when they met the flak ship. The rumours of a heavily armoured ship bristling with guns had been rife over the past weeks. It sounded as if the vessel had been deliberately prepared for the job of stopping the raids that were annoying the authorities, and the Germans were going to do it with brute force.

Peter had previously encountered flak ships in the Channel, and he was well aware that they punched their weight, in fact more than their weight.

Armed with a combination of weapons from Tank .88's to .5 mm machine guns, the 20mm cannon were particularly damaging, and they had six mounted around the deck. The Germans had a habit of sending them with convoys for air defence, though they could depress the guns to take on sea-borne targets as well.

Whenever used, the MAS boat always carried torpedoes in its tubes. Peter decided that the ML should also carry torpedo tubes and that they should always be available and loaded when on patrol or raid. So one encounter between the MAS boat and the flak ship had been interesting since, in the first place, the MAS boat was flying the Italian flag,

Peter was there after a frustrating night on Santorini, where everything that could go wrong had done its best to go wrong. Had he not been there the situation might have come out differently. As it was, since there were fish in the tubes, Peter had elected to attack the flak ship. With flags flying and speed in-creasing, the boat entered the zone for which it had been created. As they lined up for the attack Peter ordered the Italian flag lowered and replaced with the battle ensign. Then, with the throttles opened wide, he began the run. As the range closed the captain of the flak ship obviously became suspicious, though it was only when a flirt of wind revealed the White En-sign that he reacted and ordered the guns to fire.

The side being approached by the MAS boat burst into a hail of fire as it neared its target. Both torpedoes ran true but the flak ship managed to turn in time to cause one of the fish to miss. The other hit with a thud and did not go off. It caused a breach in the hull, but it did not explode and therefore failed to stop, or even slow down the barrage aimed at the MAS boat. Despite the twisting and turning the boat took damage. Since the armament on the MAS boat was light, apart from its tubes and depth charges, Peter reluctantly turned away. Mentally, he decided that they would find where the flak ship was moored and pay it a visit in the near future.

They returned to the grotto subdued and disappointed. It had been almost a wasted effort, though they had punched a hole in the flak ship there was little else to celebrate.

The repairs to the MAS boat were undertaken immediately. Peter sat down with Phillipo to discuss the enemy's possible location. Kat came in to join them and suggested that, since the ship was armoured heavily she was probably slow. She would also have limited endurance unless she carried extra fuel. Her appearance in the vicinity must be the result of their efforts to keep the enemy on the hop.

Peter, re-assured by the positive attitude of the team, also suggested that Milos might well be the base of the German ship. Phillipo had already put out the word that any information about the German ship would be appreciated.

The repairs to the MAS boat took time.

***

It was three days later. The fishing boat had been commandeered to take weapons to Agios Pathos. The partisans were creating real trouble for the occupation forces and it seemed that the German presence had been increased because of the lack of success of their Italian allies.

The German response to the partisans was typical. They rounded up the people of the small town of Lakos, and warned that any further activity by the partisans would result in the deaths of the people by firing squad in the town square.

The next demand was the surrender of the partisans. Since this would not be considered, people would die.

Weapons were needed, so that they could make sure that the Germans paid dearly for any deaths from the detained townspeople.

Peter thought about the situation. He knew Lakos personally from earlier operations and, while he realised the German garrison was a more significant problem than the Italians, they had their weaknesses, as had everyone.

The people were being detained in the only building big enough within the town, the church in the town square.

"What about access to the church?" He asked Kranko who had come to collect the weapons.

"The priest has said there may be a way to open the crypt from the house across the garden. It used to be the home of a small convent. They looked after the priest at the house behind the church. The Germans took the building over for their mess room. If we can get access to the cellar we should be able to reopen the passage to the crypt and get the people out." Kranko looked a little uncertain.

Phillipo smiled grimly. "You know of this place? How many troops will there be in the mess at one time?"

"It depends on the time, certainly anything from 5-16. But if the men are busy elsewhere.....?" He shrugged.

Peter spoke. "Two things. This is worthwhile if we make it work. So we make it work. Agreed?"

They all nodded or murmured agreement. "We need a distraction to start with. What can we blow up to stir things up? Truck Park. Stores depot. Magazine? Think, people. We need a dramatic incident to give us time to take over the house while we rescue the people."

Phillipo spoke, "The leader of the partisans has been talking of a face-off with the Germans as soon as he has enough weapons. He has the men. The delivery of arms we have for him could be enough. Whatever happens, I will ensure there will be a diversion to lure the troops out of Lakos. If you use Kranko's transport with trailers, we should be able to shift the people to safety, even if it takes more than one trip."

"That makes sense. I'll leave it to you. I will be in Lakos to open the tunnel. Finally, we need to cover our retreat. So, ideally, we need a bombardment, maybe an air raid?" Peter paused looking thoughtful. "What size is the garrison on the island?"

Kat answered. "The German contingent is 250 men based at Lakos and Yeraki, approximately half and half, plus the 300 Italians. They, incidentally, have all been shoved out to Zante, in the north. The rumour is that, now Mussolini has been deposed, they are leaving the alliance with Germany. They have not been disarmed but they are pretty disillusioned, especially with the way their so-called allies have been treating them."

"Is there any chance of them helping in this situation?" Peter asked the question, looking around the group. "I have the feeling that the new Italian government will declare war on Germany. Up to now they haven't. But at a guess it won't be long. The Germans have treated the Italians badly."

They all looked at Kranko. "Why are you looking at me?" Kranko said, sounding aggrieved.

Phillipo smiled evilly. "Probably because you have been supplying them with services throughout their stay in the island."

"That is just business. I use the opportunity to get information for the partisans."

"Well?"

Kranko looked thoughtful. "Maybe...I think they just might help. I will need some time. Can you get me there fast. That bastard German boat was spotted heading towards the island, so I need to get back before she arrives."

Peter looked at Phillipo with a grim smile. "Are you thinking what I am?"

Phillipo grinned back. "I guess so, with both boats."

***

The MAS boat had been repaired. Some of the patches looked a little raw, but otherwise she was fine, fully rearmed, alongside the ML, also armed and ready to go. Peter assembled both crews and his dirty tricks team to brief them on the project.

"We will be sailing at dusk. First drop will be near Lakos for Captain Phillipo and the Greeks. They should meet the Partisans with the weapons." He looked at his watch. "The fishing boat will be there by the time you get there. The second drop at Zante, Kranko and Kat with Harry and his lads. Both boats will rendezvous near Lakos; Hopefully we will find and sort out the flak-ship between us.

"Whatever happens next, may depend on the Italians. It will be a gamble, but I think it worth taking. Is everyone clear about what they will be doing?" He looked around at the assembled people, then nodded to Jerry Lawrence. "OK, Jerry. Take Captain Phillipo and get on your way."

The MAS boat led the ML out of the grotto. Both boats opened throttles and made for the island of Agios Pathos. Working up to full speed, Peter, in the ML, was deep in thought. There were a lot of holes in the rough plans they had made. It would be up to Phillipo to get the people out of the church safely. The partisans would create a diversion to occupy the German troops, while Phillipo and his party broke into the cellar of the nun's house and got through to the crypt,

He would still need to get them away. For a moment he thought of the enormity of the decisions he was making, the cost in lives if he guessed wrong?

He was reminded that he had other problems, with the sight of the MAS boat, having dropped the Lakos party, approaching from starboard to take up station on the ML. He turned to Wells, the signals Leading Seaman. "Send by lamp to Lieutenant Lawrence. 'Take a swing out to the West to see if the flak ship is in the area yet. Do not make contact. Rendezvous, as briefed, in one hour thirty'."

The MAS boat acknowledged and swung around the stern of the ML, to make off to the north and west in a big circuit.

Chapter twenty-one

Attack

As the ML approached Zante to the north of Agios Pathos, it throttled down and motored quietly into the harbour. The town was quiet but Peter decided that Kranko would need company in addition to the three soldiers. He spoke to CPO Smith quietly. "Keep an eye out for Mr. Willis, Chief!"

"Will do, sir. But would you like a few of the lads with you, sir. You're taking a bit of a risk."

"Chief, it's a risk I must take. I'll be with you in 45minutes. Otherwise get the hell out to the rendezvous with Mr Lawrence." Peter looked at Arthur Smith for a long moment.

Arthur Smith looked back and nodded. "Depend on me, sir."

"I know I can, Chief. Shore party away!" He turned and stepped off the boat along with Kat and the others.

***

Captain Phillipo moved silently through the streets of Lakos to the square. The church was lit with subdued lights. There were guards in front and, as he watched, sentries appeared from both sides and crossed, presumably to meet and cross behind the church before returning to the front.

He withdrew and made his way round the square to the street behind the church. The small green area was quiet and looking a little overgrown.

The Nuns' house was showing a light, as men opened and closed the front door. The partisans had been waiting for the consignment of weapons. They had agreed to create the diversion needed to clear the area of soldiers, or at least reduce their numbers.

A siren started, causing Phillipo to jump at the sudden noise. The house door opened and light streamed out. Eighteen men tumbled through the door, equipment in hand. The watchers waited. No one else came through the door. Phillipo moved over to the house. Anthony peered through the open door and Aristotle stepped through gun in hand, followed by Phillipo. Anthony waited at the door to keep an eye open for returning soldiers.

The other two went through the house carefully. There was a man working in the kitchen alone. Otherwise the house was empty. Aristotle joined the man in the kitchen and tied him up.

Phillipo found the door to the cellar and went down the stairs. In the basement there was gear stacked around the walls. He could just make out what looked like a piece of architrave poking out from behind a stack of boxes. Not bothered about the noise, Phillipo grabbed the nearest box and heaved it to one side. It took a few minutes to clear the area and reveal the door which had been obscured by the boxes. There was a handle He gripped it and turned, to his surprise the door opened without more than a jerk to unstick the slightly swollen wood.

Beyond the door the tunnel was dark. Phillipo took out his torch and went cautiously along the passage. The air smelt earthy but was cool. There was a slight current brushing his skin. After twenty five paces, at the far end there were stairs and a door. He climbed up and tried the door handle. The door was locked. He had a crowbar with him for just this eventuality. So he inserted the end in the door jamb beside the lock, and eased the sneck away from the jamb. The door popped open, revealing more boxes stacked to above-the-door height.

Aristotle joined him. Between them they removed the boxes and entered the church crypt.

The murmur of voices came from behind another door, where the light was leaking between the bottom and the uneven floor. Phillipo knocked at the door. There was a sudden silence and steps approached. A key turned in the lock. The door opened revealing the local priest. He stepped back in astonishment.

Phillipo did not hesitate. He said, "I have come to release you all, please follow Aristotle through the tunnel to the nuns' house."

The priest was quick on the uptake. He started shepherding the people through the door. The number of people within the church diminished rapidly. Aristotle went with them. Once through the house, he led them through the back of the town to the beach where he instructed them to sit and wait.

Phillipo left the priest to close and lock the door from the crypt and bring the remainder of the people through. He then called on the hand radio to Maria, Kranko's daughter.

Two trucks and a jeep appeared on the road opposite the beach, all towing trailers. With the arrival of the transport the people boarded both the vehicles and trailers.

They departed, leaving two thirds of the people behind. They returned within the hour having delivered the first load. The remainder of the people had arrived along with the priest. He supervised the loading of the next group, waiting himself for the transport to return for the last of the people. All the time the transfer was taking place, the popping of small arms fire could be heard from somewhere beyond the town boundary.

Phillipo left with the final truck and was dropped off at a rendezvous where the brothers waited. They were fully armed and had extra weapons for Phillipo. The three departed in the jeep immediately, to the scene of the diversion created by the partisans.

***

At the scene, a German patrol had been ambushed. What had started as a minor incident had now escalated to a full-scale conflict with the majority of the troops from the Lakos garrison. The partisans were firmly entrenched on high ground. The ambush point had been carefully chosen. The intention was to draw in reinforcements from the Yeraki Garrison and, in effect, engage the entire German presence on the island.

The radio Phillipo was carrying squeaked. He answered, "Phillipo!"

"This is Kat. We are on the way with reinforcements. How are you fixed?"

"No sign of re-in.........Just a minute. It looks as if the unit from Yeraki had arrived."

"Good, we have most of the Italian troops here with us. They know that Mussolini has been deposed. They also believe that their Government has turned on Germany. They agreed to jump the gun, because the Germans treated them like rubbish. They are looking for payback! We are now within five miles of you. Where do you want us?"

"Straight up the road to Piles. Debus before you get there. We are in high ground to the east of the town. Take on the Germans from the flank.

Peter had returned to the ML, much to the relief of Sub Lieutenant Willis.

They were now offshore racing to join the MAS boat off Yeraki. The radio crackled and the voice of Jerry Lawrence came through. "I have the flak-ship in sight. She is offloading troops into boats."

"Wait until all the troops are on the water, and then attack the boats. Sink as many as you can. The more you sink the easier the task. I will be with you shortly, I do have the silhouette of the flak-ship to go by. In fact it has just come into view. I need to slow down while I get into position."

The flak-ship was still offloading troops when Peter loosed his first torpedo. It ran true. It caused the ship to lift out of the water, smashing the boats still alongside. Men fell into the water from the deck and from the damaged boats. Peter called to Jerry to sink all the shore-bound boats. The wounded ships' guns opened fire in all directions, obviously not aware of the current position of the ML. Peter steered in a big arc and fired his other torpedo. The enemy ship was not moving under control. The second torpedo hit further forward causing it to settle, sinking rapidly. The guns stopped firing. There was no sign of a radio message for help. CPO Smith pointed out that the radio mast had gone with the first torpedo strike. Most of the troops in the water sank, loaded down by their equipment. The lucky ones, who had been able to get out of their webbing in time, struggled to keep afloat.

Jerry had the task of sinking the other troops in their boats. Soldiers were now firing at the MAS boat as it approached. Jerry kept his distance, and opened fire with the 20mm on the hulls of the boats. The wood shattered, the bullets gouging lumps of wood and creating holes in the hulls. The boats to filled rapidly and threw the unfortunate soldiers into the water.

Two boats reached the shore. A hail of fire from the machine guns on the racing MAS boat mowed down most of the survivors. The three who made it off the beach were attacked by a crowd of local people, attracted to the shore by the noise of gunfire. They were beaten to death with shovels and picks.

The ML cruised around the wreckage. They pulled six survivors from the sea, including one of the ship's officers from the flak-ship.

The enemy had lost 123 soldiers and 24 seamen in the skirmish.

***

On the island, the troops from Yeraki debussed from their vehicles, and confidently started moving up to support their comrades in what had become a pitched battle.

The two hundred Italian soldiers settled down on the ridgeline and waited as the German reinforcements moved up the valley in column toward the firing line of their compatriots.

A machine gun, at the extreme end of the Italian line, opened fire on the leading file of German soldiers. The rest of the Italian troops opened fire immediately. In the next ten seconds nearly half of the troops on the road were down. The others were scattered searching for cover which was not really there. Kat, who was on the ridge with the Italians, was amazed at the sheer vindictiveness of the former German allies. It was now being made clear that the Italian soldiers had hated their so-called allies.

For Phillipo, who was able to witness the slaughter of the reinforcements, it was heartening. But for the beleaguered German troops below it was a shocking blow. For the partisans it was the icing on the cake. The diversion had provided them with the opportunity to remove the Germans from the island. As soon as the extra weapons had arrived, the leader of the partisans, who had some time ago worked out an ambush plan, realised that it could now be used.

It had worked perfectly. The arrival of the reinforcements could have been a problem. But the intervention of the Italians, unforeseen by all, had turned a probable German victory into a rout.

In the valley the surviving Germans were throwing down their weapons and raising their hands in defeat. Kat and the Italian Tenente had difficulty in stopping the men shooting the surrendering Germans. As it was, the Italians came down from the ridge and collected the prisoners and their weapons.

They then advanced up the valley and took the surviving Germans from the rear. The partisans came out of the rocks and down into the valley, collecting the abandoned weapons of the hapless German troops. The transport which had brought the troops in was taken to go out to the towns, and take over the German bases set up there. No word of the defeat was allowed out at that time. The island went off air for a week.

Though the German prisoners were treated correctly as soldier POW's, the two Gestapo officers were found hanged, alongside the graves of some of their victims.

It was the beginning for the Greek islands.

Chapter twenty-two

Tunis

The base had been shifted from Alexandria to Tunis in Tunisia. The ML flotilla had been reassembled and for the moment, at least, Peter was back doing what he had been originally trained to do, only now as half leader of the flotilla. His acting rank as Lieutenant Commander had been confirmed. He was now number two to Danny Oliver, who had made the step to Commander.

The base at Tunis used temporary buildings provided by the American Army. The Quonset huts were adequate for the purpose, and as good as any available buildings in the battered town.

The feel of the boat powering through the waves in broad daylight was exhilarating for Peter. The crew were relaxed and easy in their jobs. Even Sub Lieutenant Willis was now more relaxed than he had been since he was promoted.

Jerry Lawrence had been given command of an ML. His beloved MAS boat was still with special operations, now transferred to Malta for operations in the Aegean and Tyrrhenian Seas. An enemy convoy of ships had departed from Marseilles to supply their forces in Anzio. Having made it safely to the passage between Sardinia and Corsica, they now set out in the early evening for the final dash to the Italian coast. It meant they would face the final part of the voyage in daylight. The convoy had been spotted by an Allied aircraft and the flotilla had been despatched to intercept them.

The number eight boat, on the starboard wing, sighted the convoy and reported over the TBS (Talk between ships) now supplied to all the boats .

Danny Oliver ordered a course change and the flotilla turned toward the five cargo ships, escorted by three E boats and a destroyer. Danny's voice came over the radio. "I will take the destroyer with No. 2. No's 4, 5, and 6, the E boats. Peter, take 7 and 8 and hit the cargo ships.

Peter and his group peeled off from the flotilla, and then started the wide swing around the escorts to get to the supply ships.

The others made direct for the escorts. The destroyer was not one of the newest in the German navy, Danny saw as h e approached with his partner. The destroyer started to turn toward the two MLs. Danny and No. 2, under Lieutenant Matt Parry, separated, each taking their own side and splitting the gun power of the ship. The two boats, jinking and swerving, targeted the destroyer with one torpedo each. The unfortunate destroyer was hit by both almost simultaneously. It split into two parts which rose up into the air, the propellers still turning in the aft section. The foredeck gun fired into the water, as the bow section rose, tipping forward before plunging back into the water and sinking swiftly beneath the surface already littered with the shattered bits and pieces of the broken ship.

The impact of the devastating explosion was dramatic. Time seemed to stop for a moment with the shock. Peter, despite his concentration on the targets ahead, was shaken because of the sudden impact on his ears. "All guns standby, E boat on the starboard beam." As he spoke No. 4 boat interposed itself between them and the E boat, all guns blazing. The Fairmile had had the 3 pounder gun mounted in addition to the torpedo tubes. And the concentrated firepower was impressive.

Peter's task was no pushover. All of the supply ships were armed and manned by trained gunners. The main armament seemed to be a 100mm (4 inch) gun on the foc'sle, and an AA quick-firing gun, trailer-mounted, on the forward well-deck. Though the AA gun did not have as wide a field of fire as the 100mm, it gave cover on both beams and had a rapid rate of fire, being of similar design to the Bofors gun, beloved of the British army, which could be used at flat trajectory as a tank killer as well as an AA gun. Like the Bofors, it was loaded by clip magazine, five shells at a time. It was only by jinking erratically that Peter managed to keep clear of the alarmingly accurate fire of the lead ship.

The tanker was third in line. It had a well-served 75mm gun on her foc'sle. She was low in the water, but still travelling at 14 knots along with the other ships, which meant that she was as up to date as the others. Peter swung to port in a wide arc, to make space for a run up to the tanker from abaft her starboard beam. The tanker started to swing away but the battle going on that side of the convoy changed the captain's mind. Willis's voice came over the intercom from the torpedo control position. "Steer five degrees to port! Steady. Fire One!"

The fish in number one tube leapt out ahead of the boat and plunged into the water, the trail of bubbles appearing on the surface indicating it was running to its set course. The torpedo struck the tanker with an initial flash, as the ambient gas in the air ignited in response to the explosion of the torpedo. The tanker immediately slowed down, without the power of the damaged engines to maintain its movement through the water. The freighter in line behind her swerved toward Peter's boat guns blazing, and scored several hits with the 20mm cannon fitted to the bridge wing.

Peter suddenly became aware of the racket as his ears cleared. The guns that would bear were firing at the ML, which received more hits as they broke off, using their agility to outmanoeuvre the cargo ship.

Surveying the other ships in the convoy, he called across to the other two boats to take the lead ship and the second ship while he took the last in line, a freighter which seemed the best armed and also most modern of them all. She was sparkling with gunfire, from small calibre to the 88mm on her fore-deck and a similar gun on her after-castle. The real problem was the 20mm cannon mounted both sides of the bridge, and at the after end of the centre super-structure. The guns, firing together, made a cone of destruction which they had to avoid. The high rate of fire made them lethal with their range. Both Oerlikons on the ML concentrated on the gun posi-tions. The 3pounder targeted the 88mm forward as the boat manoeuvered to stay out of the arc of fire of the after 88 mm. A single torpedo would be sufficient in the right place, and Peter decided that the engine room just forward of the after gun mounting, was the target. He called Willis and told him what he had de-cided. Willis acknowledged. "I'll need 30 seconds steady on course, to have a chance, skipper."

Peter acknowledged and swung the boat clear to line up on the target with as little hassle as possi-ble. To the two Oerlikons, both reloading preparing for the next run, he said, "This time I want those

20mm suppressed. We will be straight and level for thirty seconds to get the fish in."

Both the gunners nodded. Peter called, "All guns ready for the main attraction. Stand by for torpedo attack."

The boat turned and the speed started building. Peter stood behind the screen as the wind whipped past. "She is all yours, Mr Willis." He refrained from urging speed. Willis had enough pressure on him without adding to it.

The speed built and the bow started to crash into the waves as the boat powered up to her top speed,

The guns suddenly opened fire as the range closed, and Peter realised the shells had been hitting the waters on either side and ahead for the past few minutes. One of the 20mm found the range and a row of holes ran across the foredeck missing the foremost Oerlikon, though it sprayed splinters over the loading number crouched with a spare magazine in his hands. The gun on the ship stopped as their own fire found the 20mm position and took out the gunner and his loader. The cry, "Torpedo away," was the signal to start jinking. Peter surprised the gunners at the stern of the ship by swinging and giving his own gunners a chance at the gun crew aft and the smaller weapons mounted there. As they shot behind the target ship the torpedo hit. The big stern gun was dismounted, as the force of the explosion drove up through the deck and buckled the reinforced framework, canting the gun to an impossible angle. Peter made a return run back across the stern and dropped depth charges under the already weakened stern. As they stood off they saw the charges blow it off completely. This opened the hull to the greedy waters of the Mediterranean. Ahead of the convoy, the sole survivor was being hurried by two E boats, one of which trailed a line of diesel in the water behind it, mirroring the trail of smoke from her ruined funnel.

The tanker was still well afloat and not on fire, though she was dead in the water. Three of the other ships were sinking. There was an ML on fire. The destroyer was gone and there was no sign of the third E boat. Jerry came alongside and called across that the CO's boat was bent but still mobile. The burning boat had been abandoned. They had lost their skipper and three of the crew, but the others were all on board No. 2 boat. Peter had three casualties. The loader on the forward Oerlikon, Paddy McGuire, had splinters from the near miss by the 20mm. The TGM, Will Farquher, had been struck by debris from the stern of the final ship. He was awake and swearing, which was good sign. But Able seaman Wright, who had operated the Browning, would no longer be entertaining the long string of ladies he was reputed to be servicing. During the last run beside the sinking freighter, a bullet had hit the housing of the chamber on the Browning. It ricocheted and struck Wright between the eyes. The hole was small at the front and the bullet had remained within his skull. CPO Smith commented rather unsympathetically, "He always had a thick skull, and was tight as a tick. Never gave nothing away."

"There would be a more formal epitaph," Peter mused. "But probably not as apt."

***

They towed the tanker back to Malta, the nearest port and one which could use the fuel anyway. It also gave a short respite to the tired crews.

It gave Peter a chance to see Amy, who was now Third Officer Lucas in the Comms section in Naval HQ in Valetta. As temporary supervisor, while she awaited the arrival of the Admiral in Malta, she reported to the Wren Second Officer in charge of the cipher office.

It was there he found her and managed to arrange for her and any other off-duty Wrens to come to the impromptu party, arranged for that evening to celebrate their victory over the convoy and the acquisition of the tanker. There was some question of it being a prize of war. Therefore, its value might be apportioned to the captors?

*　*　*

The organisation had been left to CPO Smith, who had found a building in the area, suitable and private, where the officers and other ranks could gather together to say farewell to absent friends and celebrate their own survival.

The officers, having begun proceedings with the men, departed and foregathered in the Phoenicia Hotel for their own party. Peter and Amy took the chance to share the first private moments since Peter had returned to the grotto from Alexandra, months ago. Amy was already in Malta by the time Peter was transferred to Tunis.

In the room Peter had booked, with the door closed and the key turned, Amy turned to Peter and put her arms round his neck. She whispered, "I have missed you!"

He kissed her and, as he came up for breath, "I missed you too."

She wriggled loose from his arms and held her hand up to stop him coming forward. Then she undid the buttons of her uniform jacket, kicked off her shoes, then proceeded to unzip her skirt and let it drop to the floor. This performance was followed by the abandonment of the remainder of her clothing, piece by piece, shirt, tie, stockings and bra and finally, her panties, non-regulation, accompanied by a blush which interestingly seemed to suffuse her entire body. Finally she did a twirl. "Will I do?" She said with a little smile.

"You certainly will do for me." He said fervently. He started to step forward.

She held up her hand. "Your turn!"

He stopped, confused for a moment, then got the message. He went through the same routine as she had, even down to the blush as he removed his underpants. He twirled in turn. "Will I do?"

She giggled and leaped on to the big bed. "Let's find out, shall we?"

Chapter twenty-three

Salerno

The flotilla was detailed to become part of the invasion fleet for the invasion of Italy. They sailed from Palermo, having fuelled there before cruising north to join the main fleet. Their scheduled station was on the north side of the invasion fleet, to screen the ships from warship and submarine activity.

The size of the fleet astonished Peter. They seemed to take hours to get in position. In fact they did, due to the changing shape of the invasion fleet, with the ships altering position for strategic reasons. They finished up motoring abreast of a line of landing-craft transports with the rows of LCAs hanging ready to launch. The sea was choppy and grey with the land growing closer. The boats lowered. The troops embarked, the landing craft full of men crouched against the motion of the ugly oblong boxes. They smashed their way to the beaches. It was 01:00 a.m. in the morning when the first landings took place. They continued with supplies and reinforcements, as they took advantage of the surprise achieved and consolidated the beachhead throughout the day. The enemy finally reacted and fierce fighting began. Over the next few days the battle raged. At one stage British cruisers made the trip from North Africa, at full speed and packed with troops. They were landed and went straight into action. The Germans massed tanks in a counter attack. The big guns of the fleet sailed nearer the shore to add the power of their guns to the action, and smashed up the tank's attack .The response was with aircraft and glider bombs from the Axis forces.

All this was the background against which the ML's operated, coping with alarms of submarines and giving aid to landing craft with lost power, as well as acting as general dogsbody to the fleet in general.

***

A rather curious incident for Peter occurred, when he was called to take a platoon of American soldiers, including a male War Correspondent up-coast to Naples. At the approach to the port they slowed and cautiously motored into the harbour. It was only then that the Lieutenant in charge of the platoon told Peter that an informant had said that the Germans had moved out of Naples, and the Italian authorities were concerned that the city would be smashed in the approaching battle.

Peter took part in the landing and verified that they met no opposition. Nor did they see a single German soldier while they were there. They returned to the battle, leaving the correspondent in Naples, at his own request.

Speaking to Danny Oliver, Peter said, "That was the scariest operation I have ever been on. It was weird."

Danny grinned. "While you were prancing about up the Appian Way, the Italian Fleet sailed from Spezia to Valletta on the 11th of September, and officially surrendered. But for you, sir, the war goes back to the cloak and dagger."

The MLs were moored, waiting to be called to refuel and re-provision. They were currently along-side a pontoon linked to their mothership. *HMS*

Bramber had once been a cargo-passenger liner on the East Africa run. Now she serviced the flotilla of MLs and any submarine that might be in the vicinity. She had just completed her move to Ajaccio in Corsica, now liberated.

***

The two officers were making their way up to the suite allocated to the MLs, where they would receive their orders for their next task. Danny had been told that he would lose the services of Peter who would be required for a hush-hush operation. In the briefing room there were several officers present. To Peter's surprise Commander Lancaster from Special Operations was one of them.

When he saw Peter, Roger took him to one side and muttered, "We will talk afterwards. We need you for a special job, I'm afraid. So you will not be part of the operation they will be briefing just now."

Chapter Twenty-three

Commando

Seated with three others in the briefing room was the elegant figure of Samantha Brown. Roger Lancaster was flanked by an army officer whose green beret sat on the table in front of him. The badge was a dagger in a shield. Peter did not recognise it, but he realised that he did recognise the flash the soldier wore. He had heard of the Commandos. The major in front of him was the first he had actually seen.

The Naval Captain was also a stranger. It was only when the door opened and Amy appeared following the Admiral that formal introductions were made.

Amy seated herself and opened her brief case.

She withdrew a file and stood up. Taking a sheet from it she read. "Meeting held in *HMS Bramber* 21 September 1943. Present Rear Admiral Sir David Hardcastle KB Royal Navy, Captain Martin Dewar RN, Commander Roger Lancaster, RNR, Lt Commander Peter Woods DSC RNVR, Major Kenneth McLean, No1,Commando. Major Samantha Brown, SOE and Acting Third Officer, Amy Lucas. WRNS.

"You are advised that this meeting is top secret and any disclosure to anyone outside this group, will be an act of treason and will be treated as such."

Amy sat down and withdrew a notebook and pencil from the case.

The Admiral coughed. "Thank you, Lucas." He cleared his throat again then said "Ladies and Gentlemen, forgive the cloak and dagger approach, but what I have to tell you is only known otherwise to the very top echelon in our Government. The knowledge that we have here in this room could lose the war and destroy life on Earth.

"Courtesy of Major Brown, we are now aware of the progress made so far with the German experiments on a super-bomb known as the Atom bomb."

"Captain Dewar and I will leave you in the competent hands of Commander Lancaster for the planning and briefing of this mission." He left the room

Peter looked mystified. He had never heard of an Atom bomb. He looked around the group and realised that he was the only one who did not know such a bomb was in train.

Roger Lancaster explained, "The scientists, and all the necessary equipment, are in process of being shifted to, we believe, South America. Due to the secrecy involved and to prevent panic, any action we take must be completely hush-hush. We cannot allow such a devastating weapon to exist in the hands of the Western world's worst enemy.

"To re-assure you, the British and US Governments are both working on similar projects. However, our task is to hijack the enemy's attempt to shift the work to South America, Paraguay, I believe, and stop their effort in one go. We are aware there are other research projects working on similar projects. This appears to be the most advanced and we do not wish it to drop out of sight." Roger looked up from the paper in front of him. He turned to the others of the group. "You are all here for a reason, as you are undoubtedly aware.

"First: Major McLean, I understand that you have been briefed on the handling of the materials involved in the manufacture of the Atom bomb?"

"I have, Commander, though I think it highly unlikely the materials with be shipped with the scientists involved."

The Major spoke in a clipped Scottish accent, reflecting a cultured background, Peter thought.

Roger continued, "Major Brown, I understand we are indebted to you for the information we are sharing. Could you please tell us what is actually happening?"

Samantha stirred in her seat and, without referring to any notes, spoke, "I have been in France for the past four weeks. During that time I have seen the Germans take over the Vichy section of the country completely. You may be aware there was a section of the country that was seen as still ruled by France. As you probably all know, that was—in some ways—true, in others a myth. Escaping prisoners found to their cost that capture in Vichy was not to be contemplated. The gloves have come off. Now the face of occupation is clearly shown. However, it had only just been discovered that a secret research establishment in the Massif Central, unknown to us until recently, has been working since France fell in 1940 on the so-called Atom bomb.

"The scientists involved, taken from whatever source, were allowed to work in the establishment as long as they produced. I came onto the scene when the move to South America was discussed. The Jewish scientists still working at the Centre were suddenly faced with imprisonment and death. There was no question of sending them to South America. My contact was related to a scientist and thus the news got out to us before the serious security blanket dropped.

"Through my informant I learned that the Jewish scientists have now been removed and sent, either to other projects or Dachau, a prison camp where, we are now discovering, they exterminate Jews and other lesser beings such as gypsies and dissidents.

"My contact tells me her relative has been told to prepare to leave France on the 28th of September, by special flight from Hyeres. She is terrified that the Focke Wulf Condor will be shot down, and she will lose her father and mother, both of whom are research scientists. All will assemble in Toulon. The consignment of equipment and material goes by sea and the scientists by air. No destination has been mentioned. They are guessing, Paraguay.

"We need to stop the ship and capture the scientists if that is possible." She turned to Peter. "That is where you come in. We hope the ship will be identified by that time. We would expect you to sink the ship. Capture is unlikely to be an option. Though if capture is possible we would obviously welcome it. The Commandos would be sent to take the air passengers and expect to be collected by you in the ML.

"The whole operation is very important, not just because of the likelihood of the bomb being used in the war. But if they lose the war, and are able to complete the bomb in some banana republic, who knows what blackmail or devastation could be created?"

The Admiral rose. "I will be leaving you all to it. The only notes to leave this room will be those taken by Third Officer Lucas. Is that understood?"

The group all nodded and stood as the Admiral left.

Roger took over the chair and the discussion became general with maps and charts of the inshore waters in and around Toulon. The fact that Toulon was a French Naval Base meant that there was no problem for the ML approaching the coast there. But it would be well guarded. The small port at Hyeres, where the airfield was situated, was another proposition altogether.

Peter took up the discussion, "I think we should use Hyeres as our starting point. If I land the Commandos at Hyeres, they can make for the airfield and capture the party due to fly out.

"If the ship can be identified, I will do my best to sink her before it can get far enough to lose itself in the traffic. I must stress the urgency of this. If they are using a submarine for the transit it would be better that I know I advance. It would be much more difficult to sink, and even more elusive to catch.

"What about a guide in Hyeres for the Commandos? Do we have a trustworthy man or woman in mind. I ask this because I know the place pretty well. Racing in the Med pre-war, we based ourselves in Hyeres away from the other teams. I should say each of the teams had a favoured base for the races. Hyeres happened to be ours."

Major McLean leaned forward. "A local Maquisard would be enough, I think. This will not be a job for amateurs."

Roger Lancaster roared with laughter at this comment. "Major, you should be aware that one of the reasons Commander Woods is here is because of his experience and skills in covert operations. He has spent more time in action behind enemy lines that you have."

The Major looked at Peter with new respect. I apologise, Commander. I did not know."

"And why should you. I was trained in Hamworthy, in 1940. Major McNeil RM was a hard taskmaster."

The Commando sat back. "Was that Stuart McNeil, by any chance?"

"You know him?"

"He was my instructor for commando training at Achnacarry. I'll not argue with a fellow sufferer." He grinned. "Did he start with the gunbelt?"

Peter grinned back at him. "Live with it, sleep with it, and eat with it." He paraphrased.

"I think in that case we should keep it in the family. I would be happy to be guided by one of us. At least there would be no trouble with the lingo."

Chapter twenty-four

The French

Roger took the briefing over once more. "The main problem is Toulon. Sam, er Major Brown, any comments?"

"Yes, please. Amongst us, Sam is fine. Since we are all working together, can I suggest first names, and drop the 'sir' and 'madam' bit?"

They all agreed and Sam carried on. "The party will be detained in a hotel which is currently in use by the Gestapo. Getting in touch will not be easy. However, the docks are a far simpler proposition. Because of the secrecy involved, the materials and the equipment are packed in standard-appearing cases, crates, and boxes. Peter's suggestion about the submarine is probably right, There has been no sign of a suitable ship coming into Toulon and, as you know, the allied blockade is fairly effective against surface ships. Submarines are another matter. I have been informed that one of the milk-cow submarines, a type X1V, used for resupplying smaller U boats at sea, has been in the Naval Dockyard under cover for the past three weeks. It makes sense that they would use her for the task. She has the range and, though she is not an attack U boat, she carries 1x2cm AA gun and two 3.7cm , and she has a range of 12, 350 nautical miles. She can carry 430 tons of cargo, comfortably."

Sam sat back.

Roger looked around the group., "We can identify the dock at least. If Sam is right, possibly get a bomb in among the goods?"

"That could be difficult." Sam suggested, "Perhaps we could sabotage the dock gates?"

Peter said, "First, we need to find out if the submarine is the carrier. Not because it would not make a good target, merely because we have not got the time to waste getting it wrong. Which means we need to confirm what vessel will be involved? Sam, can your contacts help?"

"I'll give it a try, but I cannot promise anything. Sadly, the people who would have known have been pushed out of their jobs to make places for collaborators. They are more difficult to cultivate. However, I will try and see what I can do."

Roger asked the Major, "How many men can we call upon for this exercise?"

"I have a full company of one hundred and thirty men. But I was thinking a platoon might be a better number, maybe twenty-five men."

Peter asked, "If you need more men we will need two boats—which may well be the best idea anyway. It would mean we could station one boat to cover the docks while the other looks after the Hyeres end of things. What do you all think?"

Ken McLean grinned. I like your thinking. It struck me that we may need to send a group in to Toulon to sort out the cargo on the spot. In which case we would need more people. How many are we due to pick-up?"

Sam said. "Seventeen altogether. I will stay clear in case I am exposed."

Ken looked at her critically. "You can come and join my party if you like."

Sam said, "Ask me in six months. I'll be back in England by then."

Ken smiled. "I'll be in touch."

Roger looked at Peter, who looked at Amy. She said, "We have got as far as thinking about using more people to conduct an attack in Toulon. Two boats, more men, possibly sink the sub, possibly put a bomb on it. The only certain part is the uplift of the people from the airfield. I think that is all, apart from Sam's contribution. Her information so far is fine The rest is conjecture. I think that sums it up." She smiled at Peter.

"I will stay with the group from now on." She said quietly. "It's a security matter, of course. I will keep a record of all the plans and decisions taken to the best of my ability. I should point out that the eyes of Whitehall are on us. This is the first operation of its kind. undertaken, planned and implemented entirely by the actual team performing the task. In addition, I am here to record the entire process from beginning to end."

She sat back, flushing, obviously embarrassed at dominating the room so decisively.

Sam said, "It's Amy, isn't it?"

Amy nodded, wondering.

"Welcome to the team, Amy. Feel free to take part in our discussion on equal terms as a member." She looked around the faces at the table. "I believe I speak for us all. We are all here for the same purpose. So let's get on with it."

***

The western docks in the city of Toulon were entirely dedicated to the Naval base, many now occupied by deactivated French naval craft. The eastern section of the base had been commandeered by the

German Kriegsmarine, the docks occupied by division, E-boats at the finger quays, heavier craft at the inner harbour quays. The submarines used the inner quays, and the X1V milk-cow occupied the covered maintenance dry dock.

To gain access to the docks required identification and a special pass. When Vichy had been in charge the access was very strict also, but there was more than one person involved who was a sympathiser to the Free French cause. It simplified matters, now the entire security staff was German, SS not Kriegsmarine. This had caused resentment among the naval personnel stationed there.

Annette Moreau was enjoying the attention of the Kaptainleutnant who seemed besotted with her. It had been her intention to entrap him, and she had gone out of her way to do it. Now she had accomplished this, she was reaping the benefits. Stretching, she luxuriated in the feel of the silk nightdress on her smooth skin. She sighed and rose from the rather dishevelled bed. Johan was singing in the bath, his voice quite pleasing she thought. She opened his case, the combination being his birthdate, and she set it easily, having done it many times before.

Inside the case was a gun. it was an automatic and lay on the file of papers, black and menacing. With a pencil she slipped the end into the trigger guard and lifted it out. The file beneath was in German beyond her minimal capabilities. The small Minox camera was sufficient for the job and, while the singing went on next door, she took a photo of each of the documents in the file. Then she skinned through the rest of the case. She nearly missed a single sheet near the bottom. The word in red 'Vorsicht' on the top caught her attention, so she photographed that as well. Carefully, she replaced the papers and file, placing the gun exactly where it had been, on the slight impression it had made on the file cover below it. Closing the case, she returned the numbers to their original sequence. Wiping off any suggestion of her intrusion, she went to the bathroom door and tapped on it, saying "Have you been a good boy and washed everywhere, as I told you to?"

There was a mumbled reply from the bathroom. She opened the door and went in. "I can see I am going to check on everything myself. The door closed behind her, shutting off the sound of her giggle.

***

The photos were lying on the table in front of Sam at the safe house in Le Pradet four hours later. The papers from the file were fairly innocuous. She went through them one by one. Putting aside one sheet, she placed the rest inside a file cover, for the attention of the specialist analysts who would examine the papers at length.

The single sheet she was looking at now had a list of items to be delivered to the maintenance dry dock. They included items she had never heard of 'photo-sensitive badges, interim, if a model 247 had not been obtained'.

One sentence, 'What the blazes was a model 247?' She had some idea that the photo-sensitive badges were to do with X rays? That was radiation, wasn't it? That warning notice, what was that all about? She scrabbled through the other papers on the desk. There, the red warning at the top said 'Vorsicht'. She translated the wording of the notice unbelievingly. It was obviously a notice placed to warn people that dangerous materials were in the vicinity. 'Don't touch.' People working near these materials should report sick if they feel any unusual symptoms of illness.

Written in ink across the top of the notice was a handwritten note. 'Dock 18.'

Sam sighed. She sat back. Now they knew!

Collecting all her things together she lifted the telephone. She said, "Merde." It was the signal. She left the room and went down to the street door, and waited, dressed in an old pair of overalls, her other things in a sacking carrier bag.

As the rubbish truck came down the street she emerged from the house, a lighted cigarette in the corner of her mouth, her hair dusty and awry. As it drew abreast of her, she reached out and took one of the hand-holds on the side and stepped onto the foot-plate. Her bag went into the body of the truck. They trundled slowly along the street turning at the end into the Lotissement l'Artaude, the main road, and gained speed in the direction of Hyeres.

***

Amy said, "We now have information which makes it pretty sure that the submarine will be the shipping method, we have been examining ways of getting close enough to stop it without the boats being involved. It seems the only practical way will be underwater, possibly with a timed limpet mine, or two." She smiled. There is a naval team working on the landing beaches who have the gear. I have called on the Commander to get in contact. We can find limpets from the ship's magazine."

Peter said, "The sub is in dry dock! We would need to wait until it was in the water."

Amy asked, "What about the Italian torpedo things, the manned ones? Can they be used? I know we have captured some."

Peter mused aloud, "We would have to worry about the submarine nets at the harbour. They must open them to let the sub through. Would that be a possible way of doing things?"

Ken suggested getting an expert, to see what he had to say on the subject.

Roger interrupted at that point. "OK, folks. That appears to be the best idea at present. Peter, why don't you and Amy go out to dinner, relax for a while. You have both been at it for the past three days. I have called Amy's underwater specialist to come and discuss our problem. He will be with us later. Ken and I can deal with him. Sam should be back by tomorrow morning. We can sort out your part with Ken at that time. Then we will decide the method of dealing with the sub."

***

In the wardroom of *HMS Bramber,* Peter and Amy sat facing each other across the table. The food was eaten unconsciously as they relaxed, alone once more after their brief get-together in Malta just over a month ago.

Peter touched the single blue ring on the sleeve of her uniform. He said "You never did get round to telling me how this came about."

"I am still cannot quite believe how it all came about. It was in Alexandria." Amy said quietly. "Admiral Hardcastle appeared in the office. He wanted someone with cipher experience, preferably an officer. I was the only one there with most of the qualifications. When he discovered I had been a crew member on a racing yacht, he said, 'Just the ticket, perfectly qualified. Acting Third Officer. What is your name?'

"I said, Amy Lucas, sir.

'That is it, Third Officer Amy Lucas. Get properly dressed. The promotion will be promulgated as field promotion on my instruction. Report yourself to the seaplane base at Alexandria by 13:00 hours tomorrow for transfer to battle zone, with your gear. Go straight to the Comms office and check in with them until I arrive; that way you'll be up to date with the local setup.' He turned to his aide. 'Get that order promulgated today. Amy will give you her details.' He then disappeared almost at a run."

Peter grinned, "Just like that. I could not believe it when I saw you in Malta. I am delighted for you, and it does mean that we can meet socially here if we wish to."

"What is your cabin like?" Amy asked. "Mine is, I believe, part of the royal suite in the poshest hotel in Ajaccio. Sam and I have individual bedrooms with a private lounge and our own stewardess to look after us."

"Sounds good. When do I get the grand tour?"

"I thought you would never ask?" Amy giggled. "How about now?"

Chapter twenty-five

The Raiders

Samantha Brown sat and surveyed the others around the table. She had to admit they all looked better for a night off. "Ken. Two boats, two platoons. Yes?"

"Yes. Have you decided about the use of the second platoon? I am not aware of any suggestions so far."

Roger came in at that point. "I have a notion that the Germans regard this matter very seriously. It seems the Fuhrer has taken a personal decision to maintain a thousand year Reich. Even he has seen that it will be unlikely to work in Europe, thus the interest in South America where, for whatever reason, he appears to have allies in more than one of the countries. It is also the reason why we are still not sure of the destination, or if, indeed, there is more than one?"

Peter interjected, "Is this the only shipment?"

Sam answered. "It's the only one we know about!"

There was silence throughout the room at this comment. It was broken by a knock on the door. Amy rose and opened it. Captain Dewar was there with a Lieutenant Commander RNR beside him.

Everyone stood as they came in. "Sit, please. I have only come to introduce Lieutenant Commander Hatcher. He will tell you himself what he can do. I will merely say he is an underwater expert. Good luck." He turned and left the room.

Sam looked at the newcomer who just stood waiting. Then she held her hand out and said "I'm Sam. What do we call you?"

"Spike! It seems I can never live down my nickname. So let's get it over with. Then we can get down to the business of whatever you have planned for me."

Sam took her hand back and waved at the others, calling their names off one by one. Then she waved to a chair and said, "Sit and listen. We are in the middle of something at the moment.

"Right. How do we know if there is another shipment? The simple answer is we don't! That's it. We get on with what we know. If it comes up while we are involved in the present operation, we will deal with it at the time. Agreed?"

She looked around the table. One by one they nodded their agreement.

She turned to Peter. "Your turn to lay out the naval problem for Spike, and update the rest of us at the same time."

Peter thought for a moment then began. "We are agreed that the big submarine in dock 18 in Toulon will be used to transport materials and equipment for the development and production of what appears to be a super bomb. The entire operation has been developed, using, in many cases, Jewish scientists to handle the materials involved. These produce lethal levels of radiation. One of the effects of such a bomb would be the irradiation of a huge area around the actual explosion. This would be lasting and could taint the area for up to hundreds of years."

The others in the group looked at him in surprise. These things had not been in their initial briefing.

Peter explained, "Before the meeting today, the Admiral sent a man to speak to me about this 'atom bomb'. He was quite explicit. I thought we should all know and understand what this was all about." He paused while the others took this all in. Then he said, "The other thing that became apparent was that, if possible, the Germans should not know what we are up to. In other words, they must not know that we are aware of their plans, so all must be under cover.

"We must make it appear that the aircraft is lost over the sea, possibly a mayday message with a location over the Atlantic, a bit of frantic reporting of engines failing one by one, and sudden cut off in the middle of a word. It leaves them faced with the mysterious loss of the aircraft over water and a submarine which did not make it through dangerous waters. We lift the personnel and the aircraft disappears on the one hand. The submarine is fitted with a timed limpet, and it disappears. All we have to do, is work out how we do it. Spike, we thought an underwater approach to the sub might answer one question. What do you think?"

Spike thought about it. "Toulon is a naval port and dock 18 is within the base, I presume?"

"It is," Peter acknowledged.

"There will be anti-intruder nets in place all around the docks."

Peter said, "Dock 18 is an undercover dry dock."

"It gets worse. That will be especially protected after the Dieppe raids. We would need to get inside the submarine nets, at least."

Peter said, "An Italian MAS boat left Greek waters last week for an operation on the Italian coast. Its orders have been altered and it will be in Ajaccio by lunchtime. It has a German-speaking skipper driving it. Will that help? We need it for the lift operations anyway."

Spike was thoughtful for a few moments. Roger went to speak and Spike held his hand up to stop him. "My partner and I will need to be at the lock gates, ready when the sub leaves the dock. If we are in place, we have an underwater tug to save energy, and match speed with the sub while the limpets are fitted. Then we need a way out. That is where the MAS boat would be of use. If the gate is open and the sub is in the water we have a different scenario. We may be able to mine her in situ, if you get my meaning. That would be the ideal situation."

"What about the mines?" Ken asked.

"There are plenty in store on this ship. It is a sub-mother as well as for the MLs. The underwater tug is here too. It's under test at the moment."

"So, the snatch is the other subject to iron out." Roger sounded relieved.

"That's probably the most difficult to arrange." Amy said diffidently.

They all looked at her. "Taking into account what we have been told about the secrecy of the entire operation, we have to get hold of the aircraft and either fly it out of there with all the correct signals and protocols, then conceal it on some out of the way airfield, or blow it up over the sea, out of the sight of prying eyes." She sat back and let them think about it.

Peter said, "Is there any way we can find out in advance the signal set-up for the aircraft?"

Sam said, "We are lucky we even know it's a Condor."

Ken said, "We have SS uniforms and one of my people is a German Jew. He will love shouting orders at us."

Peter said, "I Have a Gestapo uniform, rescued from Agios Pathos."

"That's a start," Ken said. "Now, do we just march through the town to the airfield or what?"

Sam said, "We do have a Wehrmacht truck. It will have to do."

Ken put in. "My second platoon will not be needed in the main event hopefully, so they will land and create a diversion raid on the dockyard at La Seyne sur Mer. It is at the far side of the harbour. They will time it in advance. The raid will give Spike cover for his excursion to Dock 18.

"Peter and the other platoon, all dressed up, will collect the truck and drive to the airfield. We will take over the aircraft, and crew, and welcome the passengers aboard. We will also take care of any security they send. I will need gas masks for all my men travelling with the aircraft, including the pilot. One of my group must be a pilot. All we'll need then will be an escort and a secure destination. Peter and the rest of the men will use the truck to return to the boat."

Peter took up the story "Both boats will rendezvous somewhere off the harbour mouth if possible, and shoot our torpedoes at any visible ship. Then we depart at high speed, under cover of darkness for Corsica.

Ken then continued, "We will report an emergency while we are apparently over the ocean, on fire or something. Landing possibly in England?"

Amy said, "Both boats to report back here for re-assignment, damage assessment, as well as care for the wounded, if any.

"The team will be dispersed if there is no other activity scheduled. I will be here to co-ordinate communications."

Spike offered his contribution. "My sea sled will be loaded. I will include several limpets as there will be targets of opportunity there. All other limpets will be timed subsequent to that of the submarine. I need to have the re-assurance that the sub is in the water before we set out on this caper. This whole part of the exercise will be pointless if the sub is still high and dry.

Roger looked around the table. Ladies and gentlemen, tomorrow is the start-point. 19:00 hours at Toulon and Hyeres."

Sam said wryly, "I will travel with the Hyeres party. I have things to do in France for a week or so."

As the party left the room, Ken lingered to speak with Sam, before leaving to give his men their final briefing.

***

The atmosphere was tense as the two boats set out. There was no specific air cover although aircraft were about for the daylight hours in that part of the Mediterranean. It did mean there was no real interference in the passage from the mothership to Toulon. They arrived after dark on schedule. Parting company at 19:00 as specified, Ken and Peter to Hyeres in the ML, and Spike and PO Dai Davies, plus the diversion raiders under the command of Lieutenant Pat Nevins in the MAS boat commanded by Lieutenant Max Kramer RNVR along with the German-speaking officer promised by Peter.

As they coasted alongside at the quay at Hyeres, the platoon disembarked and formed up on the concrete quay, Oberleutenant Braun strutted in front of the men and proceeded to point out that they were a disgrace to the German nation, but he would make do with then nonetheless. The truck trundled down the quay and stopped, the driver dropping the tailgate to allow Ken and the assembled men to clamber aboard.

Peter and Braun sat in the cab with the driver. The Ml quietly drew away offshore and hooked to one of the mooring buoys, offshore.

A swastika ensign flapped from the rigging.

They drove in the truck through the township to the airfield, a matter of a few minutes only since the airfield was in close proximity to the quay.

The aircraft was standing on the apron in front of the hanger. It dwarfed the two Me 109f's standing beyond it with men working on them.

The truck entered the field without questions. The pass used by the driver was standard and genuine. Nobody questioned the troops in the rear of the truck, so they were able to proceed without interference onto the field itself.

There was a collective sigh of relief as the truck turned toward the big aircraft standing with the air stairs in position, waiting for the passengers.

They came to a halt beside the hanger. The troops debussed and formed up in ranks under the eagle eye of Oberleutenant Braun.

He snapped an order and the men doubled to take post around the big aircraft. Braun strolled over to the plane and climbed the stairs and entered the aircraft. In the fore cabin the stewardess was preparing a meal. In the cockpit the pilots were arranging their gear for a long flight. The passengers were due within the hour, only fourteen, plus four guards.

***

Klaus Wendt, the chief pilot, smiled. His aircraft had been fitted with airline seats for this trip so they must be important. He wondered who they were. His flight-plan was to Quito, Ecuador. But he had been warned that the destination could be changed. Michael Hasselhof, his co-pilot, was fussily checking his safety gear.

Klaus did not like his co-pilot. He had a habit of referring to the Fuhrer as if he were a personal friend. He suspected he was the one who had had their co-pilot arrested for questioning the intelligence of their Reichsmarshall, who had ordered men into the air with unserviceable machines and short of ammunition. He had been transferred to fly on the eastern front.

Klaus thought the man had been an idiot to talk in front of the obviously untrustworthy co-pilot. He shrugged mentally. Nobody was going to survive this war, not on the German side anyway. Now that the Americans had joined in, it would soon be all over. The Russians were already destroying all in their path from the east. He had never really thought about being an orphan, but seeing others with families in the path of the Russian army, and meeting people who had lost family members, he was glad to have no parents to worry about.

There was a bustle of activity in the rear of the aircraft. Klaus opened the door and stepped through to see what was happening. An SS officer was discussing the arrangements with the cabin crew.

Hanna Fromm stepped back into the crew quarters nearly tripping over Klaus's foot. He caught her before she could overbalance. "Steady, girl. What's the panic?"

"We have four more soldiers and an officer added to the flight, so I will have twenty-one to cope with, instead of fifteen."

"We knew this would be 'one of those flights'. Any news of the other passengers?"

"They are crossing the field at the moment. They do not look happy."

Klaus peered through the window. "I'm not surprised. Their escort look more like prison warders than security men."

Hanna put her hand to her mouth. She gasped, "You should not say things like that. Look what happened to Eric."

Eric had been the co-pilot sent to the Russian front.

The party arrived and Hanna became busy seating the fifteen passengers. The security men were intercepted by the SS officer, who suggested their place was beside the door. One of the men raised his voice asking why the SS were here. Why was he not told?

Whatever the SS officer said, the man shut up in a hurry and sat without further comment.

What Braun had said to the guard was simple. "My orders were personally issued by the Fuhrer himself. Feel free to question them. They need recruits for the Russian front."

Braun went to the door and looked out across the airfield. All was clear, so far! He called to the stewardess, "The door, Miss. We are all here."

Hanna came down the aisle and stood in front of the SS officer. "Sit down, sir! On this aircraft the pilot is the Captain and he gives the orders. Be seated and fasten your seatbelt!"

The two people stared at each other neither wishing to give way. Then Braun shrugged and gave a wry grin. "As you say, Miss. I am merely a passenger." He seated himself and fastened his belt.

Hanna swung the door closed, locked it, took the phone from the bulkhead and called the captain. "All passengers accounted for. Door closed and locked. Clear for your orders, sir."

Hasselhof answered, "Acknowledged, Frauline Fromm. Take your seat for take-off."

The port outer radial engine spluttered, then started, the propeller speeding up. As the other engines started in turn until all were running smoothly. Klaus waved the chocks away. The big aircraft rolled forward to begin its epic flight, the extra fuel tanks locked into the bomb racks under the wings ready to be jettisoned, when their fuel had been expended. They would add six hundred miles to their range. Klaus lined up the aircraft for take-off, and ran through the check list with his co-pilot.

As he opened the throttles for take-off, he heard Michael calling off the code words to the control tower, and receiving the release code for the flight.

They climbed in a gradual turn, gaining height before setting out across the sea, climbing all the time, to reach their maximum height of nineteen thousand feet needed while they over-flew the danger zone of enemy-occupied territory. Once over the Atlantic they would reduce height to normal cruising altitude, between fourteen and fifteen thousand feet.

Chapter twenty-six

Night moves

Max Kramer steered the MAS boat through the jaws of the huge harbour of Toulon. The naval base spread in all directions ahead, but his way was to port, the western end of the harbour.

La Seyne-sur-Mer was an area behind another set of quays, mostly in use for E boats and captured MAS boats, like the one commanded by Kramer. The same ensign flew from the rigging and the men on board were all in the same uniforms, though they spoke a different language. They had entered the harbour in the wake of a cargo ship. The flag and uniforms of the crew seemed good enough for the tug boat operating the nets. Within the harbour, he dropped off the dinghy with Commander Hatcher and his Welsh companion. The loaded rubber boat paddled off and was lost in the darkness in seconds. The MAS boat made a turn to port and motored serenely along to the target for their diversion.

There was no alarm raised as the boat lay alongside an unused quay. His passengers slipped ashore and melted into the darkness. Two of the crew presented themselves in uniform with weapons and regulation gear for guard duties.

Both were from Jewish families lost in Cologne during 'Kristallnacht'. They had been part of a Jewish unit working with Special Operations in North Africa. They and their fellow crew members risked their lives wearing the uniforms of the enemy, knowing that, if they were captured, they would suffer death, merely for being Jewish. They had been operating successfully for the past two years, though this was the first time on European soil.

The two men stepped onto the quay and took up guard positions next to the short gangway now in place.

Two tense hours later, Pat Nevins's second in command appeared with the message that his boss would back in five minutes.

Max ordered the boats cables singled up and withdrew the sentries. The engines started with little fuss. The boat waited, poised to move off as soon as Lieutenant Nevins appeared with his remaining men. The returning platoon appeared and boarded silently. Assured all were present, the MAS boat left as unobtrusively as it had arrived.

The explosions began with a roar as four E-boats burst into flame, shortly accompanied by ammunition firing off in the heat. As they motored quietly out of the complex of docks and quays into the main harbour area, they were able to see the extent of the diversion they had created. The skyline behind them was lit up with fires and there were still odd explosions occurring.

***

The dinghy with Spike and Dai Davis made progress toward the dry dock. It had taken an hour to reach a point where Spike decided to hide their boat, while they began placing mines on the other ships and submarines in the base area. The first explosions echoed across the harbour as the commandos started their diversion

Spike's first mission was to see that the milk-cow was in the water. Having loaded the sea-sled with limpet mines, the two men checked their breathing apparatus and set out.

As expected, they encountered the anti-submarine net across the entrance to the docks. This was less trouble than it might have been, as no attempt had been made to make it difficult for free swimmers to get past. They stopped the sled motor. Dai clambered over one of the floats supporting the net. Spike heaved the bow of the sled onto the float and Dai hauled it, using his weight to tip it into the water on his side of the net. The two bags of mines, each with neutral floatation, were passed over the float one at a time, finally followed by Spike. They entered the zone which they expected would be patrolled.

They dropped the sled beside the entrance to the dry dock. It was plain to see that the dock had been flooded and the big submarine was afloat.

With the sluice gate open, Spike took the opportunity and selected two limpets set for eighteen hours. He attached a small tell-tale beacon, to show up on sonar when a HF signal was sent. *Fail safe!* He was told. In case the mines don't work or were discovered. Dai took one and Spike the other and each took a side to place their charge. Spike located a point above the screw and attached the beacon firmly.

They moved off seeking other ships. Under a submarine they found alongside dock seventeen, there were still signs of damage, possibly a depth charge. The killer U boat had been repaired and readied for sea. Dai put a 24 hour limpet on the hull, under the pleat where the shafts for the screws were fitted.

On their way across the basin Dai encountered an enemy frogman. At first neither realised they were facing an enemy. Spike, who was swimming at an angle to Dai, saw the other man and recognised that he was wearing what looked like an adapted, escape re-breather. Dai, like Spike, was wearing a tank. Spike came up behind the man, who had drawn his knife and was swimming at Dai knife raised. Dai was back-pedalling as fast as he could go, while trying to release his knife, which seemed to have been caught under one of the straps on his mine sack harness.

Spike, still unseen by the enemy, swam up behind the man and wrenched the breather from his face.

Taken by surprise, the man reacted. He had been caught between breaths so sucked in a great gulp of sea water instead of air. He struggled, reaching blindly for the absent face mask. But the damage had been done. His struggles were of a dying man. Spike removed the set .from the man's belt, the other part of the re-breather, and stuffed it in his mine carrier bag, in place of one of the expended mines. He waved Dai on.

They reached the ship on the other side of the basin to find it had a moon pool. In the pool was a floating platform with diving gear on it. The chamber around it was empty of people. Spike gestured Dai to grab the side of the platform to haul it down between them, dumping the gear into the sea.

Between them they managed it with great difficulty. As the gear floated to the bottom, Spike grabbed two more of the re-breathers. They went into the bags for examination later. They set a mine under the rudder of the ship, then left her to find four more victims for their remaining limpets.

Elsewhere in the basin, they found places for their other mines. Then, satisfied they had created as much mayhem as possible, they followed their sea-sled out to the small tug which opened the net for craft entering and leaving the harbour. It had hauled the net open to release an armed trawler, obviously a patrol boat. They were able to pass through the open gate in the wake of the trawler. They had not seen the boat supposedly patrolling the basin. Spike heaved a sigh of relief as they began the trek across the open waters to Cap Garonne.

They eventually reached the rendezvous at the Royal Tower.

***

Max collected the exhausted swimmers and met up with Peter in the ML. Together they made for their destination in the approaching daylight.

The bay in the small uninhabited island of Grande Ribaud was ideal. Both had camouflage nets and spread them as they lay close to the beach on the island. The explosions throughout the western dock area of Toulon ceased, the activity cleaning up went on all day. Boats and ships moved about the area, while in the bay the two crews relaxed and rested, awaiting the onset of the other set of explosions due that night.

***

Klaus Wendt was wearing his oxygen mask. to test it in case the pressurisation failed. His co-pilot was resting in the bunk at the back of the cockpit. The door of the cockpit opened and Braun, the SS man, appeared. He was carrying a gun. He saw the mask and spoke. "Good. It will save time. You may remove the mask." It was an order not a request. Klaus took the mask off. "What are you doing?" He asked, quite reasonably he thought.

Braun smiled, and said in English, "Actually, I am hijacking this aircraft." He stood to one side and one of the other SS men came into the cockpit. "This is Stephen. He is also a pilot; Lancaster's, I believe. He can take over if needed, but I am hoping you will carry on with just a small alteration in course to Gibraltar and then turn northward to Britain."

Klaus looked at him in astonishment. "Really. You want me to fly to Britain?"

Braun nodded. "Exactly. Britain. I will obtain an escort for the last part of the journey."

***

Braun left the cockpit to Stephen and Klaus. Two of the SS men carried Michael through to the main cabin where he was gagged and handcuffed alongside the two security men.

In the cockpit, having turned the Condor on to the course dictated by Stephen, Klaus said, "You have obviously done your homework?"

Stephen Crane, who spoke German, answered in that language. "Of course, we would not undertake an operation like this without researching ways and means, and also without knowing who we were hijacking."

"You can speak in English. It is good for me. I do not get enough practice these days." Klaus had relaxed. For some reason he was feeling better about his chances, flying to England rather than South America.

Stephen smiled grimly. "Had you worked out that this would be a one-way trip, for you and all the crew, apart from your co-pilot, that is?"

"Not actually, though I was not feeling too happy about the set-up. My normal co-pilot, suddenly sent to the Russian front, and all the secret goings-on was rather worrying."

"This was mostly guesswork, until we took over the aircraft, finally. We went to attach a gas bottle to the air re-circulation system. There was a bottle of gas already attached, only it was not sleeping gas. We removed the bottle which I understand is carbon monoxide. We also discovered that someone had fitted cut-outs for the different parts of the aircraft. Since on this aircraft, the passengers are separated by a door from the kitchen, and the kitchen from the cockpit similarly. It was not difficult to work out the scenario."

Klaus paled. "You would have used the sleeping gas, knowing I would be on oxygen for the climb?"

Stephen shrugged. "We are professionals. It's what we do!"

He allowed Klaus to digest this latest information. Then. "Tell me. How does it feel? I have read all about this aircraft, but I've never flown one?"

Klaus grinned and lifted his hands from the controls. "Feel for yourself. She is a real lady. I would like to try your Lancaster." He shrugged. "But that is unlikely, I think?"

***

Peter and Max, having laid up during the daylight hours, discussed their next move. The activity at the docks in Toulon had been obvious and concentrated on the La Seyne area where Pat Nevins's commandos had really made an impact.

A signal had been sent to *HMS Bramber* that the initial mission had been accomplished. The beacon on the milk-cow submarine had been heard in the open waters of the Mediterranean by a frigate stationed between Toulon and Gibraltar. It was moving toward the strait. No attempt had been made to intercept.

As dusk fell, both boats removed the nets and moved out. Their decision had been made. They had decided to expend their torpedoes into the harbour, preferably at actual targets. As a result, they split up, Peter taking the main eastern end, and Max the west. The limpets were timed for explosions during the period 18:00-19:00 hours. Since they expected to be in the harbour at 18:40, the show should already have started.

The first of the explosions was at 18:20, the second 18:34. Then in succession the other mines started to go off. Both Peter and Max were in position outside the submarine nets to the harbour, when the gates opened to allow a freighter to leave under cover of darkness. Peter's torpedo hit the ship as it approached the open net, catching it in the bow section. The explosion blew off the fore end of the 10,000 ton ship which was under power. Its engines drove the ship under the waves, the tug operating the net did not stand a chance. The open maw of the stricken ship engulfed the tug boat, and took it under in its journey to the bottom. The two boats entered through the now open gap, and split up to use their remaining weapons on the already suffering shipping.

***

In the main cabin Hanna and the passengers were being addressed by Braun. "You were all on the way to South America, though I presume you have family still in Germany?"

In fact most had not! Two people had relatives, but none had close family there. Hanna had lost her parents months ago in an air raid.

Braun held his hands up to stop them talking. When they were silent he spoke slowly and clearly.

"First, I have to tell you, you will not be going to South America. We have diverted the aircraft to Britain. We are staging a scenario to make the German Government believe the aircraft crashed into the sea, and was lost with all hands. It means that you cannot contact friends in Germany until the war ends. On the plus side, it also means that the pilot and your flight attendant will survive after all.

"It is clear they were scheduled to die on this flight. The rest of you I can also say will be able to live pretty normal lives, rather than the lives you would face in South America. Judging by the fate of the people you worked alongside in Germany, your lives would be to stay in an enclosure until your work was completed, followed, I fear, by a sticky end. The work you are involved in is secret. They have already been quite ruthless in tidying up loose ends about your work. The staff who remained in your work-places when you left were taken to death camps. Disposed of I'm sad to say."

He once more lifted his hand for attention.

"The guards sent with you and the co-pilot of the aircraft have all been secured and should give no trouble to you. They will also be interned in England, though in a secure prison, as they must not give away the fact that you have all survived. Finally, I believe that you will be given the chance to continue your work if you wish. I am equally sure that you will not be forced to continue if you do not.

"Hanna, I think our guests could do with some drinks and perhaps food?"

Hanna rose to her feet. "Of course, sir. and the pilot too. I think." She went into her kitchen and started to sort out coffee and snacks.

They leveled off at 14,000 feet, and flew along the new course. Five hours later an emergency call announced that the aircraft was suffered an engine failure and was losing height over the sea out of sight of land. The pilot sounded panicked.

Chapter twenty-seven

…Invasion…Part One

Peter and Max made their way back to Corsica and *HMS Bramber*. They were met by Roger and Amy. Roger greeted them with a "Well done, both of you. The reports are still coming in. The docks are in turmoil. Nobody seems to know if it was a torpedo attack, or what? The Admiral is on his way here, so you have time for a wash and shave before he arrives. We'll debrief when he gets here."

The Admiral appeared one hour later, in time for the meeting of the principles from the Toulon raid.

He stood and smiled at the group. "I am happy to report that the Condor arrived safely in Prestwick, with the passengers and crew unhurt. The submarine beacon stopped transmitting off the North African coast, in the vicinity of island of Madeira. It is presumed lost, though a watch will be maintained for word in South America, specifically Ecuador." He paused. "Congratulations on an operation well conducted. There are decorations due to Lieutenant Commander Hatcher. DSM, RNR, PO David Davies RN. Also Lieutenant Commander Peter Woods DSC RNVR, and Lieutenant Max Kramer. RNVR, Lieutenant Patrick Nevins RM. Sergeant Walter Braun, RM. There will be other awards awaiting your recommendations." He paused then he removed his hat and sat down. "One thing I will stress." He spoke quietly and intensely. "I cannot stress how important this operation was. If they had got away with this technology, we could have been faced possibly with a generation who would never exist. The power that sort of bomb would have created could have caused anarchy throughout the world, whatever Governments might have to say. The secret between us must be kept. You are aware of the German solution to that problem. Our solution is to ask each and every one of you to forget whatever you have learned about the reason for this operation. Remember it as the Toulon raid, a successful combined operation."

He looked at each in turn. They nodded one by one as they met his eye. "Right. The party tonight is on me. I will leave you to your final de-brief and meet you in the ward room at 18:00 for drinks." He rose to his feet as did the entire group. He replaced his hat and saluted them before leaving the room.

In the silence that followed, Spike's voice was suddenly heard. "Well, I'll be damned. That's the first time I met an admiral who saluted me."

The room exploded with laughter as the tension of the past twenty minutes evaporated. General chatter began around the table once more.

Roger called them to order, for the serious business of the de-brief.

After sandwiches, tea and coffee, the group dispersed, de-briefing over at 16:00.

**

Peter and Amy met in her suite before the 18:00 appointment in the Wardroom. They kissed. When they broke off, Peter spoke. "I want to get married before we go any further."

Amy stood back at arm's length and looked at him. "Do you really think we should? As it is, if we marry I have to resign. At present I actually feel I am doing something positive at last."

Peter's instinct was to blurt out that he needed her, wanted her beside him. But he suddenly realised that Amy had a career, however short, which she felt mattered. Instead of saying what had been on the tip of his tongue, he took her in his arms and said. "I was dreaming. Of course we cannot marry yet. I just let my wishful thinking get in the way of my common sense. I will not ask you to forget what I said, because you know how I feel. But please understand, I am not putting pressure on you. We are both committed to getting this war over as soon as possible. Let's go and drink the Admiral's gin and boast about our past achievements.

Amy looked searchingly at him. She understood he meant what he said. She kissed him again and took his arm. "Back to the grindstone MacDuff!" She misquoted, causing both to burst into laughter and dissipating any tension that might have remained.

***

London was busy as always. The hurrying people in the Whitehall area carried umbrellas and walked determinedly, each inside their personal zone of silence. Occasionally a burst of laughter would be heard but, generally, the murmur of the odd conversation was the best anyone seemed able to do. Peter, like everyone else, walked sheltered beneath his umbrella, ducking and diving through the hurrying crowd until he reached the sandbagged entrance to the Admiralty. He retracted his brolly as he went through the door. The security man there said, "Shall I take that, Commander?"

"Thank you, Philbin. That is most kind." He passed the dripping umbrella to the Petty Officer and was already slipping out of his raincoat as he crossed the floor to the desk. With his coat over his arm, he produced his ID card and waited while it was checked. Despite attending the building daily for the past six months, they still went through the same routine every morning.

"You are clear to go up, Commander," the desk man said, "Mr. Raines is in room 61 today."

"Thank you, Parker. At least I will have a place to start today." As he went up in the old elevator, he thought his joke about having a place to start was not really a joke. Mark Raines was a difficult man to locate on occasion. His position as coordinator of resources was misleading and, in Peter's mind, deliberately so.

The collection of resources for a full scale European landing was not something to trust to many. As far as Peter was concerned, it could not be in better hands. Apart, that is, from his habit of jumping up from his seat and dashing off to another department or section without mentioning where he was going. This was downright murder on his aides. Peter had decided it was a side effect of his brilliance, manifesting itself in complete unreliability on the odd occasion. It was a case of grin and bear it; the positives outweighing the negatives in a big way.

Room 61 still contained the man he was looking for. The system worked. It was something that Peter had eventually laid on, with the full agreement of all personnel involved. Whenever Raines left the office, a call was made to the desk. At every port of call the desk was advised. Then, if anything happened, there was a record of the whereabouts of Raines, so that contact could be made.

In room 61 the charts of the invasion convoy progress were kept. Up to now they had never been required to record anything, but the finger was poised over the button, according to Paul Raines.

Peter was here essentially to say goodbye. There was a car laid on to take him to Portsmouth and his new command a Fairmile F, bigger, more powerful and heavier armed than his former command. The boat was equipped as a gunboat, and he was in command of a flotilla of Fairmile D gunboats and MLs. The D models had sculpted bows for their use as MTB's if required. The past six months had been a complete break from the tensions and pressures of command which had extended for the previous three years. The involvement in the planning for the invasion of Europe had been absorbing and the time had fled by. He had been able to get together with Amy, on several occasions both in Portsmouth, where she was now stationed, and in London.

As the car travelled south through the Hampshire countryside he thought about Raines and the last words he had to say before he left. "Watch out for new weapons. If you suspect changes to existing ones, let me know. Each would be another time marker in the progress of the war."

He pondered the words. Raines seldom said anything without some reason. It was just a question of identifying what was in his mind at the time. He gave up as the car turned into the docks. He produced his identity card and was dropped off at the Base HQ for Coastal Forces.

He stood and looked out over the basin where his command was moored alongside pontoons. He breathed the salt air and felt he was coming home.

The new boat felt like a greyhound after his old No3. At thirty-six knots she seemed incredibly fast.

Of course, he had to admit that the past six months away from all fast boats did made a difference.

The meeting in the office had gone well. Commander Henry Jackson DSC RN in command, was a re-tread, brought back into the service after a precipitate dismissal in the cuts pre-war. His attitude reflected that he was well aware of the contribution the Wavy Navy (RNVR) had made to the war effort in general and the coastal forces in particular.

He greeted Peter cheerfully. "Back to your beginnings. I believe, this was your first posting?"

"It was, and I'm happy to be back here."

"Well, as I am sure you know, there will be an invasion soon. Currently. There is no way of knowing where it will be unless you happen to be a member of the War Cabinet. I understand the information is restricted even there. We have been given the job of confusing things even more. The flotillas here are keeping the convoys running through the Channel, in both directions. We get regular visits from E-boats in Calais and Boulogne, and sometimes from ports further south. They are annoying, but as long as we keep their attention, the build-up of the invasion fleet can take place, with minimum interference.

"We also have considered raiding their bases. Think about that. I would be interested in any suggestions you might have to upset the opposition, without too much expenditure on our side, if you take my meaning." He sat back obviously inviting response.

Peter, having taken in all that had been said, took a deep breath and spoke, "I have the impression from what has not been said, that the invasion is likely to be to the southern rather than the northern end of the Channel. Which means we should concentrate on the Pas de Calais area, to encourage them to believe that is where the invasion will take place?"

Henry Jackson sat back offering nothing, so Peter continued. "I can see that a raid on the defences of Calais would give the impression we were considering an assault in that region. This would save the Germans from concentrating their forces in the wrong place, for us.

"From my own experience, I consider that a platoon of Commandos could cause a lot of damage to equipment and morale, plus the odd torpedo in the crowded harbour just to stir the pot. What sort of intelligence have we on the set up in Calais and or Boulogne?"

The Commander took a file from his desk drawer. "This might be of assistance. By the way, my comment about planning attacks was not intended for you to carry out tomorrow. let's think. Tomorrow is Wednesday, how about Friday? Perhaps an evening call might work well; after all they have week-ends, just like we do?"

***

The Second in command of the flotilla was Lieutenant Commander Basil Hawthorne RNVR. He had been through MTBs and MGBs and was now driving an MGB, a Fairmile D, carrying several extra weapons once fitted for AA duties, but now happily adaptable for horizontal targets as well.

Peter's ML had an extra in the form of a six-pounder gun aft, in addition to the twin twenty millimetres amidships, and the two-pounder gun on the foredeck, machine guns on each bridge wing, and depth charges at the stern. The MGB set up made her more effective in the role she had been given. The

flotilla had three MTBs and two hybrid, torpedo fitted, MTBs

Finally, the minelayer sitting on its own at the
far side of the mooring. Skippered by an ex-trawler-
man from Stonehaven, he ran his ship in his own in-
imitable style. MacRae had a first name, though it
was never mentioned in public. His crew had followed him from an armed minesweeper to MLs. He
found the switch from poacher to gamekeeper perfectly acceptable and, while by no means careless,
his casual attitude to the rows of mines that sat along
their rails when he went onto action frightened the
rest of the flotilla to death.

Peter was pleased to find that Lieutenant Jerry
Lawrence had found his way to the flotilla, commanding the other MGB. His own number one was
newly promoted Lieutenant Colin Willis, RNVR who
had served with him in the Mediterranean.

Amy was now stationed in the Admiral's office
in Portsmouth. Her position was as his Aide, where
she performed as his PA, keeping his diary and
scheduling his visits and appointments. She had her
own apartment off base in Portsmouth. Peter was in
contact with her and had telephoned as soon as he
had arrived back in Britain. Clearing up after the
Toulon raid had taken time. His new posting had
come through while he was back at sea operating in
the Adriatic Sea.

His return had included a week's leave, taken
at Chichester where his boat was out of the water, but
still hooked up to the facilities. Amy had managed to
wangle a long weekend which meant they could relax
and visit the pub where they had always stopped
when they first met. The landlord looked a little older
but was just as friendly, and delighted to see them
again. He spotted the ring on Amy's finger. "Thought

you might be doing something like that," he said with a smile. He insisted on toasting them both from a private bottle of brandy, brought quietly from the back room.

***

Peter's parents had never been mentioned and, when Amy had brought the matter up previously, something else had occurred and she never did get an answer from Peter about them.

She asked as they lay together on the night before she returned to Portsmouth. "Will you be seeing your parents this week?"

Peter was silent for a moment. Finally, he said, "I meant to mention it before. My parents are dead. They were on their way home from America at the beginning of the war. They arrived in Southampton when the first air raid on the place occurred. They were caught like others, wondering what the wailing sirens meant."

"You have never mentioned other family, no brothers, sisters?"

"Not a single one, I'm afraid. You will have to provide all the relations in this family."

"Where did they live? Your parents, I mean." Amy asked.

"In Berkshire, near Reading. Midgham is a village alongside the Kennet and Avon Canal."

"What happened to their home?"

"It's rented out, one of the 17th century cottages which has been extended somewhat. I will have to do something about it one day. I have not really thought much about them, I'm afraid, though I am driving their car at the moment. It sounds terrible, I know, now I think about it, but I knew little of my parents really. I was sent to boarding school as a boy, while they travelled. When holidays came around I saw them sometimes. Sometimes they were too far away for me to catch up with them. Sounds odd, but they seriously intended seeing the world and they could afford to do it too. As I grew older I shared a little more of their travels. But it was never the way it is with your family. I never actually felt close to them. Don't get me wrong. I'm sure they loved me and I was always cared for. But it always felt at arm's-length. I never ran short of money. In fact they were well off by any terms. In turn, so am I since I am their only heir. So there it is. You have landed a rich fish."

"You mean you fell hook, line, and sinker." Amy giggled.

Peter laughed, "Hooked anyway, and I'm quite happy about it.

I have an appointment with the lawyers in Reading on Tuesday. I will then know exactly where I stand. I'll call and let you know on Tuesday evening at the flat. In fact if you are about we can have dinner somewhere and I will tell all. How about that?"

"I can promise nothing. But if I'm available, you are booked."

Amy leaned across and kissed him. "Good-night, love. I'm working in the morning."

***

Peter dropped Amy off at the gate in time for her duty. He then drove off to Bournemouth, to see if he could see someone at the RM base at Hamworthy. He presented himself at the gate and asked if the Royal Marine commandant could spare him a few minutes. To his surprise, Ken McLean appeared to escort him into a familiar office.

"Well, we always like to see old boys here. Are you coming to sign on for a refresher course?"

"Nice to see you too, Ken. In fact, much though I would enjoy a refresher session, I came to have a chat about a repeat performance of the Toulon raid, only in a channel port this time."

"Is this an official request or just a fishing expedition?"

Peter could not help smiling, as he thought of his conversation with Amy last night. "A fishing expedition, I suppose."

"All right. What did you have in mind? A one platoon job, or something a little more elaborate?"

"I was actually thinking of Pat Nevins's, La Seyne-du-Mer sort of job. Lots of bangs, some damage, and minimum casualties.

"Had you anywhere specific in mind? Also, is this an attention grabber, or is there a specific target? I need to know."

"I think an attention grabber, and I wondered about Calais or Boulogne?"

"Right. I'll need a little time to think about this. When your name was announced, the boss wanted a word." He picked up the telephone and said, "Come in, Sgt Major."

The familiar figure of Sergeant Edwards, now Sergeant Major Edwards, appeared through the door.

Peter stood up and held out his hand, "Good to see you, Sergeant Major."

Edwards took his hand and shook it, testing Peter's grip, then released it. "Good to see you looking so well, Captain Cotton. Sir, if you would like to come this way?"

He led Peter to the office marked Commandant, and stood back. "Please go in. You are expected."

Peter knocked and entered.

The man seated at the desk turned, looked at Peter and smiled.

Peter stared, then, "Colonel McNeil! What a pleasant surprise."

The Colonel waved at the chair opposite his desk. "Please sit and tell me all."

As Peter began to sit, the Colonel reached into the drawer in front of him. Without thinking, Peter reached behind and drew the automatic from his waist band. It was lined-up before the Colonel had his own gun out of the drawer.

McNeil looked surprised. "You learned your lessons well, Peter."

"I had good teachers," Peter said with a smile.

"While Ken takes a look at your little problem, we can have a chat. Then Sgt Major wants to see you on the range. Now, what happened to our best driver, Amy Lucas. She suddenly began to agitate for promotion, and left us in a cloud of dust to be a Petty Officer. I now hear she is a Third Officer no less and the Admiral's PA. Did you have anything to do with that?"

"If you are saying, did I know about it, the answer is not until she was a PO. I met her in Alexandria. We became engaged there. But the next promotion was out of the blue. In Malta Admiral Hardcastle needed a cipher-trained officer as his PA. Amy was the only Wren there with cipher training. She was promoted on the spot and that was that. I learned about it in Ajaccio."

"Did you say you were engaged to Amy? I thought she was engaged to the yachtsman who was in the Air Force?"

"She was, but he sent her a 'Dear Amy' letter and married a WAAF Officer. Amy and I got to know each other driving back and forth. I had actually met her in 1938 at the yacht races at Cowes."

McNeil shook his head. "I think maybe some men are born lucky. Look, give me a ring next time and we can have a work out together. I have things to do, so I will put you in the capable hands of Sgt Major Edwards for now. McLean will call you when he is ready. I'll see you in the mess for lunch anyway." He rose to his feet and held his hand out. "I'm pleased you did not forget us."

In the pistol range, Edwards checked over Peter's automatic, and they shot six targets together, then Edwards produced a Frontier Colt .45, "Try this for size!" He said with a grin.

Peter lifted the big handgun feeling the balance. It sat in his hand easily, so he raised it and fired with the same smooth action as he used with the automatic, only between each shot he had to pull the hammer back to cock the gun. It made no difference, the six holes in the target were within a two inch group.

Edwards was impressed. "You've been practicing!"

Peter shook his head. "This is the first time I have used a gun since I was in Crete last year, and I only used it in action, I'm afraid."

Edwards inclined his head. "I guess the boss will want to see you about now, shall we go?"

In the office Ken had worked up a scheme. Using a blackboard he illustrated his suggestions with diagrams and map directions.

When he finished, Peter said, "What you are saying is, it can be done?"

Ken nodded. "Specifically, with a platoon of twenty-eight men plus leader. That would be me in this case." He grinned. "When do we start?"

"Hold your horses. One thing at a time. I will now take the suggestion to my masters, and we may be able to get the show on the road." Peter stood. "Thanks, Ken. I'll be in touch."

The two men shook hands. "As an alumnus of our academy here, you are always welcome to come and see us."

Peter returned to the boat for the night before making the journey to Reading and the lawyer in the morning.

The family Rover made light of the ninety mile journey. Having parked the car, Peter found the lawyer's office and made himself known.

He left at lunchtime stunned at the information the lawyer had revealed. He had been aware he was the sole heir, but he had not realised just how valuable the travels of his family had been. The information on the various mining ventures they had shares in had been time consuming and difficult to obtain. Because of the war and the initial delays in verifying the deaths of his parents in the first place. Peter had been aware that he was wealthy from their British interests alone. It was a shock to realise that their overseas interests had been so varied and extensive. Added to the cash and shares held here in banks, he was very wealthy. The shock was beginning to wear off when he reached Portsmouth that evening. He looked forward to telling Amy all about it.

***

Over dinner with Amy, he mentioned what the lawyer had told him.

She went pale, "My god! I did not realise there was that much money in Britain!"

Chapter Twenty-eight

Invasion part two

With throttles opened the flotilla swept out into the Solent, rapidly falling into the well-tried formation for travel through hazardous waters. They entered the Channel proper and divided into their pre-established sections.

On the bridge of the lead boat, Peter leaned against the throbbing rail, thinking about the last three weeks. The planning of the assault on Calais had been accelerated by the fact that Peter and Ken McLean had prepared a scenario in advance. When it was presented to Admiral Hardcastle he had seen the sense of the idea, especially in the light of information that he alone was in possession of at the presentation.

May was over. Now, at the beginning of June the weather was not pleasant, but no worse than it has been for the past several weeks. In Peter's boat, and Jerry Lawrence's boat beside them, the platoon of RM Commandos were poised to go ashore on enemy territory to raise their own brand of trouble in the port of Calais. Two other boats were with them, a minelayer, and an MTB.

The remainder of the flotilla under the command of Lieutenant Commander Basil Hawthorne, Peter's second in command, had the task of eliminating a convoy attempting the dash south from Calais to Le Havre.

The group of four boats made for the French coastal town of Calais through the early darkness. Radar was operating. Sonar was not effective because of the speed of the boats.

Ken McLean joined Peter on the bridge, "I understand I am expected to collect the delectable Miss Brown on this trip."

Peter smiled. "Sam is due to be there. are you going to be fast enough to keep up with her?"

"No worries, as my Australian colleagues would say. We'll be there for her."

The briefing had made it clear that Samantha would be in Calais when the raid took place. One of the reasons was that she had been helping to spread the rumours that the invasion would be in the Pas de Calais. The reality was that there was a real danger that this time she could be caught. In fact a team of Gestapo had been after her for the past several weeks. They were now close on her heels. Both the SOE and OSS had received the word of a crackdown and both organisations had adopted a low profile as the invasion date approached.

Preparations had been set up for weeks with misinformation and operations to mislead the enemy, and keep them unaware of the actual invasion time and place.

***

As the ML approached the harbour entrance, the speed dropped and the exhaust became almost completely silent. The second boat drifted past the sea wall to a point off the beach. The commandos dropped into their dinghies and silently paddled, one party to the beach – the other through the harbour entrance.

The party at the harbour reached the boom defence ship undiscovered. They boarded and took control without a sound. The boom was opened and the ML slipped through into the outer harbour. There was a patrol on the each of the quays. Observing the boat, they called quietly to each other, asking what it was doing there. The commandos spotted the patrols, locating them by their voices. They silenced them. The quays became quiet once more. The men ashore seemed to melt into the darkness, slipping through the dim shadows cast by buildings and equipment. The beach landing group was already on the other side of the beach and heading for the rail yards.

Ken McLean and five men made for the port offices, the rendezvous where Sam Brown was scheduled to be. They carried silenced SMGs and pistols, in addition to their Fairburn knives.

Peter turned the boat to face the sea gate and moored alongside the outer quay. He stepped ashore to stretch his legs. As he did so a commando approached with an agitated civilian. The Commando said "He said had a message for you!"

"What is it?" Peter asked in his rough French.

"The lady has been trapped. She is waiting at the rendezvous with Gestapo men to trap your people."

"Have you any men here armed and ready?" Peter asked.

"I have six, ready in perhaps ten minutes."

"What do I call you?

"Paul!"

"Okay, Paul. At the lighthouse, ten minutes?"

"The man nodded and ran off."

Peter said to the commando, "How many men do you have?"

"Just five, sir. A corporal and four others. We are looking after the quay."

Peter turned to Lieutenant Willis. "Get the Chief and take over the security for the quay. Open the arms locker and make sure they know what they are doing. "What's your name, soldier?"

"Cannon, Sir!"

"Right, Cannon. Let's go. We'll pick up the rest of the lads on the way." Peter picked up the MP40 from beneath the windshield. The gun, acquired during his service in the Med, had remained with him ever since. With the gun slung over his shoulder he followed Cannon along the quay to the inner harbour wall. There he found the corporal and the other three men.

"Corporal, my men will take over here. We must go and sort out Mr. McLean and the agent. We rendezvous at the lighthouse if we get split up. Let's move now!"

They trotted off down the wall of the inner harbour, their rubber soled boots making no sounds.

At the Lighthouse the partisans were waiting. "I have found eight." Paul said, "What now?"

Peter indicated. "Opposite the doorway. Two men. Watch and wait. Warn us if reinforcements arrive."

The door was flanked by two armed men in leather coats. They were laughing at some private joke.

Peter turned to the corporal. He signalled cutting the throat, drawing his knife to emphasise the move. The corporal turned to one of his men. "Poacher." He pointed to Peter. The man nodded, and handed his weapon to his neighbour, Peter handed the MP40 to the corporal. They split up and crossed the road, using the shadows of the buildings to cover their movements. The corporal watched from across the road as the two raiders drifted up to the two Gestapo men. Suddenly both were slipping to the ground.

Peter waved the men to cross the road and join him.

Inside the door there was a reception desk. Peter donned the long leather coat of one of the dead men. With his hat under his arm and the MP40 on its sling over his shoulder he walked into the lobby of the building. There were noises coming from up the stairs. The man at the desk hardly looked up when Peter indicated the stairs.

The receptionist said, "Room twelve," as he looked up. Realising he did not know the man in front of him, he opened his mouth. The bullet from Peter's silenced automatic hit his forehead, he died without a sound.

Pointing to the Corporal and lifting three fingers, Peter ran up the stairs. The noises from room twelve made it clear which it was. In room eleven two guards stood chatting and mocking Sam Brown, who was seated strapped to an arm chair. Gagged and with her blouse half open revealing a bruise on her partially exposed breast, Peter did not hesitate. Two shots. He caught one and Poacher the other.

The corporal released Sam, who took off the gag and said quietly. "Ken is in there with three thugs and their boss. The others are down stairs with my man."

The corporal said, "Take me there," he pointed to two of his men and two of the partisans. "Lead the way," he said to Sam.

Peter and Poacher went to the door of room twelve. One other commando and two of the partisans stood by as Peter opened the door. Inside, Ken was seated in a chair, stripped naked, Two big men stood, one each side of him. Facing him was a dapper man in Gestapo uniform, a Sturmbannfuhrer, Peter guessed. Two others were there, a woman in a uniform and another leather-coated man. Peter did not hesitate. He opened fire with the MP40 and swept the room. All four men dropped to the floor. Only the dapper man had managed to reach his gun, which was half out of his holster. The woman fell, sprawled. The bullet had wrecked her shoulder. otherwise she was alive and squirming, skirt riding up, showing the scarlet slip beneath it.

Poacher looked at Peter, knife in hand?

The dapper man stirred. Two bullets in his chest, he had tried for his gun anyway. Poacher's knife flashed. He stopped moving. The two bruisers were both very dead. The woman looked at them and spat. Peter unbound Ken McLean. Helping him up, Ken made it, but he had been hurt. There were bruises beginning to show all over his body. They had left his face alone. With a wry grin he said, "They told me they would begin on my face, after they took my balls off. You can imagine that I was worried you might not get here in time."

He painfully climbed back into his uniform. "Is Sam alright?" I was worried that they might have started on her. When we arrived she was unhurt, to lure us in, I suppose. But they took her out when they started on me. My boys are in the cellar. they were saving them for later."

The boys arrived on cue, re-armed and ready. Sam came with them. She faced Ken. "I am sorry. They had two girls under the knife when you arrived. I could not let them slaughter them."

"I do understand. Though it will cost you a date in England." Ken said.

She smiled. "It's a deal."

Ken turned to his men. "We have work to do." He set off down the stairs, ready to carry on where he left off.

At the street door, the partisans warned that a truck was coming, probably loaded with soldiers. Ken called to his corporal, "Ambush, with grenades."

His men disappeared.

Peter took Sam's arm and urged her to the harbour wall, "We are going back to the boat, while Ken gets on with things."

"What about that dreadful woman?" Sam asked.

Peter thought for a moment, '*What woman?* Then he realised, Sam meant the woman in the Gestapo offices. He looked back. It was still clear. Two of the partisans were still with him. He turned and went back to the office. The others followed. Peter turned to Sam. "Let us collect their records while we are here. Ken is busy outside. I'll check-up upstairs." He left them rummaging in the offices and ran up to room twelve The bloody scene had not altered much. The dead men lay around the floor where they had fallen. He collected the half-drawn hand gun from the officer. The woman's face was still snarling, but her throat gaped where a single swipe had stopped the acid tongue permanently. "Poacher did not leave loose ends!" Peter said aloud. He was startled at the sound of his own voice.

"Good. Served the bitch right." Sam spoke from the doorway. She had followed him up the stairs. "We're done!" She said. "It's mostly rubbish, but it will worry them anyway."

Carrying the paperwork between them, they made their way back to the boat.

Peter suddenly remembered the truck with rein-forcements. He turned to Sam "What about that truck?"

She grinned. "It has been diverted., Apparently someone blew-up the railway yards. So they turned around and went there. Ken's boys are booby-trapping the lock gates on both sea locks."

Peter called up MacRae. The minelayer had been standing off waiting for orders.

At the call he made for the harbour and the open boom. Inside, he dropped two mines, one at each of the locks, both with proximity fuses for the maximum effect.

"Anything else I can help you with." His Aberdeen accent calm and re-assuring as he leaned across the bridge rail alongside his leader's ML.

"Nothing I can think of offhand, MacRae. Take the rest of your babies and see if the convoy group needs you. Otherwise. home to bed."

"That's the story of my life. They ask for help. Once given, they cast you aside like an old riding boot." His mutter could be heard as the engine in-creased its revs. The minelayer motored out of the harbour once more, looking for trouble elsewhere.

Peter could not help a sigh of relief as it drew out of range. He always felt apprehensive when he was alongside the minelayer. He had seen one ex-plode with mines on board. There had been nothing left of the boat at all, or the crew. All had disap-peared completely.

***

The commandos returned by sections, two wounded, the remainder, apart from the odd cuts and scratches, unharmed. Ken and his section were last, having been delayed at the outset by the Gestapo episode.

They drew away from the quay and motored out. Finally the German soldiers got organised and started sending relief guards to the quays.

Ken commented, "I would like to see their faces when they discover all their guards are either dead or tied up."

***

Peter caught up with the convoy raiders off Eastbourne. The flotilla made the passage home without further incident.

As they tied up in the base, word came down for Peter to report immediately to the Commander

Commander Henry Jackson DSC RN was seated at his desk reading papers when Peter reported.

"Come and sit down, Peter. this won't take long. Then you can get on with your de-brief."

He finished reading the paper he held, and put it on the desk. "Peter, it's on. The invasion fleet has moved off."

"But what about the weather. I thought…"

"They found a window or something. The planes can fly. So the fleet has moved out, heading for the Caen area. You are to refuel, rearm and stand by for deployment tomorrow at 08:00. Now, get your de-brief and get your boats ready. Get some sleep, if possible."

Peter rose and left for the briefing room, wondering what tomorrow would bring.

He encountered Sam and Ken in the de-briefing room. Ken looked at him keenly. "You have heard, I presume."

Peter smiled grimly. "So have you, obviously." Sam looked at both of them curiously. "Can I share the secret?"

Peter shrugged. "The invasion has begun."

"Where are they aiming for?"

Ken said, "I thought you, of all people, would have known."

"And why do you think that? Is it because I am a spook, a spy, perhaps?"

Peter interjected, "That is why you do not know. In case you get caught."

"Exactly. Now everyone else knows. I can be told. Until then no way."

"They are landing on the beaches around Caen. That's all I know, apart from the fact that I will probably be going tomorrow to back them up."

"If you are done here, I think a drink is in order. my treat." Peter led the way to the Mess and ordered drinks for them all. From there he rang Amy, who came and joined them. They all piled into Peter's car and Amy drove them to the pub at Ringwood, where the landlord's wife produced a game stew with wedges of home-made bread. All was received with all the genuine pleasure and complements it deserved.

"What do you intend doing after the war, Sam?" Amy asked innocently.

Sam took her time answering. Then, "I'll be honest. I've never given it a thought. In this game. It is not something you normally think about, basically. I suppose, because of what nearly happened last night."

Amy suddenly realised that she was unaware of what had happened last night and probably, she would not like to know, for her own peace of mind.

Sam stepped in before Amy could say anything and turned to Ken. "What have you got planned, Ken? Anything in particular?"

"I suppose I always thought I would continue at what I set out to do. Follow the law, either a solicitor in my father's practice, or as a barrister in the Law Courts. Get married, have kids and settle for that."

"What about you, Peter? What rings your bell?"

Peter grinned. "Get married. Yes. I'm already working on that." Amy blushed. He continued, "I will carry on with the racing. But also, I think I will set up, or buy, a boatyard and build boats. That is provided my wife agrees."

Sam looked at the others, "Meanwhile.......?"

The landlord came through and announced to the pub clientele in general. "The invasion of Europe has begun, just heard it on the news. It is happening now as I speak. They will issue bulletins from now on."

"Meanwhile, I'm afraid it is back to the base. Tomorrow is a working day."

Chapter twenty-nine

Protect and Serve

The boats left the base, and rounded the Isle of Wight in a double line. As they passed into the Channel they spread out into line abreast to cover as much water as they could on their way to join the invasion fleet.

As they progressed down channel to the location of the invasion the shipping began to come into view through the grey light. Peter was astonished at the size of the fleet as ship after ship came in sight. The assault ships close to the shore were centres of activity. Landing craft shuttled to and fro between ship and shore. A lamp flashed from one of the command ships moored out at the seaward side of the armada.

"Acknowledge" Peter said.

The clack of the lamp beside him followed the "Aye, Aye, sir."

"To O/ic flotilla. Report on board the flagship, sir."

"Acknowledge."

As the lamp clattered the acknowledgement, Peter ordered the change of course. Then he spoke to Basil Hawthorne. "I've been called to the flagship. Have the lads run a patrol along the flank of all these ships. Take a squint to seaward as well, just in case."

"Okay, boss. I'll do that, treasuring every moment of independent command. Don't hurry back!"

"Cheeky bugger." Peter said, before he cut off.

"Course for the flagship," Peter told the helm, turning to Willis, who had joined him on the bridge. "Colin, please do not bash my boat, especially not in front of the Admiral!"

A hurt look on Willis's face expressed what he thought of Peter's remark.

***

Seated in the Admiral's cabin, Peter was not alone. The Captain in command of the destroyer flotilla was also present. He was a regular officer, and in Peter's opinion, young for his rank. It meant that he was probably good at his job. The Admiral was talking quietly with his aide, and a Commodore. Peter had gathered that the Commodore was in command of the support ships. The destroyer Captain leaned across to Peter. "I'm Charles Wyngard, *HMS Kennet.* I understand those pretty speedboats are yours?"

Peter grinned and nodded. "Peter Woods, and yes, they are."

"How are they against the E-boats?" Wyngard asked seriously.

"We do pretty well, especially now we match them for speed and armament."

"I have the feeling that this meeting is about E-boats and U-boats. We had a bit of a run in with E-boats on the way over. Your arrival is timely."

"Why were there none allocated from the start?" Peter asked.

Captain Wyngard thought for a moment. "I believe, possibly," he said slowly, "I have heard it said by some, that they thought your boats were boy's toys, not real naval craft. All flash and dash, all right for torpedo attacks, but not for real fighting. Does that sound stupid to you?" He was quite serious.

Peter nodded. "I have heard similar comments, but not from the Admiral who organised this junket. I was at the landings in Sicily and Salerno with the boats. Admiral Ramsey organised both, and he forgot very little, I assure you."

Wyngard sat back, noticing the DSC and bar probably for the first time. "I have been out of things for some time, in the far-east. I am more out-of-date than I realised. Having been operating with the Aussies for the past year, returning to this part of the world is rather a culture shock. The Aussies have a rather more casual attitude to command, but still manage to get things done. I guess what happened was, there was just not enough to go round."

Rear Admiral Martin Dewar RN—Peter realised he had known him as a captain who had been with Admiral Hardcastle in the Mediterranean—raised his eyes from the desk in front of him, and waved his aide away.

"Good morning, gentlemen. Good to see you again, Commander Woods. Congratulations on the bar to your DSC. It was well deserved, I understand. Also Captain Wyngard, a change from the balmy climes of the antipodes, I am sure. You were a midshipman in the Hood when I was Commander, I recall?"

"Indeed I was, sir. A happy cruise, I thought."

"You two have a task before you. Captain Wyngard has already been involved. He will be delighted, I'm sure, to add the ML flotilla to the all-round defence of the invasion fleet. I noticed that your boats had been deployed along the eastern flank of the fleet, when you reported here."

"It seemed the thing to do, sir."

The Admiral nodded. "My intention was to introduce you to each other, and give you your orders.

The written orders are here." The aide passed them both a folder. Then the Admiral continued, "In brief, I have passed the security of the fleet over to the pair of you. Captain Wyngard will command. Your responsibility is U-boats and E-boats. A second flotilla of ML-MGBs is on its way from Harwich. They will join under your command, Woods, and, of course, under the overall command of the Captain here." He indicated Wyngard.

"My aide will take you to another cabin to let you rough-out a scheme to get things started. Good luck. I have confidence in you both."

In the cabin they were allotted, the two officers weighed each other up. On the table between them the Admiral's orders lay.

Wyngard made his mind up. "Peter, is it?" Peter nodded. "You know your boats better than I do. What would you suggest, from your point of view, bearing in mind you have two flotillas to deploy?"

Peter thought briefly of arrangements he had made in the past for protecting a large body of ships. Salerno was the only occasion. Then it was the maiale, the mini-subs they really had to worry about.

"On this occasion, I have to go with my current arrangement. All of my boats, and I presume the Harwich boats, will be fitted for anti-submarine operations. I suggest we encircle the fleet to the best of our ability. By stationing the Harwich flotilla on the Atlantic side, and your destroyers, in back-up positions scattered around the fleet, we can keep in touch and throw in support where it is needed."

"That makes sense. I found in the Pacific that sub hunting gained real results if more than one ship was involved."

Peter interjected, "Also, you carry more depth charges than we do."

"Good point. So we try and work it that one of my destroyers is within range of as many of the boats as possible. That way we will cover the fleet more efficiently with the minimum of resources."

"I had a feeling we would get on. Do you know the commander of the Harwich flotilla?" Charles Wyngard looked at Peter enquiringly.

"I have a name, Acting Commander Pat Carter RNVR, DSC. The name rings a bell, but I am not actually sure if I'm thinking of the right person. Pat Carter was foreman in the boat yard which built my boat."

Wyngard looked at Peter curiously. "Your boat? You mean your current command?"

Peter grinned. "Sorry, I forget. I live in a different world, I'm afraid. I was a racing yachtsman before the war. My boat, the *Salamander,* is laid up in Chichester harbour for the duration. That was the boat I was thinking of."

"And this man, Pat Carter, was the yard foreman, was he?"

"He was. I had heard he had joined-up and was in the 'boats'. He was pretty good at what he did. I think we are lucky to have him, provided....."

"Provided he is the man you think he is." Wyngard grinned and finished Peter's comment.

They wrapped up their meeting, both men happy with the man they were set to work with, and both impatient, to get back to their respective commands.

****

Back on board Peter handed the list of code words to be used for RT procedure, over to Colin Willis. It was prepared to ensure they did not give too much away to any enemy listening in, trying to breach the protective cordon around the invasion fleet.

***

Pat Carter arrived with his flotilla of mixed MTBs and MGBs in the late afternoon. They ran in alongside the tanker sitting deep within the fleet, to refuel after their fast run from Harwich. The leader of the flotilla came alongside Peter's boat, the 73ft White MTB seemed small to Peter against the 110ft of his Fairmile.

He grinned, as he watched Pat Carter jump over the gap between the two boats. The short stocky man looked at home on the pitching deck. He paused looking up at Peter, who was stepping down to greet him.

His opening remark was typical of the man. "Did you change the fitting on the foredeck?"

"Of course, I am a professional after all." They both burst out laughing at an old shared joke. And shook hands like the old friends they actually were. "Pat Carter, driving a stinkpot? That I should live to see the day?

"They would not let me build a sailing version." Pat said, mournfully.

Peter laughed. "Come below. I'll fill you in over a nice cup of tea."

Laughing, they disappeared below, as the White boat stood off, to wait the return of their skipper.

***

Having briefed Pat on the signals and operation plan, the Harwich flotilla, now designated flotilla B, took up their place on the far side of the fleet.

Three false alarms on the first day smoothed things out for the protection screen. They linked with the two destroyers watching with them, and found themselves helping stranded assault craft, towing two off the beach where they had overdone things slightly.

To Peter, the astonishing thing was the comparative lack of activity from the enemy. the air seemed full of allied aircraft; action from the shore-based guns had been pretty much suppressed after the first day. But the troops on the beaches still found it difficult to make progress. Whatever enemy troops there were seemed to be well dug-in, despite the fact that they had received no warning of the invasion.

For the following week, the duties of the two flotillas consisted of endless patrols. Back and forth, and occasionally through, the huge armada of ships with a multiplicity of tasks, ranging from collecting and delivering mail, to moving injured seamen to ships with better medical facilities. There was also the odd false alarm, and one genuine alarm, when a U-boat surfaced in the middle of the task force. It caused no damage itself it submerged immediately. But not until it had drawn the fire of most of the ships around it.

Sadly, the firing was more enthusiastic than accurate, with the result that several of the ships present sustained damage. Three men died when a gun blew up, killing the crew.

After the past few months, and, he admitted to himself, four years, Peter found the comparative peace welcome, at first. But it became wearing after a while. It was with some relief that he welcomed the arrival of Commander (Texas) Lee with his Flotilla to relieve him and take over the duty.

The flotilla had been back in their Portsmouth base for a week before the change in pace commenced.

Having been re-united with Amy, Peter was well pleased to be there.

Normal patrolling recommenced for the flotilla. Exercises with, RM units were undertaken in preparation for action on events already begun.

Colonel McNeil RM made an appearance from Hamworthy and disappeared into the office of the Admiral. Three hours later Peter, newly returned from patrol, was called in to join the Admiral and the Colonel. It was there that he found out that the action they had been training for had come about.

When he came out, he discovered that the fine weather they had been experiencing had reverted to the similar grim weather the month of June had started out with.

The discussion with the Admiral had been about the urgent repatriation of SOE agents from Holland and Northern France. In both places there had been an unprecedented number of arrests, and attempted arrests of agents within the areas without apparent reason. It appeared there had been betrayals on a grand scale. In view of this, the urgent repatriation of the remaining agents was planned. In addition, the release of some agents was to be attempted before any moves were made to transport them to Germany or execute them.

There was definite information that the German base at Alkmaar was being used to hold arrested agents and partisans.

Using Peter's boats, the Colonel wished to make lightning raids on known bases, as well as collecting agents at pick-up points on the Dutch/Belgian and French coasts.

Speed was the essence.

The meeting broke-up at 15:00, with a promise to move the first boats by 07:00. As Peter returned to harbour he sent a man to find his flotilla 2i/c, Basil Hawthorne.

When he appeared wearing overalls he grinned as he saw Peter's No. 1 uniform, "Socialising again, I see!" Then seeing Peter's face, he became serious. "Is something up, Boss?"

"I'm afraid so, Basil. Cast off at 07:00 for Dutch coast for me, Belgian for you. Then it's shuttle at the beck and call of our commando friends.

Basil turned around to dash back to his boat. "I'll be ready. I'll pass the word to the others."

***

Peter made his way to the office to pass the good news along. The Commander was back from his meeting at the port Admiral's Office. He looked up as Peter entered. "What news?"

Peter sat in the chair opposite the desk and detailed the results of his meeting with the Admiral and Colonel McNeil, "So you see I'm off tomorrow morning to Holland which means probably return the following day. It's 300 miles give or take, so twelve hours at a slog.

"We take commandos with us, so we'll be raiding and recovering. I've warned the boys and I'll take my gear just in case."

"Look out for yourself, Peter. It's been a long war and you've been fighting it the whole time."

***

As he walked down to his boat, Peter shivered. Henry's words had hit home. It had been a long war, with very little relief for him as an RNVR. The Regular Navy rules did not apply. So his service so far had been active the whole time. It was beginning to tell on him. He shrugged. He was not alone. The old sailor's comment came to mind. 'If you can't take a joke, you shouldn't have joined'. So that was that. He stepped on board, feeling the familiar excitement and pride as he looked down the full 110 feet length of the Fairmile.

Tomorrow they would be off again, Doing what she was designed for. Going to war!

Chapter-thirty

Keeping the Faith.

After a restless night, Peter was pleased to be back on his feet again. The morning was clear with heavy overcast but it was, he was informed, unlikely to rain.

The four boats loaded with commandos motored steadily up-channel into the North Sea. They were headed for the lighthouse at Egmond aan Zee. Two trucks would be there to convey them to Alkmaar. The partisans had been warned. The men waiting had already evaded capture in the last sweep made by Gestapo. Strangely, it was the dislike of the Gestapo which contributed to their current freedom. The Wehrmacht in the region had been sickened by the measures taken by the secret police in Holland. Many of the people of the area were related to people across the border in Germany. While this meant something to the ordinary soldiers, it apparently meant nothing to the Gestapo.

In addition the top echelon of the German army had been withdrawn to the fighting fronts, leaving the security of the annexed territories to older soldiers and young conscripts.

The young men were mainly products of the Hitler youth, they were frightened and arrogant, showing, on the one hand aggressiveness, on the other, panic-driven overreaction in any stressful situation. This had resulted in unnecessary killing of innocent people, and the utter contempt of their older, more experienced, fellow soldiers.

Early dark, the four boats crept shoreward the dinghies in the water ready to land the forty commandos.

Ken McLean spoke quietly. "See you later, Peter. I'll leave five of my boys with the boats on the shore. They will signal if they need help." He held up his hand radio. "I'll blip twice when we are getting near on our way back."

"Good luck, Ken. I'll keep an eye out for you. If we have to move, we will be at Ijmuiden. Alongside the outer wall."

Then Ken was away. The dinghies loaded and gone into the darkness to the loom of the shore, the tall dark lighthouse, an extra black finger pointing against the faint skyline.

Peter sighed. This was always the worst time. The wait, all the senses on edge. Poised for the sudden flash of light, gunfire or cry of alarm. He heard the trucks departing, the sound carrying across the quiet waters, along with the other noises of life, now apparent after the last twelve hours of engine noise.

***

For Ken, the movement of the trucks allowed him to relax slightly. The time between landing and boarding the trucks was a critical one. It was when they were most vulnerable to ambush. Despite the most careful preparation and scanning of the area, things could go wrong, and that could be disaster.

They were past that point now, so he could relax a little, and look ahead to see if he had missed anything. *So far so good.* He adjusted his sten gun, made sure the safety catch was on, and waited, seated among his men.

Colour Sergeant Billy Paget, Grenadier Guards, knew he would never go back. He had done the unforgivable, leaving the Guards to join the LRDG. It had taken a little time to get used to officers who called him Bill, and fought alongside him with rifle and sten gun. He discovered that the cheeky bugger in the scruffy clothes did not need to be told how to react in an emergency. His boots may not shine, but he could march as far. No. Billy Paget had found his place for the duration of the war. *After that, who knew? First survive. Then we'll see."*

He closed his eyes for five minutes. The boss was there. He would wake if there was a problem.

***

Alkmaar was a small town in a country area. The Gestapo used it because there was a quiet, hardworking farming community. They tended to get on with their own affairs, which suited the Gestapo well.

They had commandeered the town hall, which had a courthouse with four jail cells and an office in the basement. The ground floor area was dedicated to records and offices, with accommodation on the upper floor.

The trucks rumbled into Alkmaar and pulled up in a quiet square. The engines were switched off. They sat quietly, the engines ticking as the temperature dropped. A shadow slipped out of the back of one of the trucks. Poacher Martin took a careful look about, before moving off to the lane leading to the town square. He had studied the model of the town, produced in a hurry before they left Hamworthy. The lane was clear and he made his way to the Stadhuis (Town Hall) at the far side.

There were several uniformed men lounging around in the parking area outside. They were in SS uniforms which pleased Poacher. It probably made the job harder, but, as Poacher thought to himself, much more satisfying. He completed his survey and returned to the trucks. The men were all dismounted and concealed in the shadows around the vehicles. The two drivers were apparently asleep in their cabs. Their story would be that they were waiting for the market to open in the early hours of the morning. It was not permitted officially, but normally a blind eye was turned to the offenders.

Ken decided on the bold approach. He formed his men up into parade marching order. They set off following Poacher and another scout, to circle around behind the Stadhuis. On their rubber-soled boots they marched quietly around two blocks and crossed the main road, out of direct sight of the SS men in the car parking area.

Behind the bulk of the Stadhuis, the men relaxed. Then formed up once more. When the Major and the Colour Sergeant were satisfied, Ken returned the salute from C/Sgt Paget. "Carry on, Colour Sergeant. The order was given. They stepped away, smartly marching into the main street, wheeling left and fifty yards down to the main doors of the building. They came to a halt front of the astonished SS men. Sergeant Braun spoke in German to one of the SS men, showing interest in this strange body of men. "The spies. They are in here?" With his thumb he indicated the building.

The SS man said, "Spies?" Then grinned and nodded, "Yes, downstairs….."His voice cut off with a gurgle as he drowned in his own blood. The others around him also collapsed silently, as they were dispatched by the last file of the platoon. The men had dropped out as they rounded the corner.

The bodies were dragged out of sight, while the platoon entered the building. Ken left the Colour Sergeant to attend to the office and collect the records. He led his other men down the steps into the holding area below.

There were two guards stationed at the foot of the steps. Braun called them to attention and they responded automatically. Two knives flashed and their bodies were lowered to the floor.

The first room was the guardroom. There were several beds, a table and chairs and tobacco smoke. The men, playing cards around the table, took no notice until Braun shouted "Hande hoch!"

The four men at the table raised their hands. The three men on the beds were slower to react, but one snatched at his MP40 hanging on the back of the chair beside him. His burst of fire hit the ceiling, Braun was too fast for him, but others had taken a chance as well, grabbing at weapons in desperation. The two men with Braun opened fire, sweeping the room with guns on full automatic' none of the Germans survived.

Along the corridor, a scream shattered the silence that followed the gunfire. Ken McLean signalled three men to follow and made for the room where the scream originated. Gun up, safety off, he kicked the door open.

Inside, there was a woman standing with arms tied above her head and her upper body stripped naked. Two wires were attached with clips to her breasts, and to two terminals on a box plugged into an electrical wall-socket. Three men were in the room. Two thugs stripped to the waist, and a uniformed man with a handkerchief pressed to his mouth.

The uniformed man looked up startled at the intrusion. He saw his own death in the gun pointing at him and reached despairingly for the gun at his belt. His two companions died in the same burst of bullets that killed him.

Ken stepped forward and removed the clips, which had drawn blood, from the woman's breasts. Braun slashed the leather straps tethering her to the hooks in the ceiling.

The woman covered herself with an arm and ran to the table where her blouse had been thrown and slipped it on.

Then she looked at her rescuers. "Thank you," she said in English The others are along the hall."

As she spoke there was a single shot, followed by chatter in English and Dutch. People began to crowd into the room. Ken held his hands up., "Stop!" He turned to Sergeant Braun, "Are there any others here at all?"

The tortured lady spoke. "They took several others out to the Police barracks on the road to Heiloo, south of here. I'll show you."

***

At the boat, the shore party showed a light. A dinghy came alongside. It contained two men. The commando said, "This man has reported that there was a raid this afternoon. they have taken four agents, two SOE and he thinks two OSS. The Major said to advise you of any incidents occurring while he was away."

"Does he know where these people are being held?"

"There is a barn behind the dunes. The soldiers seized it as their base when they arrived in the area."

The partisan spoke in English. "They have several more people who are local. But I am worried that the Germans will discover the four foreigners."

"How many troops are there?"

The partisan answered thoughtfully. I believe that there are twenty soldiers, but they seem to only have ten on duty at one time, The others should be in the bar on the way to Rinnegom. It's about half a kilometre down the road."

Peter did not hesitate. "Sergeant, my men will take over the shore duties with the dinghies. You and your lads will accompany this man with me. We'll see what we can do for these unfortunate agents."

Surprised, the sergeant looked up at that. His eyes dropped to the gunbelt around Peter's waist, with the Fairburn knife sheathed next to the holstered automatic. He grinned. "Captain Cotton, sir. I did not recognise you. Of course, sir. As soon as you are ready."

Peter called Lieutenant Willis. "Send the chief and four men to the shore to look after the boats. I'll be off with the sergeant and his men. We will be back as quickly as possible." He picked up the MP40 from beneath the bridge screen, removed the waterproof cover the chief had made for it, and checked the action and magazine. A bag with spare magazines went over his shoulder. "Let's go!" He dropped down into the dinghy with the sergeant and the partisan. The chief and three men joined them. They rowed rapidly to the shore, disappearing swiftly into the darkness.

***

In Alkmaar the released prisoners boarded the two trucks while Ken annexed the half-track, with trailer, parked alongside the Stadhuis. There was a kubelwagen beside it and he decided to take it, since there seemed to be no other vehicles about. It would delay any pursuit.

In the building they left behind, the bodies of the SS men and the Gestapo man lay. The office door flapped to and fro, in the breeze from the open door. Odd papers fluttered on the floor, lending an air of abandonment to the scene.

***

Peter and Sergeant Campbell with his four men followed the partisan over the dunes to the barn standing sharp against the night sky.

An odd crack of light escaped through chinks in the corrugated iron sheeting covering the walls of the building. There were sounds from within the building, though it was difficult to identify them. Their approach over the dunes allowed them to eliminate the guard stationed behind the barn. He was spotted smoking a cigarette behind his hand, as he strolled to and fro on his rounds.

Peter moved off to the right around the building, watching to see where the other sentries were. As he made his way around the corner, a man appeared carrying an MP40 and looking annoyed. It was a mistake on his part because his annoyance caused him to concentrate on his anger rather than his surroundings. The muttering that accompanied his anger stopped abruptly, as a forearm crushed his windpipe, cutting the supply of air to his lungs. He struggled, but the effort was in vain. He rapidly lost consciousness and slumped in Peter's arms. Peter released him and left. The partisan pulled the MP40 from the fallen soldier, and followed Peter. At the door to the barn a curtain had been strung to create a light-trap when the recessed door was opened. There was a chink of light through one of the windows. Peter rose onto his toes to peer through. He saw a table and chairs with scraps of food and wrappers scattered about. A row of stalls were on the other side of the barn against the far wall. There was chicken-wire across the upper, normally open, section of the stalls. Peter decided that they must be the cells where the prisoners were kept. A man, a Rottenfuhrer, (Sergeant) was seated at the table drinking from a mug, and reading a newspaper. His MP40 was hanging on the back of the chair. A row of hay bales, stacked side by side at the back of the barn, was covered with groundsheets. Five men lay on the hay in various attitudes. Their weapons were not in sight.

Peter turned to the Sergeant. "Take a look. I think it might be worth just stepping in through the door. We will need the other guards removed first."

***

Major McLean, having sent the two trucks off with the released prisoners, drove the kubelwagen, with the English-speaking agent directing him. The half-track followed them down the road to Heiloo.

The police station was an old building built of stone with small windows and an extension at the rear, where a row of cells had been added during the years before the war.

The door of the building opened and a Dutch policeman emerged.

He saw the British soldiers and started to react. The woman with them spoke rapidly in Dutch.

He stopped reaching for the door handle, and listened to her. Then he shrugged said a few words back and stepped into the road. Looking both ways he set off on his beat.

The troops debussed and gathered round the Major. "Colour Sergeant, take a squad and secure the rear. Braun, your squad is with me. The other squad secure the area.

Margit, the agent, looked at the Major, "Ready?"

He nodded. She opened the door and walked in.

Ken listened to the exchange in Dutch. Then he nodded to Sergeant Braun and stepped in. The agent stood in front of a desk. Behind it, a concerned-looking police officer sat.

The looming figure of a black uniformed man with a swastika armband stood behind him. He had been looking at the agent with interest until Ken walked in. He seemed to suddenly realise that Ken was not a German soldier. As he reached for the holstered Luger at his belt his mouth opened. The thrown knife, hit his neck in the vee of his tunic, and the sound died in his throat. He collapsed. His Luger fell from the open holster.

Margit, the agent, turned from the shocked policeman, "The prisoners are in the cell block. There are six Germans with them, four are Gestapo, like him."

Ken said to the policeman, "Lead the way!"

Margit told him in Dutch. He rose to his feet and came forward.

He opened the cell block door with a key and stood to one side.

Ken and his men went through and scanned the row of cells. There was the murmur of voices from one of the cells. They crept along the passage. There were people in each of the cells. In the far cell, the voices lured them to see what was happening. Ken peered round the door and saw other black uniformed men seated, talking to a white-faced man, who was denying any knowledge of the subject they were discussing. In the cell opposite, sat a woman with headphones on, typing swiftly on a stenotype machine. Ken indicated the agent and pointed at the typist. He stepped in with the Gestapo.

***

At the barn, the Sergeant stood back. "I agree. Get the other guards!" He detailed two men, who set off back around the barn. As he passed the man Peter had made unconscious, the man stirred. The soldier noticed and stooped behind the man, lifted his head up, and twisted his head sharply. The neck snapped with a crack. He dropped the head and continued walking around the barn.

Both men appeared at the door where Peter and the others waited, each had an extra MP40, over his shoulder.

Cocking his weapon, Peter looked at the others. All nodded in turn. He stepped forward and opened the inner door. The light flooded out as he stepped through, the others following. They lined up, looking at the men inside. The Rottenfuhrer half-rose from his chair, then with a shrug sat down again. His hand crept toward the MP40 hanging from the chair back. The other soldiers stayed where they were. None had a weapon within reach.

The MP40 knocked against the chair back as the Rottenfuhrer's hand touched it.

Immediately alert, Peter swung the MP40 to cover the man specifically. As the muzzle of the gun rose Peter fired. He sagged in the seat with three bullets in his chest. One of the others grabbed vainly at a weapon swinging from a nail on the wall of the barn. Campbell's gun spoke. The man fell, the gun clattering to the floor beside him. His fingers opened, the gun uncocked and unfired, its owner dead.

"Anyone else?" Peter called. The remaining men held their hands up. Leaving Campbell to tie them up, Peter went to the stalls and established they were cells. One contained two women, the other had several men, He stood back and shot the padlock off each door to release the prisoners.

The two women came out of their cell. One walked up to Peter and put her arms round his neck. "Peter, my hero once more." She kissed him, and, laughing, drew back, looking at him at arm's length. "Promoted too. Have you forgotten me already?"

"Karen? How could I forget you? You are the reason I'm here."

"Peter you even tell lies nicely. Meet Rachel." She drew the other girl forward, saying quietly, "She's OSS."

Peter said, "I understand there are another two of you here?"

Karen nodded at two men who were on their way over to join them. "Carl Roberts and Joe Franks, meet Commander Peter Woods, Royal Navy."

"Peter said, "Let's not hang about. The boat is waiting."

He turned to the others. "Ready, lads? Let's move."

They switched the lights off and moved out of the building, the partisan leading the party back over the dunes to the beach.

***

Heinz Maria Hauser, was a Sturrmann (corporal) in the Waffen-SS. He was frustrated and thoroughly fed up with the bumbling inefficiency of his senior officers, from the Oberst downward. He was sick and tired of sitting on his arse in this backwater of a dump, when there was a real war going on in Normandy. He was, after all, a professional soldier, not one of these amateurs who only managed to get it up by torturing defenceless women. He did not mind using defenceless woman. The odd rape went with warriors and war somehow. But there was a time for that and a time to fight. He was walking back from the bar when he heard the shots. His MP40 was over his shoulder. Unlike his compatriots, he took his weapon everywhere. He heard voiced on the dunes, so, suspecting an escape attempt, he climbed the dune beside him and scouted the area. He came upon the party by mistake. He tripped and pulled the trigger, shooting three bullets into the ground. He realised he had targeted himself and lifted the MP. He fired a long ripping burst where he thought the people were. The combined sten-gun fire of the four commandos jerked his body into a little dance as fourteen bullets shattered his breastbone pelvis and his internal organs.

Death came swiftly for Sturrmann Heinz Maria Houser.

***

The ripping noise of an MP40, and the sudden impact of the bullet took Peter by surprise. It was like being kicked in the side by a horse, or in Peter's case, what he thought it would be like anyway. He staggered and Karen grabbed him. The four commandos all opened up at once, the MP40 was stopped abruptly as the shooter was hit several times. The two male agents grabbed Peter and hoisted him between them, and trotted the remaining distance to the beach.

Peter woke to find a familiar face leaning over him. "You're on the wrong boat, Dingle."

Dingle smiled. "No, sir. You are. Mr. Willis is waiting to collect the party from Alkmaar., Mr. Lawrence is taking the agents and the released partisans home. Since you were not feeling too well, we decided the sooner we got you home the better."

"So tell me true, Dingle," Peter winced as he moved. He gave it a few seconds then continued. "Is it really bad? Should I be writing a letter to Amy?"

Dingle started to say something then stopped. "It's bad. But I will get you back to Amy, sir. You will not be driving a boat for some time. You will be able to introduce me to your children. Now, sir. If you are up to it, I have to allow the lady to see you."

Peter grinned, "You recognised her?"

"How could I forget!"

Dingle's face was replaced by Karen's. She leaned down and kissed him. "Position reversed, Peter. Fancy getting in the way of a bullet like that. After all this time, I thought you would have learned that they could be damaging."

"Karen, had I known you were there when I set out, I would have put my armour on, and ridden my white horse. I would have been quite safe then. You were not mentioned by....." He drifted off into a morphine-induced, sleep.

***

Peter woke in hospital, in bed with tubes attached, and the late autumn sun shining through the window. He could not see anything but sky from his position on the bed.

He turned and looked to the other side, away from the window. The skirt and legs of a seated woman were in view. The rest of the person was hidden, his view blocked by the bedside cabinet.

"Excuse me," he said. His voice was a whisper, his throat dry. He worked his tongue around his mouth. It tasted foul. He tried again, louder this time. "Excuse me!"

The legs moved as the woman leaned forward. "There you are." Amy leaned in and kissed him, He tried to put his arm round her, but it was too heavy.

"Oh, Peter. You nearly scared me to death." Amy said. "Then I remembered what you said to me once, and I knew it would be all right."

For a moment, Peter wondered what it was that he had said. Then, as he lay there with his raised head cushioned on her breast, breathing her scent, with her arms about him, he knew he didn't care. He was where he belonged.

Also by David O'Neil

Action/Adventure/Thriller series
Counterstroke # 1

Exciting, Isn't It?

O'Neil's initial entry into the world of action adventure romance thriller is filled with mystery and suspense, thrills and chills as *Counterstroke* finds it seeds of Genesis, and springs full blown onto the scene with action, adventure and romance galore.

John Murray, ex-Police, ex-MI6, ex management consultant, 49 and widowed, is ready to make a new start. Having sold off everything, he sets out on a lazy journey by barge through the waterways of France to collect his yacht at a yard in Grasse. En route he will decide what to do with the rest of his life

He picks up a female hitch-hiker Gabrielle, a frustrated author running from Paris after a confrontation with a lascivious would-be publisher Mathieu. She had unknowingly picked up some of Mathieu's secret documents with her manuscript. Although not looking for action, adventure or romance, still a connection is made.

An encounter with Pierre, an unpleasant former acquaintance from Paris who is chasing Gabrielle, is followed by a series of events that make John call on all his old skills of survival to keep them both alive over the next few days. Mystery and suspense shroud the secret documents that disclose the real background of the so called publisher who is in fact a high level international crook.

To survive, the pair become convinced they must take the fight to the enemy but they have no illusions; their chances of survival are slim. But with the help of some of John's old contacts, things start to become... exciting.

Counterstroke # 2....

Market Forces

Market Forces, Volume Two of the Counterstroke action adventure romance thriller series by David O'Neil introduces Katherine (Katt) Percival, tasked with the assassination of Mark Parnell in a hurried, last-minute attempt to stop his interference with the success of the Organization in Europe. As a skilled terminator for the CIA, Katt is accustomed to proper briefing. On this occasion she disobeys her orders, convinced it's a mistake. She joins forces with Mark to foil an attempt on his life.

Parnell works for John Murray, who created Secure Inc that caused the collapse of an International US criminal organisation's operation in Europe, forcing the disbanding of the US Company COMCO. Set up as a cover for money-laundering and other operations designed to control from within the political and financial administration, they had already been partially successful. Especially within the administrative sectors of the EU.

Katt goes on the run, she has been targeted and her Director sidelined by rogue interests in the CIA. She finds proof of conspiracy. She passes it on to Secure Inc who can use it to attack the Organization. She joins forces with Mark Parnell and Secure Inc. Mark and Katt and their colleagues risk their lives as they set out to foil the Organization once again.

Counterstroke # 3....

When Needs Must...

The latest action adventure thriller in the Counterstroke series opens with a new character Major Teddy Robertson–Steel fighting for survival in Africa. Mark Parnell and Katt Percival now working together for Secure Inc. are joined by Captain Libby 'Carter' Barr, now in plain clothes, well mostly, and her new partner James Wallace. They are tasked with locating and thwarting the efforts of three separate menaces from the European scene that threaten the separation of the United Kingdom from the political clutches of Brussels, by using terrorism to create wealth by a group of billionaires, and the continuing presence of the Mob, bankrolled from USA. An action adventure thriller filled with romance, mystery and suspense. With the appearance of a much needed new team, Dan and Reba, and the welcome return of Peter Maddox, Dublo Bond and Tiny Lewis, there is action and adventure throughout. Change will happen, it just takes the right people, at the right time, in the right place.

Young adult action/adventure/ romance thriller series
Donny Weston & Abby Marshall # 1

Fatal Meeting

A captivating new series of young adult action, romance, adventure and mystery.

For two young teens, Donny and Abby, who have just found each other, sailing the 40 ft ketch across the English Channel to Cherbourg is supposed to be a light-hearted adventure.

The third member of the crew turns out to be a smuggler, and he attempts to kill them both before they reach France. The romance adventure. now filled with action, mystery and suspense, suddenly becomes deadly serious when the man's employers try to recover smuggled items from the boat. The action gets more and more hectic as the motive becomes personal

Donny and Abby are plunged into a series of events that force them to protect themselves. Donny's parents become involved so with the help of a friend of the family, Jonathon Glynn, they take the offensive against the gang who are trying to kill them.

The action adventure thriller ranges from the Mediterranean to Paris and the final scene is played out in the shadow of the Eiffel Tower in the city of romance and lights; Paris France..

Donny Weston & Abby Marshall # 2

Lethal Complications

Eighteen year olds Donny and Abby take a year out from their studies to clear up problems that had escalated over the past three years. They succeed in closing the book on the past during the first months of the year, now they are looking forward to nine months relaxation, romance and fun, when old friend of the family, mystery man Jonathon Glynn, drops in to visit as they moor at Boulogne, bringing action and adventure into their lives once again.

Jonathon was followed and an attempt to kill them happens immediately after his visit. They leave their boat and pick up the RV they have left in France, hoping to avoid further conflict. They are attacked in the Camargue, but fast and accurate shooting keeps them alive. They find themselves mixed up in a treacherous scheme by a rogue Chinese gang to defame a Chinese moderate, in an attempt to stall the Democratic process in China.

The two young lovers, becoming addicted to action and adventure, link up with Isobel, a person of mystery who has acquired a reputation without earning it. Between them they manage to keep the Chinese target and his girlfriend out of the rogue Chinese group's hands.

Tired of reacting to attack, and now looking for action and adventure, they set up an ambush of their own, effectively checkmating the rogue Chinese plans. The leader of the rogues, having lost face and position in the Chinese hierarchy, plans a personal coup using former Spetsnaz mercenaries. With the help of a former SBS man Adam, who had worked with and against Spetsnaz forces, the friends survive and Lin Hang the Chinese leader suffers defeat.

Donny Weston & Abby Marshall # 3....

A Thrill A Minute

They are back! Fresh from their drama-filled action adventure excursion to the United States, Abby Marshall and Donny Weston look forward to once again taking up their studies at the University. Each of them is looking forward to the calm life of a University student without the threat of being murdered. Ah, the serene life.... that is the thing. But that doesn't last long. It is only a few weeks before our adventuresome young lovers find that the calm, quiet routine of University life is boring beyond belief and both are filled with yearning for the fast-paced action adventure of their prior experiences. It isn't long before trouble finds the couple and they welcome it with open arms, but perhaps this time they have underestimated the opposition. Feeling excitement once again, the two youths arm themselves and leapt into the fray. The fight was on and no holds barred!

Once again O'Neil takes us into the action filled world of mystery and suspense, action and adventure, romance and peril.

Donny Weston & Abby Marshall # 4....

It's Just One Thing After Another

Fresh from their victory over the European Mafia, our two young adults in love, Abby Marshall and Donny Weston, are rewarded with an all-expense-paid trip to the United States. But, as our young couple discover, there is no free lunch and the price they will have to pay for their "free" tour may be more than they can afford to pay, in this action adventure thriller. Even so, with the help of a few friends and some former enemies, the valiant young duo face danger once again with firm resolve and iron spirit, but will that be sufficient in face of the odds that are stacked against them?

And is their friend and benefactor actually a friend or is he on the other side? The two young adults look at this man of mystery and suspense with a bit of caution. Action, adventure and romance abound in this, the latest escapades of Britain's dynamic young couple.

Donny Weston & Abby Marshall # 5

What Goes Around...

Just when it seems that our two young heroes, Donny Weston and Abby Marshall are able to return to the University to complete their studies, fate decides to play another turn as once again the two young lovers come under attack, this time from a most unsuspected source. It appears that not even the majestic powers of the British Intelligence Service will be enough to rescue the beleaguered duo and they will have to survive through their own skills. In the continuing action adventure thriller, two young adults must solve the mystery that faces them to determine who is trying to kill them. The suspense is chilling, the action and adventure stimulating. Finding togetherness even among the onslaughts, Donny and Abby also find remarkable friends who offer their assistance; but will even that be enough to overcome the determined enemy?

Donny Weston & Abby Marshall # 6

Without Prejudice

Donny Weston and Abby Marshall, on their way to park their beloved boat *Swallow* in Malta to be ready for the summer, encounter the schooner *Speedwell* at La Rochelle, where problems arise for Commander Will and his wife Mary Pleasance. Tom Hardy and Lotte Compton, both from the *Speedwell* join forces with Donny and Abby to oppose the threats to the Commander. From Valetta the four follow up the threat, only to find themselves faced with a plot to use a famous mercenary in an assassination that will rock the foundations of the Euro community, and the western world. Backed by Russia and with the tacit approval of the head of MI6, a rogue CIA operative has set things up for a public shooting at a Euro summit.

The four foil the plot and the assassination fails, but ironically the CIA agent, is credited with foiling the coup and promoted. He wants revenge, and comes after the four with blood in his eye and his guns loaded. The outcome is decided in a action-packed shoot-out in high speed boats in the cold waters of the Thames estuary.

Sea Adventures

Better The Day

From the W.E.B. Griffin of the United Kingdom, David O'Neil, a exciting saga of romance, action, adventure, mystery and suspense as Peter Murray and his brother officers in Coastal Forces face overwhelming odds fighting German E-boats, the German Navy and the Luftwaffe in action in the Channel, the Mediterranean, Norway and the Baltic – where there is conflict with the Soviet Allies. This action-packed story of daring and adventure finally follows Peter Murray to the Pacific where he faces Kamikaze action with the U.S. Fleet.

Distant Gunfire

"Boarders Away!" Serving as an officer on a British frigate at the time of the French Emperor Napoleon is not the safest occupation, but could be a most profitable one. Robert Graham, rising from the ranks to become the Captain of a British battleship by virtue of his dauntless leadership, displayed under enemy fire, finds himself a wealthy man as the capture of enemy ships resulted in rich rewards. Action and adventure is the word of the day, as battle after battle rages across the turbulent waters and seas as the valiant British Royal Navy fights to stem the onslaught of the mighty French Army and Navy. Mystery and suspense abound as inserting and collecting spy agent after spy agent is executed. The threat of imminent death makes romance and romantic interludes all the sweeter, and the suspense of waiting for a love one to return even more traumatic. Captain Graham, with his loyal following of sailors and marines, takes prize ship after prize ship, thwart plot after diabolical plot, and finds romance when he least expects it. To his amazement and joy, he finds himself being knighted by the King of England. The good life is his, now all he has to do is to live long enough to enjoy it. A rollicking good tale of sea action and swashbuckling adventures.

Quarterdeck

As a boy, abandoned to look after himself at the age of thirteen, Martin encountered Captain Bowers RN and his family. Adopted by the Captain he entered the Navy as a Midshipman. Now married and a decorated Captain himself. He returns home to find his wife Jennifer at death's door. Prompted by his safe return, her recovery is assured and is followed by a return to work for 'plain Mr. Smith' with clandestine excursions and undercover trips to France. . At sea once more, he is involved not only with preventing treasure ships from falling into French hands, but also with events on the east coast of America in the run-up to the war of 1812.

Action, battle, romance, adventure and thrills abound in O'Neil's latest venture into the world of sea battles with France, Spain and American pirates.

Sailing Orders

For those awaiting another naval story of the 18/19th century, then this is it. Following the life of an abandoned 13 year old who by chance is instrumental in saving a family from robbery and worse. Taken in by the naval Captain Bowers he is placed as a midshipman in his bene-factor's ship. From that time onward with the increasing demands of the conflict with France, Martin Forrest grows up fast. The relationship with his benefactors fami-ly is formalised when he is adopted by them and has a home once more. Romance with Jennifer the Captains ward links him ever closer to the family.

Meanwhile he serves in the West Indies where good fortune results in his gaining considerable wealth person-ally. With promotion and command he is able to marry and reclaim his birth-right, stolen from him by his step-mother and her lover.

The mysterious (call me merely Mr. Smith) involves Martin in more activity in the shadowy world of the secret agents. Mainly a question of lifting and placing of people, his involvement becomes more complex as time goes on. A cruise to India consolidates his position and rank with the successful capture of prizes when returning convoying East-Indiamen. His rise to Post rank is followed by a series of events, that sadly culminate in family tragedy.

While still young Martin Forrest-Bowers faces and empty future, though merely Mr. Smith has requested his services????

Adventure thrillers

Minding the Store

O'Neil scores again! Often favorably compared to America's W.E.B. Griffin and to U.K.'s Ian Fleming, and fresh from his best-selling action adventure, "Distant Gunfire," O'Neil finds excitement and action in the New York garment district. The department store industry becomes the target of take-over by organized crime in their quest for money-laundering outlets. It would seem that no department store executive is a match for vicious criminals, however, David Freemantle, heir to the Freemantle fortune and Managing Director of America's most prestigious department store is no ordinary department store executive and the team of ex-military specialists he has assembled contains no ordinary store security personnel. Armed invasions are met with swift retaliation; kidnapping and rape attempts are met with fatal consequences as the Mafia and their foreign cohorts learn that not all ordinary citizens are helpless, and that evil force can be met with superior force in O'Neil's latest thriller of adventure and action, romance and suspense, mystery and mayhem that will have the reader on the edge of his seat until the last breath-taking word.

The Hunted

David O'Neal, UK's answer to W.E.B. Griffin and Dean Koontz strikes again with his newest suspense thriller filled with action, adventure, romance and danger. When the Russian Mafia joins forces with other European and Asian gangsters to take over a noted worldwide charity organization to smuggle guns and drugs into unsuspecting nations and begins to kill innocent people, one man – Tarquin Gilmore – Quin to his friends – declares war on the Mafia. To achieve his goal of total destruction of the criminal gangs, he surrounds himself with a few dangerous men and beautiful women. But don't be fooled by their beauty, the girls are easily as deadly as any man. On the other hand, there are a lot more gangsters than Quin and his friends and it's a battle to the finish. A stirring tale of crime and murder, mystery and suspense, passion and romance, guns and drugs... but that is war!

The Mercy Run

O'Neil's thrilling action adventure saga of Africa: the story of Tom Merrick, Charlie Hammond and Brenda Cox; a man and two women who fight and risk their lives to keep supplies rolling into the U.N. refugee camps in Ethiopia. Their adversaries: the scorching heat, the dirt roads and the ever present hazards of bandit gangs and corrupt government officials. Despite tragedy and treachery, mystery and suspense while combating the efforts of Colonel Gonbera, who hopes to turn the province into his personal domain, Merrick and his friends manage to block the diabolical Colonel at every turn.

Frustrated by Merrick's success against him, there seems to be no depths to which the Colonel would not descend to achieve his aim. The prospect of a lucrative diamond strike comes into the game, and so do the Russians and Chinese. But, as Merrick knows, there will be no peace while the Colonel remains the greatest threat to success and peace.

****